"I didn't want you to be mad." She didn't look up. "I didn't want you to send me away because of my clumsy mistake."

"You should have asked someone to help you." The anger lacing his voice was a direct contrast to the gentle way he held her hand cupped in his. She stared at the sight of his enormous fingers on her pale skin, and warmth crept into her cheeks. Her breathing constricted as it had while looking at his unclad body earlier.

With the other hand he reached up, and she stoically kept herself from flinching. He tucked a knuckle under her chin and forced her head up until she had no choice but to look at him. "You're the damned stubborned-est woman I ever knew."

Linnea's heart hammered from his closeness and the fervent look in his storm-grey eyes.

THE TENDERFOOT BRIDE

BY

CHERYL ST JOHN

MILLS & BOON

First published in Great Britain 2007
by Mills & Boon, an imprint of Harlequin (UK) Limited.
Large Print edition 2013
Harlequin (UK) Limited, Eton House,
18-24 Paradise Road, Richmond, Surrey TW9 1SR

© Cheryl Ludwigs 2003

ISBN: 978 0 263 23845 7

Harlequin (UK) policy is to use papers that are natural,
renewable and recyclable products and made from wood grown in
sustainable forests. The logging and manufacturing process conform
to the legal environmental regulations of the country of origin.

Printed and bound in Great Britain
by CPI Antony Rowe, Chippenham, Wiltshire

Cheryl St John remembers writing and illustrating her own books as a child. She received her first rejection at age fourteen, and at fifteen wrote her first romance. A married mother of four, and a grandmother several times over, Cheryl enjoys her family. In her 'spare' time, she corresponds with dozens of writer friends, from Canada to Texas, and treasures their letters.

Chapter One

Colorado, Spring 1875

"This beef chews like shoe leather."

Will Tucker scowled at his aged stepmother as he crossed the kitchen toward the back door and grabbed his hat. Listening to the old woman's complaints had become as tormenting as being staked to an anthill in the blazing sun. She hunched over her dinner plate, the red shawl draped across her bony shoulders drawing attention to her curved spine. "The hell it does."

"You cooked it too long."

"Yeah, well, the new cook will be here any time, then you can quit yappin' about my cooking and every other crotchety thought that crosses your mind."

Aggie pushed the plate away, distaste twisting her wrinkled lips. "Can't be too soon."

He snorted. "You've rowed me up Salt River

so many times, your arms must be as tired as your tongue." Will stuffed his hat on his head and slammed out the door.

Behind him the old woman cackled her gleeful response to driving him stark raving mad.

There were chores that had to be done before dark, and his time would be better spent tending to those.

A squealing pig shot across the dusty yard in his path, followed by two red-faced ranch hands covered with dust. Will placed both fists on his hips and glared. "What in Sam Hill are you doing?"

"Don't think the critter wants to be bacon, boss," Nash Winston called, out of breath.

"You're supposed to keep him tied up."

"He got away."

The men chased the pig toward the clothesline, where Will's drying shirts flapped in the breeze. Will followed at a half run. "Don't—!"

The pig dove under the clothing and Nash followed none too gracefully. The result was a clumsy tangle of squeals, arms and legs, and half a dozen shirts—an hour and a half's worth of work.

"You're no smarter than the slop-sucking pig!" Will cursed and grabbed his shirts before they were dragged all the way to the Colorado border.

From his sprawled position, Nash winced at the dressing-down and shrugged. "Sorry, boss!"

"You're the sorriest son of a bitch I ever hired on! Either catch that pig or get on your horse and ride out of here!"

Nash scrambled up from the dirt and ran full chisel after the escaping animal. After a shame-faced glance at Will, the other cowboy followed.

Will tried to brush dirt from his shirts, giving up in a fit of anger and heaving them toward the back porch with a groan of frustration and several creative curses. The garments landed in a heap near a dried-up bush. The hired woman couldn't get here soon enough.

Weeks ago he'd wired his sister, Corinne, asking her to place an ad in the Saint Louis paper and find him a cook and housekeeper. Five days ago he'd received Corinne's telegram, informing him she'd found the perfect worker. The widow McConaughy had simple needs and would do a good job. With barely enough notice, Will had sent his young hand, Cimarron Northcoat, to pick up the woman at the railroad station, a two-day ride each way. They should have been here by now.

From beneath the brim of his hat, Will squinted at the descending orange sphere of the sun.

Abruptly he focused his attention. A distant swirl of dust heralded someone approaching from the east. About doggoned damned time.

The cattle he'd herded all the way from Texas, and the buildings and the fences on the Double T needed his undivided attention, and so far he hadn't been able to give them more than a promise.

A year ago when he'd started this spread and discovered his aging stepmother was unable to live on her own, he'd brought her along. Now she was alone except for the few hours he was at the house to sleep. Why he cared, he didn't know, but something had to be done.

He and his men were almighty weary of doing double duty, ranch work as well as cooking and laundry. He had jobs lined up for this widow woman that would last her till Christmas. A sturdy, sensible middle-aged woman was just what he needed.

The wagon drew closer and Will made out Cimarron's form, hatless in the late-day sun. Fool kid, was he trying to give himself heatstroke? Beside him, a diminutive figure draped in drab brown bounced and swayed with the rocking of the springed seat. Cimarron's companion wore his hat.

A sinking feeling churned the stringy stew and cold biscuit in his belly. He didn't like the looks of this one bit. Not one damned bit.

Will stalked toward the front of the yard to meet the wagon. Cimarron halted the horses and jumped down. The girl he turned to assist from the seat couldn't have been more than five feet tall and looked as skinny as a scarecrow beneath a baggy, ill-fitting dusty dress and shawl.

Cimarron set her on the ground and she jumped away from his touch, then swayed, gathering her shawl about her shoulders and casting Will a wary glance.

She wasn't a girl, however; surprisingly, her face showed the maturity of a young woman. The frail little sparrow gave Will a hesitant, wide-eyed glance before removing Cimarron's hat and handing it to him. "Thank you."

"My pleasure, ma'am."

She turned her skittish attention back to Will as though facing a judge and jury. She was.

Will stared in disbelief. This was the sturdy middle-aged widow his sister had found to take up the slack? Taking a step to the right, he sized her up from another angle, like he would a horse he was considering buying.

She watched him from the corner of her eye,

without turning her head, and her chin raised a notch.

Her generous auburn hair had been twisted and pinned up on the back of her head. Her slender white neck didn't look as if it could hold up the coiled mass.

Her shoulders were as small as Old Aggie's and her frame didn't appear strong enough to carry her own bags, let alone heft washtubs and pails of water and bags of potatoes. No, not a sparrow, a mouse, he decided, moving back to stand in front of her.

"*You're* the widow McConaughy?" he asked, not believing his eyes, his sister's misleading description or his luck. He clenched his hands into fists, anger simmering in his gut.

The young woman cast her frightened brown gaze from his hands to his face. She turned to Cimarron, as if hoping he could protect her. Her gaze wavered to her left, perhaps gauging an escape route. After swallowing hard, she raised her chin again and spoke in a squeak. "Yes. Um—Linnea McConaughy, sir. And you're Mr. Tucker?"

A year's worth of frustration rose up in Will's belly. He thought of his shirts lying in the bushes, the pile of musty laundry inside, the garden that needed planting and a dozen other chores that he'd expected a housekeeper to do, all the tasks that he'd planned to finally turn over. He had a springhouse to build and a root cellar to dig, now that fair weather was here.

The full force of his ire turned on Cimarron. "What the hell were you thinking, bringing her here?" he roared. "Huh? Couldn't you see she's a bony little stick that will blow over in a stiff wind? You should have taken one look at that—" he jabbed a thumb toward the young woman "—that insignificant wisp of a girl and sent her packing right back to wherever she came from. What am I going to do with a nuisance like her on a cattle ranch?"

He paused, and the ache in his jaw told him he was clenching his teeth again. "I need a cook! I need someone who can do the wash and hoe the garden and pacify a cranky old woman! I do not need another lame piece of baggage!"

The girl clasped her hands to her breast as though she'd been shot through the heart. Colorless as her face already was, he could have sworn her sallow cheeks grew even paler. She clutched her thread-bare shawl to her scrawny chest and her mouth moved, but nothing came out. She blinked from

Will to Cimarron and back, putting Will in mind of a sparrow again. Her chin quivered.

Cimarron's tanned complexion took on a deep tinge of red not caused by the sun. "You didn't tell me to approve of the cook," he said thinly, "you just said to go get her. I did what you said."

Will scrubbed a palm down his face in vexation. "You could see she wasn't right for the job," he accused. He stared off at the distant mountain range for a full minute before turning back and declaring, "She's going back."

The girl's expression clouded over, a tremble reaching her delicate fingers where they clutched her shawl.

He noted the position of the sun, observed the dark circles beneath her eyes and her apparent lack of stamina. She would obviously have to eat and rest before heading back. He only wanted to be rid of her, not kill her. And to get the job done right, he'd have to do it himself this time. "I'll take her back myself. Tomorrow. For now, show her to the room across from Aggie's."

He turned his back and strode toward the barns.

Humiliation burned through Linnea's skin all the way to her bones. The trembling that had begun in her knees as Cimarron had lowered her to the ground now shook her entire body. She bit her lower lip and watched the huge surly ranch owner stride away, relieved to be out from under his condemning glare, but appalled that he'd assessed her as so much rubbish and dismissed her. She should have been used to it, but her heart hammered so hard she was sure the young ranch hand could hear it.

Cimarron took her single bag from the back of the wagon and strode to stand beside her. "He's not as bad as he seems," he assured her. "He's really not that mean, and I've never seen him hit no one who didn't deserve it."

Alarmed, Linnea swung a startled gaze to Cimarron's lean face. Will Tucker was an intimidating bear of a man, with hands the size of dinner plates, a loud voice and a thunderous expression. How many people had deserved to be beaten by him? She swallowed hard. How many had lived?

Cimarron led her toward the house, a solid two-story wood structure with an inviting front porch and two chimneys. The rich mountain timberland provided building material and water was plentiful. Quite obviously, Colorado was a fine place for a ranch.

"You'll see," the hand said. "He's not so bad."

"I don't suppose I'll have time to see," she replied in a weak voice. "He's taking me back tomorrow." She straightened her sore back and shoulders and hid the discomfort shooting through her aching body. "Do you think he might change his mind by then and let you take me?"

Cimarron cocked his head with a regretful expression. "Never have known him to change his mind about much of anything."

He opened the back door and ushered her into an enormous kitchen. Linnea blinked as her eyes adjusted. A long table ran down the center, and one end of the room held a stove and storage places, as well as a worktable. The savory aroma of beef and vegetables permeated the room, and Linnea's empty stomach clenched painfully.

A cackling sound made her jump. She peered into the dimness and spotted an old woman in a rocker beside a cold fireplace, a basket of sewing at her feet. "So you're the cook, eh?" she asked in a gritty voice.

"I had hoped to be."

The woman laughed again, the source of her mirth a mystery to Linnea. "Wish I coulda seen his face."

"That's Aggie," Cimarron explained. "Come on, I'll show you to your room."

After a nervous peek at the uneaten plate of

food on the table, Linnea followed him down a hallway and into a long narrow corner room with windows on two walls. The space was furnished adequately with a bed, a chest, a trunk, a chair and a wash stand. She stood silently, feeling awkward and unwelcome and completely lost for anywhere else to turn.

"I'll bring you some water," Cimarron offered. "You look plumb tuckered out."

She nodded her appreciation.

A few minutes later, he returned with a kettle and poured water into a pitcher. "Appears they've already had supper, but there's some stew in a pan on the stove. If you'd like some, I guess you can help yourself."

"Thank you. For being…kind."

He blushed and backed out of the room, closing the door.

A small block of wood nailed to the doorframe sufficed as a lock. Linnea hurried forward and turned it, staring at the inadequate protection. Anyone who wanted in could shove the door and dislodge that nail. Especially someone as big and angry as Will Tucker.

This was his house. She was at his mercy—for food, for a place to sleep, for her very future.

That was the risk she'd taken in traveling all

these miles to work for a man she'd never met or seen. He was nothing like his sister, Corinne Dumont, whom she'd met in Saint Louis. The beautiful dark-haired mother of two young children had been kind and helpful. Linnea didn't want to rethink her opinion. The person she'd trusted had let her come here, knowing what an awful man her brother was.

Since Corinne was a young widow herself, Linnea had believed she'd sympathized and truly wanted to help. Surely Corinne hadn't sent her here knowing how unwelcome she would be.

Removing her dusty shawl, Linnea rolled back her sleeves and unbuttoned her shirtwaist. She scooped a handful of water to drink first, not caring that the water was warm and not very refreshing for her dry throat. The liquid felt so good, she dared remove her shoes, stockings and shirtwaist to wash more thoroughly. She'd lain on the ground for the past two nights, and before that she'd dozed sitting up on a railcar. Colorado was beautiful country, but strange and vast and frightening.

Will Tucker's disapproving words rang in her mind, and a rush of fear numbed her senses and brought tears to her eyes. She had nowhere else to go. This job had been her last hope for survival.

Taking her only clean dress from her bag, she ineffectively brushed the wrinkles and donned it. After untangling her hair and rolling her dirty clothing into her bag, she stared at the bed with its plump mattress and comfortable-looking worn quilt. The last time she'd lain on a soft bed had been at Mrs. Dumont's in Saint Louis, and before that she couldn't remember when she'd had the luxury.

With her sore feet still blessedly bare, she padded to the bed, tested its thickness, and tentatively stroked the soft cover. Giving in to temptation, she stretched her aching body across the quilt and stifled a groan. Her stomach rumbled, but the thought of abandoning this indulgence just to eat while the old woman watched prevented her from giving in to the hunger.

Instead she closed her eyes and let her body relax.

It was dark when she woke to the call of a screech owl. Linnea sat up, her back and hips shooting pain. First, she oriented herself, remembering the ride and the churlish reception she'd received from the man in whose home she'd just slept. Her stomach clenched painfully.

Grimacing, she stood and peered out the window near the bed, guessing the time. Surely everyone was in bed now and she'd be alone to find something to eat.

After pulling on her stockings and pushing her swollen feet into her boots, she grabbed her shawl and made her way through the narrow hallway to the kitchen.

Light flickered from the coals in the stove, barely enough to guide her to the lantern on the table. She found matches beside the stove and lit the wick.

The stew still sat in the pan on the stove, now thick and congealed and unappealing. Just seeing it nauseated her, but she found a bowl and a spoon. Driven by painful hunger, she devoured the tasteless vegetables and stringy meat, spotted a wrapped loaf of bread and sliced a dry chunk. The food made her stomach hurt. She hadn't eaten properly or much at all for weeks, and her belly was probably trying to adjust.

Hunger appeased, she studied the room. In addition to the remains of supper, dinner and breakfast dishes had been neglected, too. The stove was crusted with grease and scorched food. Will Tucker's hurtful words about not needing another lame piece of baggage struck her afresh.

She had eaten his food. Slept on his bed. She

had nothing to pay with, but she could earn her meal. She could show him she wasn't as useless as he'd accused. Linnea located a broom, a bucket, lye soap and rags, and set to work. As the sun peeked over the horizon, she peered bleary-eyed through the window glass she'd just cleaned with vinegar and water. Overhead a floorboard creaked.

At the thought of the surly rancher awake and angry, her heart lurched.

The old woman shuffled from the back hallway, relying heavily on a cane. Her silver-gray hair hung in an untidy knot over one bowed shoulder. She blinked at Linnea with surprise. "You up already, girl?"

Then, with faded blue eyes, she surveyed the clean stove and scrubbed floor, the straightened shelves and the row of shiny pots hung on the wall. Even the stone hearth had been swept and scrubbed.

"Land sakes, you've been busy!" With an audible creak of her bones, she lowered herself into the rocker and took a hairbrush from the pocket of her apron. She sighed as if the trip to the kitchen had worn her out and raised the brush with a grimace. "Damned old shoulders won't let me raise m' arm anymore."

Linnea moved forward. "Here, let me help you."

She took the brush and slowly worked the knots from Aggie's hair. The old woman hadn't come out for water that morning. "Do you want me to take warm water to your room?"

"I washed with the water from yesterday. What I'd really like before I die is a bath."

Linnea hurried back to the room she'd used, gathered a few hairpins from her bag and brought them back. Pinning up Aggie's hair, she said, "If I'm here long enough this morning, I'll warm you water for a bath. Now I'm going to make coffee and breakfast. How many men eat in here?"

"I'm thinkin' there's ten."

Linnea nodded and set to work. She did know how to cook, no matter what Will Tucker thought. She'd cooked for her father and she'd cooked for her husband and the men with whom he rode. Cooking for more shouldn't be so difficult. After gathering eggs from the henhouse, she inquired as to where supplies were kept and sliced bacon and grated potatoes.

Maybe when the man saw how capable she was, he'd change his mind and let her stay. He had to let her stay. She had nowhere else to go. And time was running short.

Chapter Two

William wiped lather from his face and rinsed his freshly shaven cheeks with last night's cold water. He imagined he smelled coffee, and his mouth watered. As he shrugged into a stiff, wrinkled shirt, he smelled the appealing aroma of frying bacon drifting up the stairwell. After only five hours of sleep, his weary brain could probably conjure up anything.

As if he wasn't behind enough in his work, today he had to take that presumptuous girl back to Denver. He'd lose another four days. This time he'd find a man to cook for the hands. That shouldn't be so difficult. But that still left him with the problem of Aggie.

Aggie had been a thorn in his side since he was thirteen, and things hadn't changed. His father had married her only a year after Will's mother died. Will had resented him bringing her to their home, just as he'd resented being forced to work in his demanding father's lumber mill from a young age. And Aggie hadn't helped the situation. She'd never liked him, and she'd never pretended she had. Will was Jack Tucker's flesh-and-blood son, and she'd never given Jack children.

The older he got, the more Will realized she was afraid of him, thinking he had more influence as Jack's only son than she did as his second wife. Damned foolish thinking, because all Will had ever wanted was to get away from the mill to work with horses and cattle. At fifteen he'd had enough of his father's bullying and took off on his first cattle drive.

The first couple of years he'd gambled and whored his pay away like all the other drovers. Finally he'd considered his future and decided to save for a spread of his own. Riding herd was hard work. He'd taken a few winters off to marshal and had spent three years as an army scout during the war. He'd been breaking horses in Abilene when news of his father's death had reached him.

He'd made it to Indiana for the funeral, and he could still remember the fear and loathing on Aggie's face when he'd gone to the house. She had promptly ordered him out. "You never cared enough to show your face when your father was alive. Don't come sniffing around like a vulture now that he's gone."

Will had stayed at a hotel, attended the funeral, and tolerated Aggie's glares until the day the will was read.

Jack Tucker had left the house to Will, huge shares of railroad stock and other investments to Corinne, and the mill to another son—an illegitimate son none of them had known about.

Aggie's shock and indignation had been unleashed in a fury of bitter name-calling. She had fully expected Will to throw her out on her ear. It had been his legal right.

But he hadn't. As hateful as she'd been to him, he pitied her the scandal she had to accept. She had no way to support herself, but he was young and strong and capable. He'd signed the house over to her and returned to the cattle and horses he understood better than people.

It had taken him another ten years to earn the money for his ranch. He hadn't felt betrayed about the sawmill, because he hadn't stayed and helped his father run it. He had no right to inherit. What he felt betrayed by was the fact that the half brother he'd never known about was only two years younger than himself. He'd been born while Will's mother was still alive and had grown up in a city a hundred miles away.

Will washed shaving lather from his face and carried the bowl of dirty water downstairs. The aromatic smell of bacon struck him fully and he knew he couldn't have imagined it.

He stopped just inside the kitchen doorway and surveyed the transformed room. Every surface—even the floor—had been scrubbed. On the tabletop, steam rose from platters of bacon, grated fried potatoes and eggs fried with crispy brown edges.

Roy Jonjack hit the back door the same time that Will stopped and stared. Their eyes met over the table. It was Roy's week to cook, but he'd never put on a spread like this. His expression was as confused as Will knew his own must be.

"Is there a dinner bell?"

The timid voice came from the mousy woman in the brown dress and shawl. Will turned his puzzled gaze on her.

"I didn't know how to call everyone in to eat," she said.

"I'll do it." Roy turned for the door and whistled, an ear-piercing sound that made the little mouse cringe.

She'd done all this? Cooked breakfast, scrubbed

the kitchen? Even a cozy fire burned in the fireplace, taking the morning chill from the room. Will took in the neatly organized shelves and the gleaming pans. She must have been up all night.

Aggie's cackle arrested his attention. She sat in her rocker by the crackling fire, her clothing neatly buttoned and arranged, her gray hair in an orderly bun. Will narrowed his gaze. What the hell did the woman think she was pulling? If she thought she could kill herself for one morning and get him to change his mind, she was sorely mistaken.

Boot heels hit the back porch and noisy men entered the room. One by one, as they discovered the bounteous breakfast and the blushing young woman, they quieted and doffed their hats, crowding the table for a seat.

"Mighty fine spread, ma'am."

"Best eggs I ever et."

"Don't these biscuits just melt in yer mouth, Clem?"

Will dumped his water out the back door and returned, setting the basin down with a bang on the wooden stand inside the door.

Nobody but the mouse moved, and she jumped from her position near the stove to turn and stare.

Will glared at her and took his seat.

She served him coffee, her hand trembling on the pot she held with a scorched flour sack wrapped around the handle.

Will was nobody's fool. Her attempt to sway him wasn't going to work. But this mouthwatering food was ready and he hadn't had to cook it, so he was going to make the most of it. He helped himself to the platters that were passed and savored the best meal he'd tasted in months. Even the coffee was brewed to his liking, with nary a ground in the bottom of his cup.

"Miz McConaughy's a mighty fine cook, boss," Nash said in an attempt to appease Will. "Did you try her biscuits?"

"One meal doesn't prove she'd stand up to the workload," Will replied, unmoved by the flaky golden biscuit on the edge of his heaping plate. He didn't look over at her because he didn't want to see the edge of fear in her eyes.

He did observe his men, though, and they were cutting him sidelong looks of disgust as they dug into the feast, their displeasure no secret. It was obvious they all thought a delivering angel had descended into their midst. Will knew better.

And Aggie. Damn the woman! She'd been wearing an irritating smirk and rocking smugly since he'd entered the kitchen. She loved nothing more than to see him with his tail feathers in a knot.

The men lingered over their enamelware cups of coffee longer than usual, complimenting the cook and shooting daggers in Will's direction.

"This isn't a holiday," he said finally, glowering at each sun-burnished face. "You've got work to do, and I've got a trip to make."

Nash stood. "Much obliged, Miz McConaughy."

He grabbed up his hat and exited, and the others followed, grumbling.

When they were alone, Will set down his cup. "Be ready in an hour." He jerked his head in her direction to make sure she'd heard. She was placing a pan in the tub of sudsy dishwater, her back to him. "Understood?"

She turned her face so that he could see her cheek, but so that she didn't have to meet his eyes. "An hour. Yes."

Will got to his feet, and ignoring Aggie's maddening sounds of amusement, grabbed his hat before heading out into the growing daylight.

Discouraged, Linnea hurried through the cleanup, not allowing herself time to think about her fate. She had promised Aggie a bath if she had enough time, and she meant to keep her promise.

She'd been heating water, but finding the tub in

a room off the kitchen and filling it took another fifteen minutes. She added boiling water and after checking the temperature, gathered towels and soap and assisted Aggie to the room, out of her clothing and into the water.

The old woman was stooped and withered, her skin hanging on her bones and her spine hunched into an almost inhuman posture. Linnea couldn't help but feel sympathy for her loss of independence, but Aggie kept her dignity, issuing orders and cackling over Will's predicament, which seemed to please her to no end. Back aching, Linnea lathered Aggie's hair and scrubbed her scalp, wondering when she would next get a bath herself.

Aggie closed her eyes after a few minutes and Linnea allowed her to take her small pleasure in the luxurious feel of the hot water. "We'd better get you dried and dressed before Mr. Tucker comes back," she told her finally. "I have to be ready to leave."

She brought Aggie clean clothing from her room and helped her into it, running a comb through her wet hair and draping toweling across her shoulders to absorb the moisture.

Just as she had Aggie settled in her rocker again, the back door slammed open and Will

Tucker's boots stomped across the wooden floor. "You ready?"

Linnea pointed to the small side room. "I need to empty the tub."

Will's penetrating deep-blue gaze moved across Linnea's baggy dress, darkened by wet spots, to Aggie, who sat dressed in clean clothing with her wiry gray hair drying.

"I'll do it later. Where are your things?"

With resignation, Linnea nodded to her bag beside the door.

Abruptly, he turned and picked up the bag. "Let's go."

Linnea gave Aggie a timid smile. "Bye."

The old woman's wrinkled lips pursed and she returned a weak-wristed wave. "Thank you, girl."

Legs and feet weighing like lead, Linnea followed the broad-shouldered man to the wagon that sat in the yard, two shiny dark horses hitched to the traces.

He reached for her and she sidled away instinctively. Glaring, he took a deliberate step back, giving her plenty of space. She couldn't quite reach the running board, though, so it was with reluctance that she accepted his laced fingers as a step.

Settled on the seat, she waited for him to climb up. He stared at her, but she didn't meet his eyes.

"Where's your hat?" he asked.

"I lost it."

"Lost your hat?"

She nodded. The old thing hadn't been much of a bonnet, but it had protected her head. It had disappeared weeks ago during her train excursion. She suspected a young girl who'd sat beside her between Kansas towns had taken it while Linnea slept. The girl must have needed it worse than she did, she'd told herself.

"Don't you have a scarf or something?"

She shook her head.

"Don't think I'm giving up my hat," he warned.

"I don't."

Sensing him moving away, she turned to watch him stomp toward the house. His dark hair reached beneath his hat and hung in a wave over his collar, all the way to his broad shoulders. His legs were long and he covered the ground and took the stairs in half the steps it would have taken her. When he appeared carrying a straw hat, she looked away quickly. He stopped beside her and raised his arm. "Here."

Linnea sized up the hat with skepticism. "What's that?"

"Aggie has more hats than she needs."

"Did she say that?"

"She said you could have it. So take it."

Knowing that wearing a head covering was wise, Linnea accepted the hat. Briefly, she admired the artificial daisies decorating the brim, then placed it on her head and tied the wide sash beneath her chin.

He seated himself beside her and released the brake.

"Tell Aggie thank you," she said.

Flicking the reins over the horses' backs, Will pretended not to notice Linnea wincing as the animals jerked the wagon forward.

The little mouse said nothing. For miles she said nothing, just rode in silence, stoically gripping the side of the wooden seat for balance when the wheels hit stones or ruts. Aggie would have given him a tongue-lashing for her discomfort, and even Corinne would have kicked a time or two. But not this one. She rode with her gaze straight ahead, her lips clamped shut.

He thought about how clean the kitchen had been and wondered how early she'd gotten up to accomplish that—or if she'd ever gone to bed at all. "Just because you cleaned the kitchen and cooked breakfast and gave Aggie a bath doesn't mean I'm obliged to hire you."

She didn't flicker an eyelash, just dispassionately studied a hillside forested with cedar and piñon trees. "I know."

He wasn't used to silent acquiescence. If she had argued with him, he'd have been able to make his point and convince her he was right. If she thought the silent treatment would make him change his mind, she was wrong about that, too. She was all wrong. Period.

She sat as far to the right as she could, trying ineffectively to keep her skirts from touching his leg. From time to time, when the wagon lurched, their elbows bumped, and each time she jerked her arm away as if his was a glowing branding iron.

Every so often, under the guise of studying the landscape, Will cast a glance at her profile. The straw bonnet shaded her face well, but he couldn't help noticing her tiredness and the circles beneath her dark-lashed eyes. She wore another baggy brown dress and the same shawl she'd worn yesterday.

He turned and glanced at their things beneath the tarpaulin in the back of the wagon, and couldn't think of a woman he'd ever known who could take a trip, let alone move to another state, with so few possessions. The provisions he'd packed for the trip occupied more space than her one small battered bag. "If you've had trunks shipped, you'll have to give me a forwarding address."

She turned her face toward him finally. "Pardon me?"

She wasn't so bad to look at, he surmised. Her features were even and her nose was small. Her eyes, beneath dark brows, were a warm golden brown. "Your things. Did you have baggage shipped separately to the train station?"

She avoided him by looking toward the purple mountains in the distance. A startled woodpecker darted from a ravine filled with wild blackberry bushes, and she watched its flight. "No. No baggage."

"You lost them, too?"

Her cheeks turned a deep pink, but she said nothing, merely shook her head.

Why the hell was he trying to talk to her? He could care less where she was going, as long as she wouldn't be a problem for him.

Shortly after noon, he pulled alongside a grove of cottonwoods flourishing beside a gurgling clear stream and climbed down. When he came around to assist her, she stared uneasily at his shoulder, so he backed away to let her manage on her own. Never had he met a woman so skittish and independent. The females he'd known loved to be catered to and pampered.

He pulled bread and cheese from a saddlebag and spread a blanket on the ground in the shade. She probably needed to rest a few minutes before going on.

He filled two tin cups and a canteen while she made a discreet trip behind a dense thicket of rabbit bush. A few minutes later, she seated herself rather awkwardly on the blanket.

Will pushed the food and drink over to her.

She glanced at it, but looked away. "I'm not hungry."

"It's a long day and we won't stop again until dark."

Accepting the cup, she took several long deep swallows, but didn't make a move toward the meal.

"Eat the food," he ordered, looking at the top of the hat which was all she presented to him.

She didn't raise her head. "I cleaned the kitchen to pay for yesterday's meal and for the bed last night." She glanced away, further avoiding his scrutiny. "I won't have an opportunity to earn this meal."

Something unfamiliar moved in Will's chest at her words and her evasiveness. "You earned more than one meal and one night. That kitchen was filthy. You took care of Aggie, too."

"Yes?" She raised her head and looked at him straight on finally, studied him as if to gauge his sincerity. In this light her eyes were the most unusual color. A hazel-like golden brown with a hint of green, fringed with thick, dark lashes.

He gave a single nod. "Eat."

She picked up the cheese with reverence. "Thank you."

The way she ate, a man would think she'd been given a king's fare. She chewed slowly, as though savoring each bite, and after watching her, Will slowed down his own eating. He hadn't noticed her sit down at breakfast. Had she eaten before or after the men—or had she eaten at all?

Not finishing her portion, she took a clean handkerchief from her pocket and wrapped her leftover bread and cheese, presumably for later in the afternoon. Will watched her tuck the small bundle away. The remains of her lunch disappeared into a huge pocket on her voluminous baggy skirt.

She wore a long garment, much like a man's shirt, that added to the impression of how skinny she was under all those dowdy clothes. Combined with the ever-present shawl, her clothing would appall a fashion-minded woman. What had Corinne seen in her? he couldn't help wondering.

The journey wore on into the afternoon and finally she removed the shawl and folded it into a neat square that she sat on when she thought he wasn't looking. She didn't even have enough meat on her bones to protect her skinny butt from the bludgeoning wagon seat.

Will didn't attempt conversation. He felt no need to entertain or befriend her. When the late sun glowed orange in the western sky, he glanced over to find her chin resting on her chest, her eyes closed.

Locating a wooded area protected from wind and weather and close to a stream, he stopped the wagon and unharnessed the horses. He led them to the grassy bank and stood holding the lead ropes until they'd drank. Then he staked them on a patch of grass.

The mouse had climbed down and was moving stiffly, gathering dry wood and moss. When he grew close, she jumped and looked up. "Is—is it okay to have a fire?"

"Of course." Why wouldn't it be okay to have a fire? "We have to make coffee, and it'll get chilly after the sun's been down a while."

She gave a brusque nod and continued her fire

building. Pausing again, she glanced up. "Do you have matches?"

He withdrew a tin from his saddlebag and lit the kindling. While he went for water for coffee, she used the supplies he'd set out to mix biscuit dough.

Will set the pot on to boil and opened a can of beans.

They ate in silence, the woman once again eating slowly and deliberately, not looking at him as she did so.

Afterward, she carried the pans to the stream and returned with them scrubbed clean. She'd obviously done this before, knew how to cook over a fire and make do with little. He hadn't had to tell her how to do anything or even ask for her help. If she'd simply sat and let him do it all, he would have considered that normal for a city woman. Her abilities proved her more capable than he'd imagined.

For the first time he seriously wondered about her circumstances and why she'd answered the ad for employment on an isolated ranch.

Taking two bedrolls from under the tarp, he unrolled them on opposite sides of the fire.

She sat on a stump, warily watching his preparations.

"This suit you?" he asked finally.

She nodded, keeping her gaze carefully averted.

An owl hooted from a nearby tree and the sounds of small scurrying animals were magnified in the dark. Maybe she was afraid of being out-of-doors at night. Coyotes, wolves and bobcats were plentiful in these mountainous regions, and on her trip to the Double T, Cimarron had probably warned her to stay close to the fire and to him.

Will placed his rifle near his bedroll, removed his boots, and stretched out with one of the two blankets, using his leather bag as a pillow. He'd slept in this manner more nights in his lifetime than he had in a bed under a roof.

The mouse moved around some after he closed his eyes, and he cracked them open a slit. She'd taken off her shoes and unbound her hair. She was sitting on the padding, using a brush to untangle the shiny mass. It wasn't really mousy hair at all, but tresses a rich lustrous shade of mahogany that the fire seemed to light from within. He imagined he could hear the crackle of the bristles running through it over the hiss of the fire. Over her shoulder, she plaited the silken mass into a long braid. When she finished and tucked the hairbrush into her bag, he told himself he wasn't disappointed.

Finally, with a grimace and a stifled groan, she eased down and covered herself with the blanket.

She glanced his way.

Will feigned sleep.

Chapter Three

After a few minutes, he peered through his lashes to see she'd fallen asleep with a frown wrinkling her forehead.

Her physical discomfort was clear, though she hadn't complained once. She hadn't said a word about the sparse noon meal or the hard bumpy ride or sleeping on the ground. But then he was used to Aggie, and that cranky old gal complained more in a day than most women could in a lifetime.

Will thought about how worried the shy young woman had looked when he'd observed her studying the countryside when she hadn't known he was looking. She had taken in the scenery, from time to time closing her eyes and inhaling, as if she wanted to remember the smells and sounds. This was beautiful country, no question about that. He wondered where she was from.

He thought over her hesitation to eat because she wasn't earning the meal. Did she think everything had to be earned? Had he given her that impression? Probably. He'd been madder'n hell when he'd seen how small and unsuited she was for the jobs that needed doing.

She was unsuited for ranch work, and he didn't have to feel guilty over saying so. He would never have chosen her, and he didn't know why the hell Corinne had. His sister was a businesswoman, raising two young children, and he'd trusted her to make a sound judgment.

Listening to the crackle of the fire and thinking he'd wake up later to add another log, Will drifted to sleep.

He awoke to an unfamiliar sound. He'd spent many a night on the ground, listening to cattle low and horses stomp and blow, to men snore and to animals gathering food in the cover of darkness, but this sound was unfamiliar to his trained ear.

It was a soft, snuffling sound, like no animal he'd ever heard. He came fully awake and lay perfectly still, straining to hear. The muffled sniff was clear.

The mouse was crying.

The knot in his stomach twisting, he listened to

her tiny sounds of misery. Turning his head, he glanced across the dwindling fire. She huddled in a ball beneath the blanket, the fringed edges of her shawl touching the dirt near her head.

The blanket quivered, as though she trembled beneath. Was she cold? Afraid of the night? What should he do?

Damn the fool woman for being a problem and a hindrance from the moment he'd set eyes on her. Damn Cimarron for hauling her across country only for Will to take her back. And damn Corinne for getting him into this. He plotted the nasty telegram he would send her when he got to Denver. Had the mouse been her idea of a joke?

The quiet crying continued until he wanted to yell for her to shut up. A man couldn't even sleep in peace with her around. What did she have to cry about? One job, one lousy job she'd been turned away from. Life was all about taking the ups and downs, and nobody was immune.

A barely stifled sob made it through the blanket.

Maybe there was more to her loss than just this one job.

What would make a woman travel across the country for a difficult position? He hadn't advertised for a wife, thank God. Just a cook and housekeeper. Shouldn't a young woman like her have better prospects?

Granted, she wasn't much to look at, at least not that he could see. She had pretty eyes and her face wouldn't exactly make a freight train take a dirt road, but she was no raving beauty. However, men advertised for brides all the time, and took them sight unseen. Didn't she want a family?

His thoughts shifted. Maybe she was still grieving. She was a widow, after all. Little more than a girl, by all appearances, but one who'd been married. Perhaps she'd lost a young virile husband whom she'd adored.

Will gritted his teeth. Damned if he wasn't lying awake in the middle of the night, wondering about the fool woman's problems.

At last the sobs subsided and eventually he fell back into slumber. When he woke next, it was full morning and she had started coffee and biscuits without waking him.

She had the shawl pulled around her against the morning chill, but at least she needed it this morning. Her hair was hidden by the straw hat she already wore.

The brim didn't hide her puffy eyes or the redness around her nose. He said nothing, ate a biscuit and drank the coffee, then stood and started toward the horses. He stopped and turned back to look at her.

She had picked up the leftover biscuits and was efficiently rolling them into a square of white fabric. She tucked the bundle in her bag.

Will experienced an odd sinking sensation in his chest. Guilt ate at his conscience. Was she afraid she wouldn't have anything to eat after they parted? She'd squirreled away a portion of her bread and cheese the day before, too.

He let himself really think about her reasons for coming to Colorado. Had she needed the work so badly that she wouldn't be able to afford to eat? The notion was unfamiliar to him. He'd always made a living, but then he was a man.

Women did things they normally would never do if they hadn't been desperate for a means to support themselves. God knew he'd paid for his share of women in his younger days, not caring why the sportin' women supported themselves in that manner. Was the widow McConaughy's situation hopeless enough that she'd do something like that?

He stepped back to where she was wiping out the skillet. "Was this job important to you?" he asked.

Startled, she glanced up. Her cheeks turned a

deep pink. "I need work," she said, rubbing her palms together nervously.

Will waited for more, some explanation, a clarification.

"Your sister assured me I would be right for the job," she said softly, then shrugged one shoulder. "I would never have come if I'd known that you wouldn't like me."

Wouldn't like her.

Damn the idiotic urge that had made him ask.

She had grit, he'd give her that. She'd come all this way, not knowing what she was getting herself into—hoping for a job. She was uncomplaining and competent.

Corinne had assured her she'd be given a job. Had given her hope. And what had he done? Growled at her like a mad grizzly and packed her back to start all over.

He wasn't caving in because of the crying he'd heard, by God. That would be foolish. And it certainly wasn't anything about her scrawny looks that gave him a second thought.

It was the doggoned damned biscuits. The bread and cheese she'd hidden away like a mouse with a cache.

She thought he didn't like her.

Well, he didn't. Why the hell should he?

Aware that the stupidest words he could ever say were doing a Texas two-step on his tongue, he pursed his lips and thrust his fingers into his hair, kicking dirt with the toe of his boot in frustration. He clamped his mouth shut.

She straightened and backed away with apprehension in her unusual gold-flecked eyes.

He groaned inwardly. She was terrified of him. What the hell was he doing? "All right!" he shouted to the heavens, causing her to jump. He glared at her. "You can stay."

She blinked, confusion wrinkling her brow, and composed herself. "What?"

"You can stay, dammit!" He gestured down at the supplies. "Pack up and get your bony behind on that wagon seat. We're going back."

She clearly didn't know what to say or think. She studied him warily. "I'm not sure I understand."

"We're going back to the ranch," he said as if talking to a three-year-old. "I'm going to give you a chance. I'll give you a month to prove you can handle the work without killing yourself. If it's too much—if it's too hard—then I'll pay you for your time and take you to Denver and put you on a train and be rid of you. Understood?"

Relief seemed to sweep her features and lessen

the tension lines around her mouth. She blinked rapidly and nodded. "Yes. I understand. I can handle the work, I swear I can."

"I'll be the judge of that."

She nodded again.

Already kicking himself for his flimsy resolve, he turned and strode toward the horses. What in Sam Hill had he done now?

She still didn't speak, but those funny little worry lines between her eyes had smoothed out some. If they didn't stop, they could make it back to the Double T by late tonight. He told her so, and she agreed with a nod.

"You need to stop, you say something," he said.

She asked twice, and he obligingly halted the horses near foliage, and while she did her business, he poured cups of water from the canteen. She brought out the biscuits, the stale bread and cheese she'd packed away and shared with him.

By evening, she swayed so dangerously on the seat that he ordered her into the bed of the wagon to lie down. She did so, and from time to time he glanced at her sleeping form in the darkness, cursing himself for his weakness.

When at last he pulled the wagon into the yard,

he got down and climbed into the back. She didn't make a move, but slept soundly.

Gravel crunched and Cimarron appeared from the direction of the bunkhouse. "Back already, boss?"

"Yep."

Cimarron discovered Linnea sleeping in the wagon bed and his brows rose in surprise. "Something wrong with her?"

"Just tired is all." Will gathered her into his arms, and stepped to the ground, her hat falling behind somewhere.

"You change your mind, boss?" the hand asked in surprise, undisguised hope in his voice.

"Not really. I decided to give her a month is all. Then she goes back. Grab her bag, will you?"

Will carried her into the house, surprised by how light she felt in his arms. She barely weighed anything, but she didn't feel as bony as he'd suspected. Through his shirt she seemed soft and delicate against his chest. He placed her on the bed where she'd slept the night before—or where she'd been assigned to sleep the night before—and looked down at her. Even in slumber, worry seemed to be keeping her from looking altogether peaceful.

Cimarron set the bag down. "I'll put up the team."

"Thanks." Will turned and met the young man's

eyes, gauging his thoughts. "She still goes if she can't do the work."

Cimarron hung the straw hat and her shawl on a peg. "I didn't say anything."

"Good. Don't." Cimarron left the room and Will turned back to the woman on the bed.

Without time to talk himself out of it, he picked up one ankle and unlaced her boot, slipping it off and moving to the other. The leather was cracked and worn and, though the shoes had been polished, the soles were scuffed nearly all the way through. He placed them on the floor by the wall and pulled the blanket from the foot of the bed up over her.

Tendrils of her hair had pulled loose during the day and lay softly against her temples and her neck, giving her a distinctly feminine appearance. Her dark lashes fanned down across her cheek, and her rosy lips were parted and soft looking.

She was so small and frail, how would she ever bear up under the grueling workload? He was going to be sorry he hadn't followed through with what his head told him was the best and carted her all the way to Denver. He'd given his word though, and there was nothing he could do about it now, but let her fail.

Will backed from the room and closed the door.

* * *

Linnea woke surprised to find herself back in the comfortable little bedroom, lying on the cushiony soft mattress. She sat up and winced at the aches that shot through her hips and lower back. That wagon ride had been torture, and she suspected that Will Tucker had deliberately guided those horses through every gully and over every boulder, just to see her suffer.

Thinking of him made her wonder how she'd come to be lying on this bed. Concern crept into her thoughts. Had she slept so soundly that she didn't remember him bringing her in? Turning back the lightweight blanket, she studied her stockinged feet with skeptical regard.

A knock sounded at the closed door. It had been left unlocked, she noted belatedly. Her heart hammered. She knew nothing about Will Tucker except his bad temperament. Maybe he had read more into her desperation than was there, and there'd be hell to pay now. "Yes?" she called, hating how timid her voice sounded.

"There's hot water out here," Aggie said in her reedy voice.

Relieved, Linnea got unsteadily to her feet. "Thank you."

Linnea found the old woman making her tedious

way down the hall toward the kitchen, and appreciated the effort it took for her to do something so simple as to come wake her.

"Will said to drink that." With her cane, Aggie gestured toward a mug on the table.

Linnea peered into the cup. "What is it?"

"Not sure. He wouldn't kill you on purpose, if that's what you're thinkin'."

Linnea picked up the cup and sniffed. The liquid looked like weak tea and smelled like a green plant. She took a sip and found the taste bitter, but not undrinkable. "What's it supposed to do?"

"It's for aches." The booming voice came from the doorway. Linnea glanced up to see Will Tucker's broad-shouldered frame blocking the opening. His sudden appearance and the statement caught her off guard. He set two milk pails inside the door. "Cover those with wet cloths."

She nodded and he left.

Surprised that he knew of her discomfort, yet more surprised to think that he might actually care to ease it, Linnea drank the tea with a grimace. Taking a bucket of hot water back to the room, she washed, fixed her hair and dressed in clean clothing. Today she had her chance to prove she could do the job and secure a place for herself.

She made flapjacks, stirring the batter smooth

and browning the cakes in perfect circles on the griddle. Cooking was delightfully easy in Will Tucker's kitchen. He had all the proper ingredients in good supply, so she didn't have to substitute or leave anything out. The walls were filled with pans, the cupboards stacked with bowls and wooden spoons and there was plenty of wood for the stove, already split and neatly stacked nearby. And he thought this job was *hard?* She shook her head. He'd obviously never lived like she had in the past.

She smiled to herself as she placed the platters of flapjacks and sliced ham on the table.

The middle-aged ranch hand who'd been in first the morning before entered and hung his hat. "Mornin', Miz McConaughy."

"Morning."

"Name's Roy, in case you didn't catch it before."

"Pleased to meet you, Roy."

"Not as pleased as I am to meet you." His handsome smile encompassed the food on the table. "You're a fine cook, ma'am."

She lowered her gaze and turned away for a stack of plates. "Would you care to do that whistle thing again?"

"My pleasure." He stepped to the door and gave his shrill whistle. Turning back, he said, "Pardon my mentioning it, but there's no jam or honey on the table."

"Oh." She glanced around helplessly. She'd thought she had everything ready.

"I've known the boss since we were just boys. He's always liked applesauce on his flapjacks."

"Applesauce?"

"Yes'm." He pointed.

Linnea hurried to the tall cupboard he indicated and took out several jars. In her experience there had never been canned fruits or jams. Those were luxuries, and she'd felt lucky to have a pint of sorghum. "Mr. Roy?"

"Just Roy, ma'am."

"Okay. Whenever you see that I've…um…forgotten something, like the jam, will you remind me?"

"Happy to," he said with a grin.

The men hit the back porch then, and within minutes the kitchen was filled with activity and the air charged with good humor.

"Mornin', ma'am."

"Works of art, those flapjacks, ain't they?"

"Melt in yur mouth, they do."

Linnea carried a plate to where Aggie sat in her rocker, and the old woman gave her a genuine smile as a reward.

The ranch owner seated himself at the end of the table and Linnea made her way toward him, pouring coffee as she went. When she reached him, he glanced up and met her eyes.

He'd carried her in last night, she was pretty sure. She didn't remember getting out of the wagon on her own. She was not comfortable thinking the man had touched her while she'd been in such a vulnerable state—removed her shoes. Warmth rose up her neck into her cheeks, and she looked away.

After setting the metal pot back on the stove, she carried the jar of applesauce to him. "Mr.—I mean—Roy said you liked this on your flapjacks."

He accepted the jar without touching her fingers. "That's a fact."

He poured a liberal amount on his stack of cakes while she watched. He glanced up to find her observing. "It's even better if you sprinkle a little powdered sugar over the top."

"Do you have any?"

"Second shelf," he replied.

She spooned powdered sugar into a cup and handed it to him.

After sprinkling it on his food, he took a bite.

Linnea had backed away, but watched him warily.

He chewed, then looked up and nodded with apparent satisfaction.

Why that nod seemed like applause in her mind, she didn't know. Her heart soared as though she'd received the highest praise. The man was not going to make anything easy for her, and he was not free with a compliment. But she'd managed her first morning as an employee of the Double T without incurring his wrath. And that must be an accomplishment for anybody, she was sure.

After the men thanked Linnea, they stomped off toward their chores. She scraped and stacked plates.

"Eat, girl," Aggie ordered. "Put some meat on your bones."

Linnea glanced from Aggie to the food left on the platters. She heated two flapjacks and a slice of ham in the oven, then seated herself at the table.

Hesitantly, she glanced at the jar of applesauce.

"Go ahead," Aggie urged.

Linnea spooned a small portion on her flap-jacks, sprinkled them with powdered sugar and tasted the concoction. The tantalizing combination of sweetness melted on her tongue. She closed her eyes to chew and swallow. The salty ham complemented perfectly, and she savored each bite. Nothing had tasted this good for a long time. Maybe never.

This was a good day, a good day indeed. If the rest of her days could be this rewarding and go as smoothly, she'd be in heaven. But after making her employer's acquaintance and experiencing his cantankerous mood, she knew better than to set her hopes too high. The way Will Tucker disliked her, nothing was certain.

Chapter Four

Linnea paused in wringing out the last shirt and admired the basket of well-wrung clothing. At the Double T every chore went more smoothly than she had ever known possible. Will Tucker owned an amazing roller wringer that squeezed water from clothing and sheets with the turn of a crank.

She'd been at it so long that she was having to use two hands on the crank now, but it was still easier than doing wash by hand in a cold river, which was all she'd ever known.

Carrying the full basket to the clotheslines strung between the house and a wooden beam, Linnea straightened slowly, realizing that whatever her employer had given her to drink that morning had assuaged her aches until this past half hour.

After hanging his clothing and Aggie's bedding, Linnea studied the drying garments and sheets, a sense of pride at a job well-done filling her now. She'd never gone to school, never learned to read or do numbers, except to count money, but she was smart and capable. All she'd ever needed was a chance to show her usefulness. She dumped the wash water and stored the tubs.

The house boasted a modern kitchen range, wall lamps, a wall-mounted coffee mill, cast aluminum ware, a box churn with a crank, sturdy furniture, rugs and various gadgets for which she had yet to figure a purpose. Linnea had grown up in a tiny two-room cabin, the youngest of three sisters and a brother. There had never been enough room or enough food. She was just another girl, another mouth to feed, and when her father had seen a way to get rid of her, he'd done so without blinking an eye—and made himself a profit at the same time.

Even though her father had called her a no-account runt and constantly accused her of being useless to him, he'd punished her severely whenever she'd tried to sneak away to school.

Many mornings Linnea had hidden on the Kentucky hillside and watched the small square schoolhouse, hungry for a glimpse of the smartly dressed children carrying lunches and schoolbooks, the girls wearing tight braids, the boys' hair parted and slicked to their heads. At noon a bell rang and the students ran out-of-doors to skip rope and play marbles and share lunches in the shade of a sycamore tree. Oh, how she envied them their freedom to learn, to join in activities, to live with families and grow up with mothers.

But their life was never to be hers, and wishing hadn't made it so. With pruny fingertips, Linnea brushed wrinkles from the neatly hung sheets and headed for the kitchen.

The busy sounds of hammering and laughing men echoed from the corrals as she checked on the beans she'd been soaking for the noon meal. Within minutes she had a fire built in the stove and the kettle simmering on top, then added chunks of salt pork and onion.

"Where you from?" Aggie asked from across the room.

Linnea stirred the pot slowly. "I grew up in Kentucky. Moved around some since then."

"I have a drawer full of aprons you might as well put to use. Go on into my room and look in the bottom drawer of the bureau. Take yourself a stack."

Linnea glanced down at her damp skirt, then turned to study the woman. She wasn't certain how to reply. She didn't have any aprons, which undoubtedly seemed foolish for someone hired on as a cook and housekeeper, but she didn't feel right about accepting gifts from a woman she barely knew.

"Go on. They're not doin' anybody any good layin' in a drawer, now, are they?"

"No, ma'am, I guess they're not." Linnea followed her directions and entered the old woman's room. Earlier when she'd stripped the bed, she had picked up Aggie's beautiful wedding ring quilt in shades of lavender and yellow, folded it carefully and laid it on a chair. Linnea admired the spread again, along with the rose-painted hurricane lamps and the silver comb and brush set on the bureau.

The aprons were just where Aggie had said they'd be, neatly pressed and folded and smelling of cedar chips. Linnea sorted the stack, deliberately taking three that appeared the oldest, and closed the drawer.

"Thank you," she said to Aggie, dropping one with a bib over her head and tying the sash loosely behind her back. "This will keep my clothing clean."

"How long ago did your husband pass on?"

Unprepared for the question, Linnea's fingers froze on the bow momentarily. She caught herself and finished tying, turning to brush butter on her risen loaves of bread dough. "It's been a while," she said noncommittally.

"You're not wearing black, so it's been over a year?"

Fact was, it had been less than a year, but Linnea didn't own a black dress. She gave a brief nod, placed the heavy loaf pans in the oven, and set about mixing corn bread.

"I remember when my husband died," Aggie went on. "Jack owned a sawmill and did business with everyone in the county. They all turned out for his funeral. Your husband have a nice funeral?"

Three hungover men and Linnea pushing Pratt McConaughy into a shallow grave somewhere between the raging muddy waters of the Missouri River and the jail in Chillicothe, Kansas, in a frog-strangling downpour wasn't her idea of nice. But then, in her opinion, Pratt hadn't deserved anything better. "It rained," she said simply.

Aggie pushed her rocker into a steady rhythm. "Seems like the heavens open up and God cries tears when there's a death, doesn't it? Ever notice how many burials are performed in the rain?"

Linnea didn't know about God, but she surely hadn't shed a tear over Pratt's passing. He'd been the most sour-tempered and demanding man she'd ever met, not that she'd known that many, but even her father's neglect and contempt had been easier to abide than Pratt's abuse. His death had given her a profound sense of relief, followed quickly by the fear of being alone with no place to live and no means of support.

As long as she could keep this job, her life had taken a turn for the better. She had the use of a comfortable bed with clean sheets, a variety of plentiful foods to eat and even a measure of peace. After being on the run, sleeping on the ground in all weather and doing without the most basic necessities, this place was like a dream come true.

Her position here wasn't guaranteed, however. She had twenty-nine days left to prove herself to Will Tucker. She was used to catering to a demanding man. She could follow his instructions and take orders. Aggie seemed to be on her side, and the ranch hands approved of her, but the owner of the Double T was the one she had to please.

"Does Mr. Tucker have a favorite meal or a dessert he's especially fond of?" she asked.

Aggie picked up an embroidery hoop and squinted at the needle. "Don't know much about

Will's likes and dislikes, 'cept he was never too fond o' me. Feeling was mutual."

Linnea stared at her in surprise. "But you're his mother!"

Aggie laid the embroidery on her lap and looked Linnea in the eye. "I am not that uncivil man's mother."

"But you're here. Living with him. I'm sorry, I just assumed."

"I married his pa. Will never approved of me or the marriage."

"It's none of my business. I didn't mean to pry."

Aggie's head seemed to teeter on her neck for a moment, while she gathered her words to speak. "Did the boy an injustice, I did. He was pretty much grown when I married his father. Will didn't want me for a mother any more than I wanted him for a son. And we didn't work at gettin' along." She twisted a thimble on her bony finger. "I should have tried, but I didn't. Was glad to see him take off on his own."

The way she'd heard Will speak to the old woman, it was no secret that things hadn't changed much between them. But still, she was here, living on his ranch. "Was this his father's place?"

"Lord, no. Jack had a real house in Indiana. A beautiful home with carpets on the floors.

Oak banisters and velvet furniture. There was a big clock in the front hallway that chimed every hour."

"Oh." This was the nicest house Linnea had ever stayed in, but she didn't want anyone prying into her past, so she wasn't going to ask personal questions of Aggie. She returned to her tasks.

At noon, as if a silent bell had rung, the kitchen filled with hungry men, smelling of horses and fresh air. "Storm clouds off to the west," Roy said to no one in particular. Linnea scooped beans onto his plate. "Thank you, ma'am."

"Roy," Will directed, "you and Clem ride along the riverbed and send any strays back this way. We'll keep 'em tight on the east side of the ridge until this passes."

"You got it, boss."

"Cimarron, you and I will check on the mares and foals in the east corral. We'll bring the skittish ones into the barn."

Linnea frowned, thinking of her laundry on the lines. She hoped the rain didn't come before dinner was finished and she had a chance to run out and bring in the clothing and sheets.

"You saving that corn bread for something special?"

At Will Tucker's question, Linnea started. Confused, she glanced toward the worktable where the golden-crusted corn bread sat cooling, then hurried to cut it into squares and serve it.

"We've got work to do. No time to dawdle," he said.

A sinking sensation dropped in her chest at the chastisement, and she hurried to serve the men and fill their cups. She accepted their thanks half-heartedly as they finished and left.

Will Tucker stood and took his hat from a hook at the back door. He turned and glanced from Linnea to his stepmother. "If the wind comes up fierce, you see she gets to the storm cellar, you hear?"

Linnea nodded. "I will."

He turned and strode out the door.

Cimarron and Nash were finishing their fourth pieces of corn bread. Linnea had never seen men who could put away as much food as these ranch hands. But then, she'd never been around men who worked hard for a living, either.

"Foul weather gets him in a pucker," Nash explained, almost apologetically. "He piled on the agony when I first hired on, too, Miz McConaughy, but don't get huffed. He's not the mean critter you might think."

"You're a fine cook, Miz McConaughy," Cimarron seconded. "Thanks for the meal."

Linnea thanked him and ran out to bring in the laundry before the rain broke.

The storm was upon them within the hour, the sky turning dark as nightfall and jagged spears of lightning splitting the heavens in all directions. Thunder shook the windowpanes and rattled the tin pans in the cupboards. Linnea lit the lanterns, saw to Aggie's comfort and went about her chores.

Will came early to supper, hanging his dripping slicker inside the door. "You're not in the storm cellar."

"It wasn't windy," Linnea replied. "I asked Aggie if she was afraid or wanted me to take her and she said no."

He arched a dark brow. "*You're* not afraid?"

"It's just some rain and thunder," she replied. He had expected her to be afraid. It probably seemed to him that she was afraid of everything, but that wasn't so. She'd never found the weather as terrifying as people.

The storms lasted for two days, but other than bad weather and bad moods, the week passed uneventfully. Linnea grew accustomed to the kitchen and the variety of food and supplies she had to work with, and enjoyed preparing meals and desserts.

At least Aggie seemed to be on her side, offering a cookbook and suggestions for ingredients Linnea had never had the luxury of using. The recipes endeared her to the ranch hands even more than before. Everyone except her employer had a kind word or a smile for her at each meal.

But he didn't have to smile at her. And he didn't have to compliment her. She didn't expect appreciation. She didn't need it. What she needed was money, and he paid her on Saturday. Her wages were worth all the dark looks and disapproval he could dish out.

That night she counted the coins carefully, placed them in a sock in the bag she stored beneath the mattress and prepared for sleep. A hard-won glimmer of hope warmed her from the inside. She'd made it a week.

Hair brushed and braided, dressed in her worn sleeveless cotton gown, Linnea crossed the room in the yellow light of the lantern. As she had every night, she studied the flimsy piece of wood that masqueraded as a lock, then moved beside the chest of drawers and leaned all her strength into it, pushing the piece of furniture in front of the door.

The barricade wouldn't hold back an angry man

for long, but at least it would slow down anyone who tried to get in. Padding back to the bed, she reached under the pillow for the curved handle of the Smith & Wesson .32, the only useful thing her miserable husband had left behind, checked the full chambers, and tucked the gun back into its hiding place.

Security measures in place, she blew out the light and lay down.

She didn't think she'd been asleep more than an hour or so when a terrible racket from outside woke her. A high-pitched screaming accompanied snarls and growls and the frantic neighs of the horses in the nearby corrals.

A loud thump sounded overhead, followed by heavy footfalls on the stairs.

Linnea peered out the window into the darkness, her heart beating skittishly. Events that happened in the middle of the night meant trouble and usually ended in someone's death. Her stomach turned over at the thought.

Finally, she made out Will Tucker's huge form as he ran from the house carrying a rifle.

A shot was fired, followed quickly by another. Horses neighed in fright. Linnea ran back to bed, grabbed the gun in shaking hands and huddled in the center of the mattress, her limbs quaking.

The house shook with the slamming of a door. "Mrs. McConaughy!"

She started at the sound of her name shouted through the kitchen and down the hall.

"Dammit, woman, where are you?" Pounding sounded on the door to the room she occupied. The doorknob twisted and the door hit the back of the bureau with a resounding whack. "What the—*Linnea!*"

The man didn't push the door open farther. She aimed the barrel of the gun at the door. Her breathing eased a little and she managed to force out a reply. "Wha-at?"

"Will you get your butt out here and heat some water? Fast! I need some bandages, too. Use sheets. Ask Aggie which ones."

Someone was hurt. Tucking the .32 under her pillow, Linnea sprang from the bed and grabbed her shawl. Had Will Tucker shot a ranch hand or an intruder?

She shoved the bureau away from the door and ran out into the hallway. "Who's been shot?"

The broad-shouldered man stopped at the kitchen doorway and turned back to look at her, a scowl on his face. "No one's been shot. A coyote got one of the foals. I need to wash the wounds and wrap him. Nash is carrying water for you to heat."

She nodded numbly.

His dark gaze took in her disheveled hair, then dropped to the shawl and the thin white cotton gown that left her lower legs and feet bare. Outlined by the dim light from the kitchen, she noticed he hadn't taken time to put on a shirt. His chest was broad and thicketed with black hair. The sight gave her a tight panicky feeling in her chest.

"Cover yourself before he gets here," he ordered, his voice deep and gruff.

She nodded, then turned and fled back to dress. When she returned, Aggie was poking kindling into the stove. Linnea touched her misshapen shoulder. "I'll do that."

Aggie moved aside and Linnea had a fire roaring by the time Nash brought the third and fourth pails.

"How much water does he want?" she asked.

Nash shrugged. "I'm just doin' what I was told. I'll carry the buckets to the barn for you."

While the water heated, he helped her tear two sheets into strips and quickly roll them. He carried the buckets and she followed with the bandages.

A mare, obviously the injured foal's mother, neighed pathetically from where she'd been confined in a stall at the far end of the barn. Two of the hands held lead ropes taut to keep her from hurting herself. She snorted and strained against the impediment, kicking the wooden enclosure.

In another stall, Will and Roy were bent over a writhing long-legged foal, the straw bedding covered with bright red blood. The young animal suffered from a long gash down the side of its neck to its shoulder point and several cuts around its front legs.

"Oh, the poor thing!" Linnea exclaimed, tears forming in her eyes at the beautiful creatures' suffering.

"I'll get the rest of the water." Nash darted away.

"It's going to take two of us just to hold him still," Roy said.

"Hand me that lead," Will ordered over his bare shoulder.

Linnea immediately found the leather strap and gave it to him. He secured the horse's head and handed the rope to Roy. When he raised his arm, Linnea saw the blood smeared across his wide chest and flat stomach, and her ears rang. She'd seen gunshot wounds before, and they weren't pretty. She stared, but didn't see a hole in his flesh or note him experiencing any pain.

It took a second for her mind to clear and for

her to comprehend that the blood was from the foal's injuries.

"Some rope now," he ordered with curt efficiency. "We'll tie his feet."

Relieved in a way she didn't understand, Linnea turned and ran.

Chapter Five

Linnea located the tack room. On the wall inside the door she discovered an arrangement of branding irons, hoof clippers, iron currycombs and implements she couldn't identify. Quickly selecting a short length of grass rope, she returned to Will.

The poor animal trembled now, trussed as he was, and his eyes rolled in fear. Will took the cloths and the first bucket, and began to gently wash the wounds.

Linnea instinctively moved between the two men and let the foal smell her hand. Immediately his ears pricked forward and he nuzzled her palm. "Maybe you should cover his eyes," she suggested, surprising herself with her boldness.

"There's a leather blinder inside the door of the tack room," Will said immediately.

"I'll get it." Nash had returned. He brought the blinder and Will covered the animal's eyes.

As Will cleaned the gaping wound, Linnea rubbed the foal's bony poll and nose, and spoke softly. "There's a pretty boy. We just want to help you."

The colt wriggled until his head was in Linnea's lap. She captured him there and gently told him to lie still.

"Keep talking to him. Your voice is settling him down," Will said. He turned to Nash. "Tell them to take the mare out of the barn if they have to. She's scaring him worse."

Nash ran to do his bidding.

"We'll have to stitch this up," Will said matter-of-factly. "He's not torn anywhere vital, but I don't think we'll get the bleeding to stop if we don't sew him."

Linnea's eyes watered at the pronouncement.

"Y'ever done it before?" Roy asked.

"Sewed up a horse that got caught in some barbed wire once," Will replied. "I've stitched my own arm."

Linnea wasn't normally queasy over wounds, but now her stomach lurched. She breathed through her mouth and swallowed hard. With compassionate strokes, she rubbed the colt's neck.

"You don't have to stay," Will said quietly, the softest she'd ever heard him speak.

She looked over at him and a glimmer of concern actually shone in his eyes. Maybe she had passed out and was dreaming it.

"I'll stay," she replied. "You said my voice calms him." No, that was her voice, and she hadn't fainted.

She couldn't watch, so after Nash brought the medical supplies and while Will painstakingly mended the long cut, Linnea stayed where she was, sitting on her knees and leaning over the foal's head. She talked and petted until her legs cramped. The barn had quieted, so she assumed the men had taken the mare out-of-doors. She told the young animal how beautiful he was, how shiny his coat was in the sun, how someday he would be saddled and trained and be a valuable mount to a lucky rider.

When she ran out of things to say, she sang. She didn't know many songs, so she went through the hymns she'd heard and the songs the children had sung while they played outside the schoolhouse.

Eventually Will had the worst injury mended, and the other cuts treated and bandaged. She turned her head and discovered Nash listening from outside the stall, Roy with a half smile on his face and Will washing his hands, arms and chest. "Nash," he said, drying off.

"Yeah, boss?"

"Got a clean stall ready?"

"Yes, sir."

"Then let's put this fella in with his mama and let them both get some rest. He's weaned, but she'll keep him calm."

Linnea discovered she couldn't move her legs. "Ooh," she moaned.

"What is it?" Roy asked.

"My legs went to sleep," she said in embarrassment.

Will tossed the toweling aside. "You two take him, I'll help Mrs. McConaughy."

Without another word, Roy and Nash lifted the foal and carried him out.

Will glanced down the corridor. "Cimarron, clean this stall out before you turn in, will you?"

"Sure thing, boss."

"Then everyone get some sleep."

The tall man bent and leaned over Linnea. She slanted a glance upward, taking in the expanse of tanned bare skin and the thatch of dark hair across his chest. Her heart thumped erratically. If she could have moved, she would have jumped away.

His hair fell forward over his cheek. "Can you stand?"

"I don't know. *Oh!*" Sharp needles shot up her

calf at her clumsy attempt. She must have been sitting with her legs under her for an hour. What a useless dolt she was.

Her boss knelt and again leaned toward her.

Immediately Linnea curled into a ball, drawing her arms in and tucking her chin down. He lifted her effortlessly and her heart stopped beating for a full minute. In the recesses of her mind she recognized that she wasn't as afraid as she would have been a day ago. She'd watched him tenderly minister to the young horse, seen a side of him he'd kept well hidden until this night. Now he meant to help *her*.

The scent and warmth of his skin assaulted her senses. A tight panicky feeling came over her, and she told herself he wasn't angry with her. He had no reason to harm her. No reason to do anything to her. She wasn't his wife. She wasn't his enemy. She was his cook.

A breeze caught his hair and blew it against her cheek. At the unexpected contact, a shiver caressed her skin from the spot where his silky hair touched to her shoulders and down her arms. Behind her back and knees his arms were solid and warm. Against her side and hip, his hard chest and belly radiated heat. His body was stronger and more muscled than her husband's had been, and she couldn't remember Pratt ever carrying her. Shoving, poking, slapping, but not carrying her. This potent reaction she was having was not fear.

In the kitchen he placed her on her feet and held her upper arm while she steadied herself with a hand on the back of a wooden chair. Linnea dared a glance up at him. He studied her in return, taking in her face as though for the first time. A muscle in his square jaw ticked.

The day's growth of beard made him look fiercer than usual. His mouth was a hard line, his jaw solid. She deliberately avoided looking at his bare chest, and her cheeks warmed at the mere thought. She could still feel his strength and heat along her body where he'd held her.

"Did you kill the coyote?" she asked.

Will returned the widow McConaughy's uncomfortable gaze. "Yes. It's dead."

She nodded.

Against his better judgment, he remembered how he'd pounded on her door with no response and tried the handle to find the bureau pushed up against the wood. Had she found him that terrifying? What did she think he would do?

He recalled her running down the hall after him, asking who'd been shot. In his puzzlement at the question, he'd turned to discover her in a threadbare nightgown, that ugly shawl around her shoulders. The sight of her slim calves and bare feet had struck him with an arousal so strong and sudden, he'd had no blood left for his brain to function.

His reaction had shocked him. She was the last woman who should have given him a physical jolt that disturbing and unexpected. She was a brown little mouse, not a seductress.

And then she had shocked him—by carrying out every order efficiently and competently, and then by turning huge compassionate eyes on the foal and unreservedly comforting the animal. Why that surprised him more than the biscuits and the roasts and the pies and the clean bedding, he had no idea.

Those other tasks were the things she'd been hired for, after all, and a middle-of-the-night emergency might have thrown her off, but it hadn't. Words of thanks were on his tongue when he caught himself just in time. He wasn't getting soft now. Her presence spelled trouble.

Her sweet singing had not only calmed the horses, but allayed the tension between the men. Will frowned. The effect she'd have on his men would be no good. An unmarried young woman on a ranch added up to trouble.

"Can you walk back to your room?"

She stepped gingerly from one foot to the other. "Yes."

She turned, showing him her thick braid and her narrow back, and moved away a bit unsteadily.

Will found a pan of water on the stove, gathered towels, and carried them up to his room. Scrubbing his hands, nails and arms with soap, he considered the fact that his cook had not failed as miserably as he'd believed she would. Miraculously, she'd held up for a week, and had even handled an emergency adequately. Perhaps she wasn't going to be as easily discouraged as he'd imagined.

Then again, the reality of the situation may not have sunk in yet. Once the isolation and the heat and the tedious labor got to her, she'd take off in a cloud of dust. And if she didn't…why, then he'd be stuck with her because he'd given his word.

As the following weeks passed, Will grew resigned to the fact that the widow McConaughy was not going to crack under the workload. He'd observed her carrying buckets of water and baskets of laundry, wrestling the steel tubs and chasing chickens she'd designated for the fry pan.

And she was a damned good cook. There wasn't anything she'd fixed that he hadn't torn into like a ravenous wolf—except maybe the turnips. She had a passion for turnips and cut them into soups, sliced them into stews, and often just boiled them as a side dish.

After Cimarron plowed a garden plot, she'd raked and hoed and prepared the ground for seed—planting yet more turnips. She always dressed in those awful baggy brown dresses, with the shirt and shawl. Though her garments were clean and pressed, she did nothing to draw attention to herself or her femininity.

All of his clothing was washed and crisply ironed—each week she placed his things in neat stacks at the foot of his bed.

His room was cleaned, the furniture and floor polished, the lamp chimneys washed and the wicks trimmed. He would have had to make up something to find fault with her housekeeping or her cooking.

One evening, as he returned from the barn, he approached the house and heard men's laughter. He came upon Ben Taylor and Nash perched on the porch railing. Their expressions when he appeared were sheepish, and he didn't figure out why until he saw Linnea sitting in a rocker. In her lap, she held a red flannel shirt, meticulously stitching it with a needle and thread.

In the matching rocker beside her sat Aggie, amusement turning up her wrinkled lips. Ever since Linnea's arrival, the old woman was always freshly groomed, with her clothing clean and pressed. And she obviously took perverse pleasure at his growing unease.

The conversation had stopped upon his arrival. "What's this, a sewing circle?" he asked.

"Miz McConaughy is fixin' my shirt," Nash said quickly.

"She's gonna do mine next," Ben added.

Will studied the group with a scowl.

"My work's all done for the day," Linnea said quickly.

"None of my concern what you do in your free time," he replied and entered the house, letting the screen door slam behind. *Except when it involved his ranch hands lollygaging about on his porch,* he thought in irritation.

Aggie's cackle unnerved him, so he didn't even pause for a cup of coffee but headed straight for his room.

A few days later he inadvertently learned that the

men were paying her to launder their shirts. Roy had picked up his stack of laundry, paid Linnea, and was admiring the crisply ironed creases when Will came around the side of the house.

He'd known Roy since their boyhood days in Indiana, and recognized a sheepish look when he saw it. He knew Roy well, as a friend, as a seasoned cowboy and trail partner and now as his ranch foreman.

"Now you're taking in laundry, as well as sewing?" Will asked Linnea.

She dropped the coins into her skirt pocket. "I haven't shirked any of my duties, and your clothing comes first, Mr. Tucker."

Roy gave Will an irritating grin and moved backward down a step.

"You're making such sissies of my men, you'll be readin' 'em bedtime stories before I know it."

Her eyes widened, but she said nothing.

"Thanks, Miz McConaughy," Roy said, tipped the brim of his hat, and loped down the stairs toward the bunkhouse, whistling.

"Would you rather I didn't do the men's laundry?" she asked. "I saw it as a chance to set aside some extra money."

"I haven't seen you spend a cent yet," he said. "There's a catalogue in the cabinet if you want to order clothing. Or one of the men can take you to town or pick up sewing supplies for you."

Her cheeks turned fiery red, but she didn't respond.

"As long as the work I pay you to do is done, I don't care if you tuck them into bed at night. Suit yourself," he said peevishly to the slip of a woman and tromped toward the barn.

Linnea watched him go, embarrassed that he'd noticed her lack of appropriate clothing and angry that he'd been rude enough to mention it. She had more to worry about than pretty clothes. She had to make sure she could provide for herself, and setting aside as much as she could earn was her first priority.

She had discovered that she could provide services that were respectable and profitable, and doing so made her feel better about herself than she had for a long time. She wished her extra work wasn't making her employer mad, but everything made him mad. Staying out of his way and taking care of herself was all she cared about. Her situation would change soon enough, and she had to be ready for it.

One breezy warm afternoon a week later, Will found her taking clothing from the line. That day she'd worn her hair in a long braid down her back, and he noticed the sun on it as he approached her. He handed her a list he'd made up that morning.

"What's this?" She frowned at the brown paper.

"Cimarron's goin' to Rock Falls tomorrow. I want you to go along and buy those things for me. And any other supplies you need. Make a list. I have an account at the mercantile."

She didn't meet his eyes, but nodded and tucked the paper into a pocket in the folds of her skirt.

A wind had come up suddenly, the gusts blowing clouds westward. Will glanced at the sky.

When he looked back, he discovered her studying the gray heavens with a funny line between her brows. "I don't think it's a storm," he said.

She turned her gaze to his finally, and the unusual tawny gold flecks in her brown eyes caught him off guard. Definitely not mousy eyes. More like a cat's eyes-—or a cougar's. Like warm spiced honey.

He didn't like the direction his thoughts had taken. Abruptly, he turned and took a few steps away.

"I'm not fixing turnips tonight."

He stopped. Turned back. "What?"

"Turnips. You don't like them, do you?"

The wind caught her skirts and flattened them

against her legs. The tails of her shawl blew back from her shoulders and the fabric of her dress was pressed against her body, clearly outlining her shape. Breasts. *Belly.*

An obvious mound protruded beneath her breasts.

Will stared, recognition dawning with surging anger.

Linnea tugged her shawl around her and turned away, reaching upward to remove a shirt from the line.

His head filled with a roar.

"What the hell?" Leaping from where he stood, he surged forward and pounced on her.

Catching his approach from her side vision, she cringed and, with a startled shriek, took a step back, dropping the shirt. Her face had gone white. She raised a hand as if to ward off a blow.

"Son of a miserable bitch…" Not paying attention to her terrified reaction, Will grabbed her with one arm around her back and spread his other hand flat over her stomach. Beneath her layers of clothing, her belly was an unmistakable hard, round protrusion.

She trembled and struggled to pull away, grabbing for his wrist and scratching him in her panic. Her braid fell over his wrist like a silky caress, and her clean feminine scent rose in his nostrils. His physical reaction angered him even more.

With his hand spread across her belly, her fingers gripping his wrist, and the wind whipping his hair toward her, their eyes met. Hers were wide and filled with genuine terror.

His anger was so sharp, he tasted it on his tongue. Fury throbbed through his veins. What had this stupid woman been thinking in coming here?

The widow McConaughy was going to have a baby.

Chapter Six

Linnea fought like a wild woman. Yanking from his grasp, she spun and turned away, and when he reached for her arm, she shrieked and clawed his hand. She started to run for the house, but then, as if thinking better of being caught inside, she picked up a crate sitting near the steps and threw it at him.

Will knocked it away with his forearm and kept moving forward. Turning, she made a beeline for the trees behind the house. With her skirt hem raised to her knees, and terror driving her, she was fast. Turning abruptly, she escaped around the back of the barn. Quickly adjusting momentum and direction, he shot after her.

Alarmed over Will Tucker's sudden moves and his furious outburst, Linnea ran as though her life depended on it. For a huge man he was amazingly agile and would be upon her any second. Heart pounding and out of breath, she found a hiding place in the dense shelter of sage brush behind the barn and crawled into a thicket, curling to make herself as small as possible.

Trying to calm herself and remain silent, she took slow deep breaths, chaotic thoughts whirling in her mind. Running had been her first self-protective instinct, but hiding was foolish. He would find her, and he would be madder than ever that she'd run.

Inwardly, Linnea chastised her cowardice. She should be stronger. This man was bigger than both her father and her husband, but he was nothing to her. He had no claim on her. She had the freedom to leave if she chose. If he hit her.

She covered her mouth, so she wouldn't give herself away with a sob of hopelessness. If she'd had a place to go, she wouldn't be here. Security was imperative, and until now this had been the best place she'd ever found.

But now he knew just how weak and vulnerable she was.

A twig snapped. Her heart stopped. The sound of someone—Will Tucker—walking through the undergrowth was unmistakable. Her trail was in plain sight, of course, a trail that would lead him right to her. He would send her away for sure now.

Knowing his demands for stamina and strength, as the next months passed, she would never be able to fill his requirements.

She had been fooling herself to think this would work. Pressing her knuckles against her mouth, her mind whirled in confusion. Now what? she thought in desperation. There were very few choices left.

"Linnea?" he called, his voice deceptively, unthreateningly quiet. "I don't know what you thought I was going to do back there, but I wasn't going to hurt you."

Was this a trick to get her to come out? She'd seen the anger on his face, and she knew just how mad he was. He was an enormous man, built of solid muscle; he could snap her in two with no effort. Lying curled in an uncomfortable ball caused her baby to move as though in protest. Instinctively, she moved her hands down to her swollen abdomen. She had to protect this innocent life within her. She was responsible for this baby.

If only she'd carried the gun in her pocket and hadn't left it in her room, thinking she needed protection only at night.

Her thoughts flew to the coins so carefully hidden under the mattress in that narrow room back at the house. Her earnings. Her future. Her baby's future. Her mind ran in a hundred directions. What did she think she was going to do? He would beat the bushes until he found her. Even if he didn't try to find her, even if he went away and left her here, what then?

Wait until dark and sneak out? Then what? She couldn't hide in the woods forever. If she tried to make her way on foot, she'd get lost. Besides, wild animals prowled this country. She was helpless on her own.

She supposed if he left her here, she could sneak into the house and get the coins and the gun. But then what?

She was hiding in the woods like a child who feared punishment. Linnea called on every ounce of fortitude she possessed to bolster her courage. She was not a child. And if she wanted him to respect her—if she was ever going to respect herself—she had to face him.

If she wanted her money, she had to face Will Tucker's music. Her heart raced again at the terrifying thought, so she fought to calm herself.

Will Tucker had made a home for his stepmother. He was good to animals. His men respected him. She wasn't convinced that he wouldn't be violent if provoked, but based on what little she knew about him and the choices available to her, she was going to have to take the chance that he wouldn't harm her.

Taking a deep breath, she pushed herself up onto her knees and crawled out into the open. Standing, she brushed leaves and twigs from her clothing, then her palms before facing him.

He studied her without moving any closer. His expression was still thunderous. His size, his scowl, everything about him made her knees quake. It took all her resolve to stand her ground and not bolt. She raised her chin and composed herself. "I'll be packed and ready to go in the morning."

She'd never noticed the color of his eyes before. They were as gray and stormy as an ominous thundercloud. He stood a good six feet away, however, and the distance gave her hope. "Where will you go?" he asked.

She had no answer, so she shrugged.

Will looked her over, trying to make some sense out of her. "Were you ever really married?"

She looked at him as though he'd lost his mind. "I sure didn't get this way by my own choice."

Will didn't understand that reply, nor was he going to try to, because he was angrier than ever and trying not to show it. Not only was the woman small and unsuited for ranch work, but she was in a delicate condition! She shouldn't be lifting buckets or standing on her feet all day. *Now* what was he going to do with her? Worse yet, he'd had completely unsuitable physical reactions to her on more than one occasion.

"How long before that baby comes?"

"Three months, I think."

Holy— She would never find a job in the fix she was in, especially the closer she got to her time. What the hell had she been thinking?

"Your trickery doesn't sit well with me," he said gruffly.

She nodded her understanding.

If she had no money and no one to help her, he knew why she'd kept that detail a secret. Nothing justified the deceit in his opinion. He had a ranch to run, and he needed someone to help him do that. He already had one helpless female on his hands, he didn't need another.

The woman wasn't completely helpless, he amended his thinking, and she did cook well. The men were content and that was important. But he'd already noticed that they carried and fetched things for her. And she had taken on the extra work of their laundry.

Experience had taught him that anger would get the best of him if he said the first things that came to mind. He took a slow deep breath and said, "I'm gonna have to think."

She studied him warily.

"I'm not inclined to send you off like this." He scratched his head and turned in a frustrated circle, surveying the woods without seeing the trees. The question finally burst from him. "*Damn, woman, what were you thinking?*"

He glared at her, not even hoping she had an explanation. Nothing she could say would change the mess she'd made of his life by coming out here. A smudge of dirt darkened her cheek, and seeing it helped soften his anger.

"If you want me to go, I'll be ready," she said. "If you let me stay, I'll work hard. You won't be sorry."

"That's just it," he said. "I'm already sorry. I can't let you kill yourself working too hard. I can't let you hurt yourself...or..." He made a gesture, indicating the baby she carried.

Linnea hunched her shoulders forward protectively. Evidenced by the way he held himself and the modulated tone of his voice, his anger was barely controlled. Should she believe he cared whether or not she worked too hard?

He narrowed a look at her. "How long has your husband been dead?"

"Six months."

"And you don't have any family?"

Oh, she had family—a father who'd sold her to Pratt five years ago to be rid of her. She wasn't about to go back there, no thank you. She shook her head.

"And your husband has no family?"

A couple of illegitimate children somewhere and a brother in a Missouri prison. She shook her head again.

He narrowed his gaze. "Did Corinne know?"

She looked at him without comprehension. Her thoughts were swirling in her head.

"My sister. Did she know about…your condition?"

Linnea shook her head. "No. No, she didn't."

Grateful that he was talking and not swinging, she chose not to mention that his sister had most assuredly known what a cantankerous man he was and hadn't bothered to tell Linnea.

A muscle clenched in his jaw and his stare bored into her. "What did you think would happen? You knew you couldn't keep it a secret forever."

Her priorities were food and a place to stay. She had hoped to earn enough money to get her through the weeks ahead when she couldn't work. She had a good start on that, too. If only he would let her stay a while longer, she could afford to pay for room and board later on—and buy whatever necessities she'd need for a baby.

"Aggie is the only other woman within miles," he said in exasperation, "and she's too old to be of help to you."

Linnea studied his face in puzzlement. "I don't need any help."

"You will. You can't have a baby by yourself."

Flustered now, she didn't have a reply.

"There's a doctor, but he's half a day's ride from here."

Her blood ran cold at that declaration. "I don't need a doctor. I don't want one."

"If you're staying here, you'll have a doctor check on you. Head back." He gestured for her to move forward.

She did, walking toward him, but keeping her distance and allowing him to lead the way. "I don't need a doctor," she told him again. "There's nothing wrong with me, and I won't spend my earnings for something I don't need."

He gave her a dark scowl. "There won't be any more argument on the subject."

In the side yard they reached the basket of folded shirts and towels. A few handkerchiefs and an apron still flapped on the clothesline. Linnea reached to take them down.

"Is there anything else I should know?"

She folded the fabric and settled the apron on the pile without looking at him. "No."

"There'd better not be."

She had deceived him, and his anger had been justified. "I knew you would never let me stay if you knew."

"You had that right."

She picked up the basket and carried it to the house, feeling his glare on her back the entire time. Hard work wasn't enough for any man, she'd learned that the hard way. She didn't dare think she could prove herself and win his approval and therefore a safe place to stay.

Resting the load on the kitchen table, she pulled the note he'd given her from her pocket and stared at it, regret and fear still her constant companions. There was more Will Tucker didn't know. But this was a secret she could prevent him from learning.

Taking a few minutes, she went to her room and pulled the sock that held her money out from under the bed. She counted the coins, hoarding them for the inevitable time when he was finished with her for sure. She would never be strong enough or smart enough to please the man who hadn't wanted to hire her in the first place; the only reason she was still here was pity. Just as her father and husband had always accused, she was no good to a man.

Her only hope was that by the time Will discovered the rest of her inadequacies, she would have saved enough to make a fresh start for her and her baby. And God help her poor child if it was a girl. Linnea closed her eyes and prayed fervently for a son.

Linnea helped Aggie get changed and tucked in to bed for the night, then she blew out the kitchen wall lamps. Instead of going to her room, however, she slipped out of the house into the darkness. She moved stealthily across the yard and skirted the corral, taking the long way to avoid being seen. With the corner of the bunkhouse in sight, she crouched in the long grass at the corner of the corral and waited.

Some time later Clem made his way to use the outhouse. Roy and another hand sauntered out to roll cigarettes and smoke them beneath the eaves. The scent of tobacco drifted to her on the night air. Eventually they returned to the bunkhouse. Her legs were cramping and she'd been bitten by mosquitoes before she finally saw Cimarron exit the doorway and head for the barn.

"Pssst!" Head low, she ran toward him.

Quick as lightning, he drew a pistol and aimed it at her.

Stopping in her tracks, she raised both hands and whispered, "It's me."

"Miz McConaughy?" Squinting into the darkness, he holstered the gun and walked toward her.

"Shhh," she said, glancing around. "I don't want anyone to see me."

"Okay." He glanced toward the barn. "Let's go in there."

"What about Mr. Tucker?"

"He's not in there."

"You sure?"

"I'm sure. He's down at that end of that paddock with a horse."

Linnea glanced in the direction Cimarron pointed.

The hand led her inside the barn, into the tack room and lit an oil lamp. "What's this about?" he asked.

She pulled the note from her pocket and unfolded it. "Mr. Tucker gave this to me today."

Cimarron accepted the list and glanced at it. "You want me to get this stuff for you?"

Relief washed through Linnea. Cimarron could read. "No, he wants you to take me to town so I can get these things for him."

Cimarron handed the paper back to her. "All right. I'll have a wagon ready first thing in the morning."

Face warm with embarrassment, she swallowed her pride. She needed this young man's help. "There's a problem, but I want you to promise that you won't tell Mr. Tucker."

Cimarron scratched his head and his expression revealed his discomfort with her request. "I—I don't know, ma'am."

"Please, you have to help me. If he finds out I can't do something he's asked me to do, I'm out of here. I *need* this job."

"I need my job, too, ma'am, and Will, well, he's a fair boss and a good man."

"Mr. Northcoat."

"Yes'm?"

Linnea opened her mouth to state her predicament for the first time ever. "Truth is…" She squared her shoulders and looked Cimarron in the eye. "I'm going to have a baby."

His eyes widened and he almost glanced down at her belly, but then he caught himself. His cheeks reddened.

"That's not the secret," she hurried to say. "Mr. Tucker knows about that already."

Cimarron swallowed hard.

"But if I can't stay here, I don't know what will happen to me or my baby. All I need is a little bit of help. Tell you what, I'll explain what I need help with, and then you can decide. That way if you think it's too awful of a secret, you don't have to promise. Fair enough?"

He shifted his weight uncomfortably, and then conceded with a shrug. "All right."

"I need you to read the list for me. And any other lists Mr. Tucker gives me."

The young man studied her, the glow of the lamp revealing his puzzlement. "You can't read, Miz McConaughy?"

Cheeks warm, she shook her head.

"Well." He glanced around. Stuck a hand in his pocket. "That's not such an awful secret."

Linnea had lived with the humiliation of being unable to read or write her entire life. Her father hadn't believed females needed an education. It only gave them notions of importance, he'd claimed, and her husband had forbidden her to learn, as well. "You'll keep the secret then?"

Cimarron nodded. "I have a better idea," he said, smiling excitedly.

"What's that?"

"I'll read the lists for you," he assured her with his palm toward her, "for now. Meanwhile I'll teach you to read them yourself. Wouldn't that be better?"

Linnea blinked at the paper in her hand, at the confusing squiggles that made no sense to her, and imagined being able to read the words. Her hand shook with a trembling anticipation. She glanced up at the ranch hand in awe. "You would do that for me? You would teach me?"

"Well, sure. Ain't that much trouble, ma'am."

"Did you go to school?"

He nodded. "My mama made sure I went every day during the winter. Spring and fall I had to help my pa with the plantin' and pickin'. I never much wanted to be a farmer, so I liked the school part. My pa said I needed to read and cipher, so I could manage on my own."

Linnea pictured him as a boy, dressed in a shirt and knickers with suspenders, carrying books on a strap, and a little smile touched her lips. "Did you have any sisters?" she asked.

"Two of 'em. Redheaded and ornery as the devil." He laughed.

"Did they go to school, too?"

Halting for a moment, as though he didn't want

to reply and make her uncomfortable, he finally said, "Yes, ma'am, they did."

Carefully, Linnea folded the note and tucked it back into her pocket. "I would like very much if you taught me to read, Mr. Northcoat."

"Cimarron."

"But it *must* be our secret. Mr. Tucker mustn't know. Promise me."

"We won't be hurtin' anyone, ma'am. Most of the hands play poker or sit by a fire and swap yarns of an evenin', and the boss don't mind. He won't mind me teachin' you to read, either."

"Just the same, I don't want anyone else to know."

"Okay," he finally agreed. "It's our secret."

"Where will we meet?" she asked.

He scratched his head thoughtfully. "We could meet down by the stream of an evening. The boss spends most of his time in or around the barn here, so we'll be out of his way."

She nodded her agreement to his choice of locations. "We'll start tomorrow night?"

"Tomorrow," he replied.

No one had ever made her such a generous offer. No one had ever really cared about her one way or another, except as to how she inconvenienced them by being alive.

"Thank you," she said, hearing how inadequate the words sounded.

"No need for thanks," he replied. "I spend my days with cows and horses. It's not exactly gonna be a hardship to spend evenin's with a pretty lady."

Those words caught her completely by surprise. Her expression must have shown her dismay, because Cimarron hastened to add, "No disrespect intended, ma'am."

"I'll be ready to ride into Rock Falls right after breakfast," she said, and left the barn ahead of him.

Since she'd come to Colorado, Linnea had been completely out of her element. Some days she stopped her outside chores just to gaze in wonder on the countryside, layer upon layer of variegated greens that blended into hues of blue and gray the higher the elevation. She would close her eyes and smell the air, feeling the sun on her face and through her clothing and simply enjoying being.

But it wasn't just the lush countryside, the crisp air and the breathtaking mountains that were different from anywhere she'd ever lived. The circumstances were beyond her experience as well.

After Pratt's death, she'd made her way to Saint Louis, hoping to find a job and a place to live far from the plains of Kansas where her husband had dragged her. It was while she was there, sleeping in a back room in exchange for sweeping floors and hauling water to a kindly old blacksmith, that she'd felt her baby move for the first time and realized she'd been carrying it in ignorance for some time.

A fierce desperation had washed over her. She experienced anger at the husband who had done this and left her destitute. Still, she never regretted for a moment that he was dead. Having another life to consider added to the burden of looking out for herself and added a time pressure. But she didn't wish him back.

She'd asked the livery man to read the ads in the paper to her, and had responded to the one placed by Corinne Dumont.

The woman lived in a well-furnished home, the likes of which Linnea had never seen until she was ushered into the parlor and served tea in a delicate porcelain cup.

Corinne had assured her of the cooking job, given her encouragement and hope, treated her with respect and dignity, and even offered her a room in which to stay until travel arrangements were made and she was on her way.

When Cimarron had picked Linnea up in Denver, and she'd seen his smile and sensed no resentment or anger, she'd felt as though she'd landed in a dream world. Even spending two nights on the trail with him, she'd never been afraid. Starved for friendship and acceptance, she'd been drawn to his easygoing manner and brotherly smile.

Will Tucker, on the other hand, was more familiar territory. He was like the other men in her life, heartless men who had never given her a chance to prove her worth. But, she thought, moving across the yard toward the house in the darkness, that was not entirely fair, because he had given her a chance. He'd given her one month to prove she could do the work.

If that was the extent of the kindness and generosity that his sister had claimed he possessed, Linnea would have to say Corinne had exaggerated.

And Linnea had done the work, that had never been a question in her mind. But she'd angered him with the secret of her baby.

She'd never had the luxury of feeling safe or wanted, and though those securities were not to be hers, it didn't seem that fate had left her out to dry completely. There was plenty of beef and chicken on the Double T, as well as milk, eggs and crates of dried apples and bags of flour and sugar. Nearby she'd seen peach trees that would bear fruit in summer, and vegetables were growing in the garden. She and her baby were well nourished.

In the little room at the corner of the house, she had more privacy than she'd ever known. And so far no one had raised a hand to her. And...

A tingling excitement combined with the fear of doing something forbidden brought a shiver to her spine. She was going to learn to read.

Chapter Seven

William Tucker didn't speak to her the following morning. At the opposite end of the table from where he sat, Linnea filled tin bowls from an enormous kettle of oatmeal. The hands passed them around and Will got his first. He helped himself to the pitchers of milk and molasses and slathered butter on bread she'd toasted in the oven.

She'd learned that the men would eat anything she prepared, and that they would eat a lot of it. Over the weeks she had doubled the amount of food she'd originally thought would suffice and the men had consumed it all.

"Cimarron and Mrs. McConaughy will be in town come noontime. Roy, you come in and slice a ham and bread for our meal."

Roy nodded. "Will do, boss."

Linnea had been wondering how the midday meal would work, but they'd obviously managed without her before she'd arrived and could do so for one meal.

"Cimarron, you see to it Mrs. McConaughy packs somethin' for both of you to eat on the road."

Cimarron glanced at Linnea. It would have been more suitable for Will to instruct Linnea to prepare their meal, but instead he'd spoken to Cimarron. She looked away and arranged places for herself and Aggie to sit, then helped the old woman onto one of the few chairs. Stools and long benches surrounded the long table, but the two women had each been designated a chair for their use. Settled in, Aggie ate her oatmeal in silence.

The conversation turned to the day's work. Will assigned chores and finished his meal in silence as the rest of the men bantered about the less desirable jobs.

Linnea had noticed that the men listened with respect when the ranch owner spoke. They accepted their duties and asked questions regarding watering, moving cattle and treating horses. When the conversation veered from work, however, the hands joked and teased, but Will didn't join in.

When he'd finished eating, Will pushed back his chair, took his hat from the rack near the door and exited without another word. The hands never seemed to notice the lack of pleasantries, but Linnea did.

A few of the others finished, thanked her and headed out.

When there were only a handful left, Linnea asked Roy, "I've been wondering how the young colt is doing. The one that was attacked by the coyote."

"He's doin' just fine, Miz McConaughy. The wounds are healed, he's growin' like a weed and frisky as all get-out. I think we'll be movin' 'im out of the barn later in the week."

Linnea gave him a shy smile. "That's good."

"Come out to the barn and see 'im," Nash suggested.

"Oh, I don't know…." she said, hesitating. "I wouldn't want to be in the way." She didn't know if her boss would want her where he hadn't invited her. Her trip out to talk to Cimarron last night had been dangerous enough.

"Sure," Roy agreed with Nash. "Come out later tonight and we'll show you the little fella."

Roy was the ranch foreman. She supposed if he said it was all right to visit the barn, it wouldn't hurt. "If you think it will be okay with Mr. Tucker."

"Heck, ma'am, you helped doctor that little

guy," Nash said. "Ain't no harm in you getting a gander at 'im now that he's better."

She would like to see the colt, so she agreed. "All right then."

The men grinned and thanked her for the meal and sauntered out.

Linnea set about hurrying through the cleanup and the dishes, then settled Aggie into her chair and gathered her sewing for her. "Do you need anything while I'm in town?" she asked.

"I'd ask you to get me some threads for my piecework, but I can hardly see the stitches any-more," the elderly woman said with a disgusted cluck. "Don't get old, girl. It's no damned fun."

Linnea hung her apron and hurried to her room to check her hair in the grainy mirror. She settled the hat with the daisies on her head, surveyed her dowdy appearance in her baggy brown dress and took one of her precious coins to knot into the corner of a handkerchief and tuck into her pocket. She didn't intend to spend it, but if she needed her own money, she would have it.

When she hurried out, Cimarron had two horses standing in the traces before the springboard. He courteously stepped forward to assist her up to the seat, his polite touch not the least disturbing. He had placed a folded saddle blanket on her side of the bench seat, and as the wagon rolled over the ruts in the road, she was grateful for the padding.

The mountain air still held a morning chill, and though the afternoon would be blazing, Linnea was glad she'd brought her shawl.

As before, when he'd brought her to the ranch, Cimarron was a pleasant traveling companion. "You comfortable, Miz McConaughy?" he asked.

"Yes, thank you," she replied. The baby gave a healthy kick just then, and instinctively she placed her palm on her belly. Embarrassed, she drew her hand away quickly.

"One of my sisters is older than me, and she has two boys," Cimarron told her comfortably.

She remembered his mention of the ornery red-headed sisters. She turned to study his profile.

"My younger sister teaches school back in Indiana."

"Is that where you're from?" she asked.

"Yup. But I didn't want to farm, and I took off on a trail drive when I was just sixteen. My pa left the land to my sister and her husband, and they farm it now."

"Your father is dead?"

"Yes'm. My mama and my younger sister moved to Fort Wayne. Ever been there?"

"No. I've only passed through the southern end of the state."

"Where are you from?" he asked, not prying, but making friendly conversation. Still, the question made her uncomfortable.

"My father moved us around when I was a girl," she said simply. "My husband did the same."

"What did your husband do?"

Linnea had dreaded being asked that question, and she wasn't a very good liar. "He worked on the railroad. What kind of bird is that?"

Her companion glanced in the direction she pointed.

"Stellar's jay," he replied. "See the black crest and the dark blue wings? Noisy birds, those are."

Perched on the limb of a spindly juniper, the bird cawed loudly as if on cue, then took off with a flap of wings.

The rest of their trip was spent in companionable silence. When they reached Rock Falls, Linnea discreetly found an outhouse behind the livery while Cimarron watered the horses.

He showed her to the feed store, where he read the list to the owner and waited on the dock while the bags were loaded into the wagon bed.

Next came the mercantile, and when they entered the establishment, he guided her toward the front, quietly naming the first five items on the list, so she could request them herself.

A small man moved out from the shadows behind a stack of denim trousers and squinted at them. A pair of round spectacles sat atop his shiny bald head, the earpieces stuck into fuzzy yellow-white hair that sprouted on the sides of his head. He wore a white shirt with suspenders and an apron. "Double T, ain't it?"

"Yes," Cimarron replied. "This is Miz McConaughy," he said. "She's our cook now, and she'll be ordering supplies for Mr. Tucker and for her kitchen."

"Pleased to make your acquaintance, ma'am," the man said. "Marcus Carmichael, proprietor, at your service."

"How do you do, Mr. Carmichael. Mr. Tucker needs kerosene, shingles, ten penny nails and a razor," she said easily.

He turned in a sprightly manner and set about gathering the supplies. "Young fella, you'll carry the shingles from next door."

Cimarron said softly, "Give him your cooking supply list next." He tapped his temple, indicating she had it all in her head, then strode away.

Linnea took a breath, closed her eyes, and recalled all the items she'd gone over during the ride, praying she wouldn't forget anything. "I need twenty pounds of coffee, a sack of flour, one of sugar, salt, a barrel of vinegar, baking soda…" She continued ticking off items as Mr. Carmichael gathered them.

"Do you have thread for piecework?" she asked.

"There's a crate over by the fabrics," he replied.

Linnea studied the orderly bolts of colorful fabrics, ran her palm over one of the soft-looking materials and admired the variety of patterns and hues.

"Like something for a new dress?" the store owner asked, surprising her with his nearness.

"Oh, no," she said, snatching back her hand and moving toward the crate which held threads. She picked out a few colors for Aggie.

Back at the counter, he asked, "Need needles, too?" He squinted at a package, then remembered the spectacles on his head and brought them down to study a card of needles through their lenses. "These should do."

Noting his action, Linnea asked without forethought, "Do you sell spectacles?"

He bent to reach under the counter and pulled out a cigar box, which he opened and showed her. "Crystalline lenses," he told her. "They're the finest. The shape of the temples keeps these from falling off." He removed his own and demonstrated. "They're steel, so they're more affordable than gold-filled. Unless you want gold?"

"No, no steel is fine."

"Want to see if they fit properly?" He picked up the eyewear and held them out to her.

"They're not for me, they're for Mrs. Tucker. How much do they cost?"

"A dollar."

"Oh."

"Comes with this nice leather case."

She studied it, thinking.

"Want me to put them on the ranch account?"

"No," she said quickly. Will Tucker had not requested anything other than his supplies and the food necessities. She had no authority to spend a dollar of his money.

Linnea touched the handkerchief tucked into her pocket, felt the hard round coin. A sense of burning independence and pride came over her. She could spend her own money any way she saw fit.

She pulled out her hanky and untied the coin. "I'll pay for them with this."

"I'll wrap up the eyeglasses for you, Miz McConaughy," he said, reaching out for her dollar.

Linnea looked at his hand. Then she looked at the coin. And placed it in his palm.

The store owner's fingers closed over it.

Linnea blinked and looked up to watch him carelessly drop it in his cash box and close the metal lid. Gone. He folded the spectacles into their case, wrapped it in brown paper, and handed her the small package, along with the wrapped thread and needles. "Anything else for you today?"

Linnea accepted her purchase almost reverently. "No, thank you."

Cimarron returned then, and with their shopping finished, he led her out to the wagon. She waited on the seat while he and Mr. Carmichael loaded the rest of the crates and bags and Cimarron covered the supplies with a tarpaulin.

"We can stop a ways outside town to eat," he told her, glancing at the sun overhead in the sky.

She nodded her compliance and the horses jerked the wagon forward. Linnea tucked the small wrapped bundle into one of her roomy pockets for safekeeping.

Chapter Eight

They were back at the ranch in plenty of time for her to start supper. She gave Aggie the thread and needles, and the old woman thanked her, setting them aside to watch Linnea peel potatoes.

Linnea glanced at Aggie, remembering her remarks that morning, and wondering how the woman would react to the gift Linnea had brought back for her. Having second thoughts about her impulsive purchase, she wondered if Aggie would even be willing to try the eyeglasses. "I got something for you."

She dried her hands on her apron, and hurried back to her room where she took the paper-wrapped case from a drawer and carried it back to the kitchen, hoping the woman wouldn't be offended. She almost lost her nerve and ran back to her room, but she'd already told Aggie she had something for her, so she had to go through with it.

Linnea approached shyly. "I got these for you when I was in town."

"You already gave them to me."

"No, the thread was on Mr. Tucker's account. This is something I bought."

Aggie sat up a little straighter. "What is it?"

Linnea unwrapped the paper, revealing the leather case. She opened it and showed Aggie the eyeglasses that lay within.

Aggie's brows shot up. "Spectacles?"

"The mercantile owner uses them. He said these are called crystalline lenses, and that they're the very finest. They make the object you're looking at bigger, so you see it better."

Aggie simply studied the contents of the case.

"Want to try them?" Linnea asked.

Aggie shifted in her rocker for a moment, as though considering. Her expression showed her interest was piqued. "Can't hurt to try," she said finally.

Linnea sat the paper and case aside and lifted the eyeglasses out, opening the earpieces and holding them toward Aggie.

Aggie accepted them, settling the spectacles on her nose while Linnea helped her get the curved metal around her ears. That done, Linnea stepped back.

"Oh, my!" Aggie stared at her and blinked in surprise. "Land sakes, you're kind of pretty, girl!"

She picked up Aggie's embroidery hoop and handed it to her. "Look at this."

"Oh, my," Aggie said again.

"Can you see it better?"

"Looks like it's right in my face," she said with a dry chuckle. "Didn't realize that was blue." She pointed with a gnarled finger to the center of a flower she'd stitched on the fabric. "Thought it was black."

Linnea had knelt down beside her and joined her in looking at the various colors of the threads.

"I used to do a better job," Aggie said wistfully.

"It looks fine to me," Linnea replied.

A moment later, Aggie looked up at her, her faded blue eyes sparkling behind the lenses. "You did a real nice thing, girl. Thank you."

Linnea couldn't remember ever being able to buy a gift. It felt good. Aggie's pleasure seeped into her and warmed a lonely place in her heart. "You're welcome."

Linnea straightened and went back to the potatoes. After they were peeled and covered with water, she glanced over at Aggie. The woman was staring at her.

"You're carryin' a child," she stated.

Uncomfortable with her stare, Linnea nodded.

"I felt your belly when you brushed up against me a couple of times," she said, "but I didn't realize that's what it was for sure. Does Will know?"

"He knows."

Aggie's blaring cackle filled the kitchen. "No wonder he's had an extra burr under his saddle lately. He gave his word he'd let you prove yourself and then he found out you were carryin' a babe. Did his face turn real red?"

Linnea nodded.

Aggie chortled. "Did his ears go back like a horse gettin' ready to buck?"

Linnea couldn't help a cringe at Aggie's apt description of Will Tucker's reaction. It seemed so strange to her that the old woman took perverse pleasure in anything that irritated her stepson. "He was upset and rightly so," she said simply.

Aggie set the rocker to moving and cast a look over Linnea's clothing. "Your husband left you flat broke, huh?"

Linnea nodded again.

Aggie clucked and shook her head as though she sympathized. "Damned fool men. Ain't a one of them have the sense God gave a mule."

Linnea stoked the fire under her potatoes and hurried to set the table.

It wasn't long before the men filtered in and seated themselves. They all showed up with clean hands and faces, most with hair wet and slicked back after their turn at the pump. She surveyed the gathering, noticing the assortment of shirts she had been paid to wash, iron, and mend. They looked mighty nice if she said so herself.

Will Tucker, too, made a habit of coming to the table freshly washed and groomed. Linnea didn't look directly at him, but took sidelong glances when he wasn't looking her way.

The hands were extravagant with their appreciation for the meal and the apple cobbler she'd baked for them that afternoon.

When she served the dessert and poured fresh coffee, silence drifted over the room, and in an almost reverent state, the men slowly consumed the warm cinnamon-flavored dessert.

"You have a considerable talent for baking, Miz McConaughy," Roy told her. "We're lucky you settled for ranch life, instead of cookin' for some fancy restaurant in the city."

Embarrassed by his excessive praise, Linnea dabbed her mouth with her napkin and folded her hands in her lap. "I doubt any fancy restaurant would hire me," she protested with a shake of her head.

Half a dozen voices rose to assure her, and Will set down his coffee cup with a loud thunk. Silence descended on the table. He had a way of squashing a good mood like one would swat a bug.

One by one, the men excused themselves and left the kitchen, until only Linnea, Aggie and Will remained.

"Looked like you bought everything I had on my list," he said in his usual gruff manner.

"Yes."

"Did you get the kitchen supplies you needed?"

She proceeded to list the items she'd purchased on his account, including Aggie's needles and thread.

"Look what else the girl bought." Aggie had maneuvered herself up out of her chair and shuffled over to her sewing basket. She plucked out the eyeglasses and held them up so Will could see them.

"Not on your account," Linnea said quickly, making sure her employer didn't think she'd done anything without his approval.

"Aggie asked for those?" he asked.

"No," she replied.

Aggie put on the glasses and inspected Will with magnified eyes. "You've been frowning so much, you've worn lines in your forehead," she told him.

He ignored her.

Her eyes twinkling, Aggie continued, "She made a *gift* of 'em," she said, emphasizing the word *gift* in a haughty manner. "Some people do kind things just for the heck of it, don't ya know?"

Will glanced from Aggie to Linnea, a muscle in his jaw jumping, and she wasn't sure if his irritation was caused by Linnea or his stepmother...or both. "You bought them yourself?"

"Yes."

"I'll pay you back," he said.

"No need," she said. "It was my idea. I wanted to get them."

His storm-gray gaze moved over her hair and clothing, and she wondered if he was looking to see if she was wearing anything new.

He finished his coffee and stood. "Appears you did a good job with the shopping. That's one less chore I'll need to worry myself over. Plan to go into town every other week for supplies from now on."

Linnea's ears rang from his words, the closest she would likely ever get to hearing praise from the man. Relief washed over her. With Cimarron's help, she'd done well. She'd shown Will Tucker

she was capable of another task, and he'd ac-
knowledged the fact in his gruff manner.

And he'd said nothing about sending her away
now that he knew about the baby she carried; in
fact, he'd said that she'd be doing the shopping!

Her heart suddenly felt as light as a feather.

Without another word, he grabbed his hat and
left the house, the screen door banging behind
him.

"Charming dinner companion, isn't he?" Aggie
remarked.

Linnea was too relived to think critically of the
man right now.

"I'm making a trip out back," Aggie continued,
"and then I'd like to take my sewing to my room.
Would you mind moving my chair in there?"

"Not at all." Linnea stepped beside the fireplace
and found the cane she'd been encouraging Aggie
to use to keep her balance. "Take this."

Aggie accepted it and shuffled out the door.

After moving the rocker, Linnea scraped plates,
and stacked and washed dishes. Although she
didn't mind Aggie's company as she worked,
it was nice to have the kitchen to herself for a
change. She felt free to move about unobserved.

All day she had debated whether or not to accept Nash and Roy's encouragement to see the

colt in the barn, but now knew she would do so when her chores were finished.

Finally, hanging her apron and the flour sack towels to dry, she carried warm water to her room, washed her face, and rebraided her hair. She wound the lengthy rope around her head and pinned it in place.

From her pathetic choice of clothing items, she selected a clean pressed skirt, brown as all of them were, and wore her oversize shirtwaist over it. Once, when she'd been married to Pratt, he'd traded stolen gunpowder for two bolts of fabric—both brown—and a half a dozen chickens.

The fabric had been new and the garments she'd sewn from it were serviceable. And she'd never had anywhere to go that required anything fancier. If she'd ever dreamed of colorful dresses in silky materials, hair ribbons or pearls, it had been long ago and in a state of hopeful innocence she'd long since lost. She hadn't minded all that much until Will Tucker looked her over, and she remembered his sister's lovely clothing and hair.

Linnea smoothed a little glycerin Aggie had given her into her hands and traveled through the darkened kitchen and out the door.

Nash and Roy lounged at the corner of the barn as though waiting for her. They straightened and smiled as she approached, touching their hat brims politely.

"Evenin', Miz McConaughy," Roy greeted her.

They led her into the barn, where lanterns were lit to guide their way. From a rear stall, the young colt pushed his nose through the gate as they approached.

"Oh, look, isn't that darling?" she asked.

"He remembers you," Roy told her.

Nash lifted an iron hook and opened the gate a mere foot. "Slip in."

"It's all right?"

"Sure, his mama's outside, and he's not afraid of you."

Sure enough the colt stretched his neck to catch her scent, and stepped nimbly forward when she entered the stall.

Linnea rubbed his bony forehead and finger-combed his coarse mane. The animal bumped his nose against her arm and nickered.

"You think he really remembers me?" she asked.

"Horses are smart critters," Nash replied. "He knows a friend when he meets one."

Linnea grinned and continued to pet and stroke the colt. She talked to him, and his ears pricked forward with interest.

The two hands allowed her to take all the time

she wanted with her new friend, and eventually, thinking she was taking them away from something else, she told the colt goodbye and stepped out of the stall.

"Join us for coffee, ma'am," Roy said. "We always have a fire of an evenin' and sometimes Clem plays his harmonica."

"Oh, I don't want to intrude," she told him, hanging back.

"You're not intrudin'," he assured her. "The fellas told me to ask you. We'd like your company. Please?"

At those amazing words, she couldn't help but allow Roy and Nash to usher her out of the barn and around back of the bunkhouse a way to where the hands did indeed have a fire built in a circle of blackened stones. An enormous battered coffeepot sat to the side. All the men stood when she approached.

Ben Taylor handed her a cup of coffee and gestured for her to sit on a short stool, which was already waiting. She took the cup and the seat, and sipped the strong hot liquid, feeling sorely out of place. The men took their seats again and gave her encouraging nods.

"Want sugar?" Roy asked, holding a tin can toward her.

She accepted a spoonful and stirred it into the black brew.

"Hope the coffee's to yer likin', ma'am," Clem said with a gap-toothed grin. "Lost a spoon in mine, I did."

Linnea pulled out her spoon and glanced into her cup.

Chuckles erupted around the campfire.

She met their amused friendly gazes and realized she'd been teased.

"Don't mind Clem, he pulls that on a tenderfoot any time he can," Ben explained.

"Miz McConaughy's no tenderfoot," Cimarron objected. "Anybody seen somethin' she didn't know how to do yet?"

Several *no*s were spoken around the gathering, and her cooking skills were highly praised.

Linnea blushed, uncomfortable with the attention.

"Now, Emory Coleville was a tenderfoot," Roy said.

Cimarron chuckled and agreed. To Linnea he said, "This Coleville fella joined a trail drive, writin' a piece for a paper back East, he says. He was watchin' us break a few horses we caught along the trail in Montana."

Clem slapped his leg and hooted. "And he asked

what made the horses so mad that they jumped up and down!"

Laughter rose and Linnea joined in.

"We got a real gully washer one night," Cimarron told her. "Emory's socks got soaked inside his fancy shoes, so he hung 'em on a stick over the fire."

"The stick burned clean in two," Roy added, "droppin' his socks into the fire and scorching them. That crazy tenderfoot had to pull 'em out with another stick and wear 'em that way."

"How about the night we told that Jenkins kid to start the fire?" Clem asked.

Another story unraveled, and in no time the men's banter and laughter had her laughing until her cheeks ached. They included her in their conversations and vied to tell the most outrageous stories about each other. She listened, enjoying their playfulness and the ease with which they spoke to one another and to her.

She hadn't enjoyed herself so much around people for as long as she could remember. She'd never felt as accepted as she did around this mismatched gathering of men, young and old, who hailed from all over the country. And she had spent many a night beside a campfire with a gathering of men.

But those men had been unkempt with cagey

expressions and glittering eyes. Their talk had been furtive, and bottles of whiskey had laced their words and their plans, and made her wary of every move and glance. Her husband had been one of them, but she'd never felt safe, not even when he was present.

Here there was no threat evident, no malice or malcontent on the lips of those who spoke. And Linnea drank it all in, like sipping sweet hot cocoa on a frosty night. A star twinkling overhead caught her attention, and she glanced up. What good fortune had brought her here? And how long could it last?

Chapter Nine

William came upon the lively scene as he left the corral and headed for the barn. Fifty yards away, from the shadows of the building, he stopped and observed the motley gathering around the fire. To his surprise, his young widowed cook sat in the midst of the men's circle, looking for all the world as though she fit right in.

At the moment, Roy and Cimarron were trying to outdo each other in a far-fetched tale about a bear attack that had happened while they were ice fishing two winters ago. The story had grown out of proportion since Will had first heard it, and now included being lost in a cavern and running into a Sioux hunting party.

Even from this distance, the expression on Linnea's face was one of pure discovery and delight. She listened with rapt attention, which only drove the tale tellers to more extended heights of malarkey, and she wore a smile that would have lit the cool evening without a fire.

That smile changed everything about her; her plainness became gentle beauty, her timidity a sweet serenity, and the amazing transformation hit him like a plank in the chest.

He'd observed his men many a night. Some of them he knew from years riding herd, others since he'd started the ranch and hired them on. He was used to being an outsider while they swapped tales and speculated on subjects from ghosts and stars to womenfolk. Roy and Cimarron continually argued good-naturedly about the best knots and the best guns. But Will had never seen them like this with a woman in their midst.

Will hadn't missed the fact that whenever he stepped into their gatherings, the men fell silent and the laughter stopped. He told himself it was because he was their boss, and bosses couldn't afford to be too friendly with their help, but he didn't fool himself. It had been this way on trail drives, too, back when he wasn't the trail boss, but just another hand.

Not so with the widow McConaughy. If anything, the men's antics had increased and the mood become more jovial than ever with her here.

In that second, as he studied her in the firelight,

the sound of her muffled crying across a camp-fire came to mind and brought with it a helpless regret, like a mistake he couldn't go back and fix. At the time, he'd wondered if there had been something he should have done. But she skittered from him like a prairie dog fleeing a fox and besides, he hadn't wanted to encourage her to think he might weaken and let her stay.

Might as well have; he'd broken down and changed his mind the very next morning. Or had it been that night? Had it been those tears?

Clem had pulled out his harmonica and begun to play "Red River Valley," a far cry from his usual saloon repertoire, and Will knew the choice was purely for Linnea's benefit.

Roy poured Linnea more coffee. Will could remember only one young woman, many years ago, who had caught Roy's attention. The girl had married another man, and Roy hadn't seemed inclined to keep company with females since. But his longtime partner was showing the same obvious weakness for Linnea as all the other hands. One after the other.

Somehow the woman had won over his sister, too. Had Corinne felt sorry for her? From day one, Linnea had ingratiated herself with Aggie. And today the eyeglasses. He would've bought 'em for the old woman if she'd said anything. Did Linnea have some deliberate ploy in mind? Get Aggie on her side. Sidle up to his men and get them soft toward her. If that was her plan, it was doggoned damned well working. Will studied each man settled around the fire and calculated their reaction when he finally had to let Linnea go.

And he would have to let her go. Wouldn't he? She was going to have a baby, and this was no place for her or a baby. Why hadn't she realized that herself? Why was he the only one concerned?

He turned and headed to the barn. After all these years, he still understood horses a lot better than he did people.

Cimarron caught Linnea's attention and jabbed a thumb over his shoulder. Instantly, she stood to excuse herself from the gathering. "Thank you for the coffee and the visit," she said.

The men stood and wished her a good-night.

"I'll walk you back, ma'am," Cimarron said, joining her. "I'll show you the spot," he told her in a hushed voice, leading her away from the house in the darkness. "And after this time, you just meet me here. That way no one will see us leavin' together."

The moonlight guided them to a flat bank beside the bubbling stream. Cimarron lit a lantern he'd left in the crook of a tree and knelt to a saddle bag at its base. "I got these today."

He showed her two slates and opened a small cloth bag containing sticks of chalk. "We'll start with learning letters."

"Is that how you do it?" Linnea was somewhat disappointed to see no book in his bag.

He nodded and made a cushion with a saddle blanket for her on the ground beside the lantern. "That's how you do it. You memorize your letters first."

Linnea placed her hands on her cheeks, and her insides jittered. "I do hope I'm smart enough." She'd been worrying about the fact all day.

Cimarron chuckled. "You're plenty smart enough."

He proceeded to draw stick and circle symbols on the slate and tell her the names of the letters and what they sounded like used in words. He had her draw the same letters, and Linnea felt like a clumsy child. She placed her trust in her young teacher, though, believing him that *A* sounded two different ways depending on the word, and that *B* was a letter, not an insect that stung, although the letter was in the word *bee*.

Head swimming, and a million questions later,

she couldn't believe the time was over when Cimarron concluded the lesson and opened his bag to pack the slates away.

Pausing, he held one toward her. "Would you like to keep it with you so you can practice?"

Without hesitation, she accepted the slate and gave him an appreciative smile. Linnea knew he had barely begun teaching her, and she was impatient to learn, but she was grateful for his time and generosity. "Your laundry is no charge from now on," she told him.

"That wasn't our agreement," he told her as they made their way toward the ranch house. "I can't let you do my wash for nothin'."

"Then I will pay you for my lessons."

"Your lessons are my pleasure, ma'am. I want to do them. For nothing. As a friend."

Linnea had never had a friend before. She rolled the word around in her mind. "And I want to do your shirts," she told him. "For nothing. As a—a friend."

She had him there, because he didn't argue any more. "All right then."

He paused fifty yards from the house. "I'll watch you from here. Evenin', Miz McConaughy."

"Night," she replied. After bestowing a grateful smile, she hurried to the house, climbed the back stairs, and entered the kitchen.

Will Tucker sat at the table with a lantern, a ledger book opened before him. He glanced up.

"Mr. Tucker!" She hid the slate behind her skirts.

He nodded and looked down at his figures.

"Can I get you a cup of coffee? There's apple strudel left."

"Got my own coffee." He gestured to a mug on the tabletop.

Removing her shawl, she draped it over the back of a chair, then walked into the pantry, hid the slate behind a crockery jar and scooped dry beans into a kettle. After carrying the pot of beans back to the kitchen, she set it under the pump.

"Here." Will Tucker's chair scraped back, and he stood, moving forward to edge her aside and prime the pump.

Surprised at his helpfulness, she stood aside and watched.

Water splashed into the kettle and he continued until the container was half-full. "That enough?"

"Yes, that's good."

He lifted the pan by the handle and set it on the back of the stove. "Set it here to soak overnight?"

She nodded. "Thank you."

When he went back to his seat, she scooped a measure of salt from the wooden box with her fingers and dropped it into the water.

She looked over her shoulder. He picked up a quill pen and dipped it in ink, then wrote something on the paper. Her attention was drawn to his knuckles, scraped and raw looking.

"What happened to your hand?" she asked, without thinking.

He glanced at the cuts. "Mare backed me against a stall gate today."

"You washed those fingers good?"

He nodded.

"You should probably put something on them or they'll be sore tomorrow when you bend your fingers."

The man turned and looked at her then, making her uncomfortable as always beneath his gaze. She glanced away.

"I suppose so," he said.

"I'll get something." She moved to the shelf beside the pantry which held salves and ointments in tins. Opening one, she sniffed the contents, then returned to the table. "This should do."

He lay down the pen.

She held the tin in one hand, the lid in the other

and stared at him for a second. For the life of her, she could not make herself move any closer.

He turned over his left hand and reached for the tin.

"Let me," she said quickly, stuffing her fear away as though she was stuffing pork into a sausage casing. Poke, poke. Get it all in. There. She took a step forward and stood right beside him. "You don't want this all over your fingers, or you'll mess up your neat pages."

He had to turn sideways, because she had approached him from the left and the cuts were on his right hand. He turned his body on the chair, so that he faced her, and placed the hand on the tabletop.

Setting the lid on the table, Linnea dabbed two fingers into the ointment, finding it thicker than she imagined, and pressed harder, getting a greasy dab. Without looking at his face, she lowered her fingers to his hand and touched the ointment to the raw places. He didn't make a move or utter a sound, simply sat stone still as she gently rubbed it in. His skin was warm, his knuckles rough. Those sensations were impossible to ignore.

The back of his large hand was dusted with dark hair, and she studiously avoided looking past his wrist. Her own hands seemed as small and pale as a child's in comparison. Seconds seemed like an hour, and she felt his gaze on her face the entire time. For some reason beyond her control, his gaze drew hers like a moth to a flame. Slowly, she allowed her gaze to ascend until she was looking directly into those storm cloud eyes.

His lashes were sooty black, and his cheeks were shaded by the growth of an evening beard. At the moment his face was relaxed, without the usual mask of anger, and the unexpected encounter disturbed her more than if he'd been scowling. The expression was so rare, his face so bewilderingly relaxed that her guard eased and her attention traveled his features.

His thick sable brows were perfect for those moody eyes. His nose was large, but not overly, just the right size for his face.

His upper lip bore a sharp bow in the center, his dark beard outlining it, his lower lip thicker. His mouth was surprisingly soft looking.

An odd feeling fluttered in Linnea's breast, a feeling like the first time her baby had moved within her. Following the warm sensation came the horrifying realization that she was studying his face—his mouth, and a mortifying warmth rose in her chest and her cheeks.

Glancing into his eyes, she saw a strange heat

returned there, but she shot her gaze to his hand, finished dabbing the knuckles she'd all but forgotten and backed away as though she'd been burned.

Flustered, Linnea wiped her fingers on a rag, and placed the lid on the tin. She dipped a small pail of warm water from the well on the back of the stove. "If there's nothing else, I'll go now."

"Nothing. Thank you."

She nodded and darted away.

Will stared at the shawl she'd left forgotten on the back of a chair. What had just happened?

He hadn't expected anything from her, hadn't asked for her aid. She'd gone for the salve, rubbed it into his sore knuckles, and before he'd known what was happening, the air had been sucked from the room and the only thing left to breathe had been her. She smelled like soap and vanilla and even a little like mountain air and faintly of smoke from the fire where he'd seen her last.

He hadn't moved a muscle, and she'd been like a mouse tiptoeing around a sleeping giant. When she'd looked up and discovered he was awake and watching her, a dozen things had crossed her face. Fear, fascination and awe were among them. He'd never seen much to brag about looking back from his mirror, and he doubted she was particularly moved by his features. So where had her fascination come from just then?

A scraping sound reached him from the hallway beyond the kitchen, and he recognized the source. She pushed the bureau in front of her door every night; he'd figured that out early on. He couldn't be offended, she hadn't known him from Adam when she arrived, and a woman probably had to look out for herself any way she could.

But it rankled that *she* didn't trust *him.* There was the rub.

She didn't seem like the game-playing type. But she could be deceptive, he'd learned that the hard way. She'd charmed Aggie, then the men. Maybe he was next on her list of people to convince to let her stay.

Will slammed the ledger shut with a snort. It would take a lot more than a little ointment dabbing to convince him of that.

Midmorning the following week, a black horse pulled a buggy up the drive to the house and stopped. A man in dark trousers and jacket, wearing a narrow-brimmed hat climbed down.

Wiping her hands, Linnea went to the screen door and looked out.

Will Tucker came from the closest corral to

greet the man. They shook hands and spoke for a moment. Linnea's thoughts ran to making fresh coffee. She'd taken cinnamon rolls from the oven earlier, and could serve those to the guest.

The man reached up to the floor of the buggy and retrieved a black bag. A medical bag. He glanced toward the house, and the two men started forward.

Linnea's heart hammered and she backed away from the doorway in a near panic. A doctor! Will Tucker had sent for a doctor.

Chapter Ten

William pulled the screen door open with a squeak and ushered Dr. Hutchinson into a warm kitchen smelling of cinnamon and yeast. His attention moved to his young cook who stood against the table staring at them.

Wearing a panicked expression, her gaze darted around as though seeking a route of escape, but apparently her feet wouldn't cooperate, because she didn't move. The look on her face disturbed him.

"Something smells wonderful," the doctor said, removing his hat. Keeping his attention on Linnea, Will took the hat and hung it on a peg.

She stood with her hands clenched in front of the apron that covered her rounded stomach, her face ghastly pale. What in creation was wrong with her?

From her rocker near the fireplace, Aggie rocked and blinked through her new spectacles.

"Mrs. McConaughy, this is Dr. Hutchinson," Will told her.

"How do you do, ma'am," the doctor said.

Linnea's stricken eyes moved from the doctor to Will with a pleading expression that seemed to ask why he'd done this to her. He got the distinct impression that she felt he'd betrayed her somehow.

The silence drew out, making her displeasure perfectly clear to everyone. "I don't need a doctor," she said finally. "I'm not sick."

Damned infuriating woman! Will felt the anger rising in him and held it in check. He took a step toward her, and she jumped sideways.

Exasperated, he silently cursed her pigheaded foolishness.

"Excuse us a minute," he said to the doctor, and took her by the upper arm and led her out onto the back porch and closed the door. She pulled away from him and glared.

"What did you jump like that for?" he asked. "What's the doctor going to think?"

"I don't care what he thinks."

"I told you that you would have to see a doctor," he said, keeping his voice low.

She wouldn't look at him.

"A woman should have a doctor when she's…

she's…" He stumbled over the words. "He'll just make sure everything's okay. No harm in that." And remembering her objections, he added, "And I'm paying the bill. You're in my employ, and I will take care of the cost."

She looked at him then, and the pain in her eyes was something he couldn't understand. His awkward helplessness frustrated him. She was like a frightened horse that didn't understand he meant no harm. "Are you afraid?" he asked finally.

Again her gaze skittered away. No reply.

He couldn't accompany her while the doctor examined her. It wouldn't be right, and she didn't take any comfort from him anyway. He didn't understand her fear, but he could try to alleviate it. "Aggie will stay with you," he said curtly.

That decided, he ushered her back into the kitchen without touching her again. She kept her distance so he wouldn't. "Aggie, will you keep Mrs. McConaughy company?" he asked.

Aggie looked surprised, but without a word of complaint, thank God, she pushed from her chair and latched on to her cane. Shuffling slowly, she accompanied Linnea down the hall toward her room. A minute later Dr. Hutchinson followed.

Will went back outside, stood in the sunshine and puzzled over Linnea's reaction to a doctor's visit. A woman should be glad to have medical care, someone of whom she could ask questions. She should be grateful to have her baby's health assured. Instead, she was obviously resentful. The widow McConaughy was the most confusing, frustrating, maddening woman he'd ever met.

Try to get rid of her, she wouldn't leave. Try to help her, she didn't want it.

His thoughts rolled back to the day when he'd been trying to take her back to Denver, and she'd said, "I would never have come if I'd known that you wouldn't like me." *Wouldn't like her?* What the doggoned damned hell had *liking* her had to do with any of this? He didn't have to like her. He'd thought he was hiring a cook. Instead he got himself into a whole peck of trouble he didn't have time or inclination to deal with.

He'd sent Ben Taylor with a message for a telegram to Corinne, but Lord, it would have been so much more satisfying to give his sister a piece of his mind in person. All the things he wanted to say to her still lashed about in his head. In the message, he had ordered her to come help out now that she'd landed him in this fix. He couldn't wait until she showed up. *If* she showed up. His sister had a mind of her own.

The back door opened behind him. "You joining us for coffee?" Dr. Hutchinson stood in the doorway, smiling.

Will leaped up the stairs and entered the kitchen.

Linnea set a plate of fragrant rolls on the table and poured only three cups of coffee. Her face was more pink than white now, but she pointedly didn't look at Will.

Aggie settled herself on a chair and Linnea handed her a plate.

Linnea set a plate and a cup in front of Will, then swept out the door.

The doctor sweetened his coffee and bit into a pastry.

"Is Mrs. McConaughy well?" Will asked finally.

"She's fit as a fiddle," the doc replied. "Mrs. Tucker tells me your cook has gained weight since she's been here. Good thing, I'd say."

To Will's stupefaction, he felt relieved at the pronouncement of Linnea's good health. He conversed with the other man who ate three helpings and then patted his belly. Finally the doctor wished Aggie a good day and stood.

Once outside, the doctor said, "Might skittish, your widow woman."

Without reply, Will handed him coins in payment.

The doctor tucked them into his vest pocket.

"You think she was really married or just made that up so's to have a name for her baby?"

Will looked at Dr. Hutchinson oddly. Will had asked Linnea if she'd really been married, and wondered why the doctor would question it. "She claims she was married. Why do you wonder?"

"Just a guess. Seems more like a girl than a woman. Maybe some scoundrel took advantage of her. Maybe someone forced himself on her." He shrugged. "'Course, maybe she's just the jittery sort."

Will took the black medical bag and placed it in the buggy, then handed Dr. Hutchinson the reins. "Thanks for makin' the trip."

"Send for me when her time comes. Or if she has any problems. I'll get here soon as I can."

Will waved him off and turned to seek out Linnea in the garden. She was wearing a cloth over her hair, and the apron she was never without no longer disguised her belly. She used a hoe with energy, hacking at offending weeds that grew among the vegetable plants.

He was tempted to go over and speak to her, but instead kept his distance. He knew what he needed to know. She was fit and her baby was fine. Talking to her would make it seem that he cared more than he should.

And he didn't.

He had a horse waiting for him in the far corral when he reached it. One he'd separated from a herd earlier in the week, and had been working with every day since. So far, he could get inside the pen and stand near the gate without the whiskey-colored stallion galloping back and forth in fear, its hooves churning up dust. Each time Will tried to get any closer, the animal reared and screamed in fright, the whites of its eyes a round circle.

Will stood inside the pen, allowing the horse to catch his scent, look him over, grow accustomed to his presence. After an hour, Will took two steps forward and stopped. The horse recognized the difference and shied away, but didn't rear. It assessed the new situation and kept its attention on Will, shaking its massive head so that its mane fluttered in the breeze.

Getting the stallion used to him gave Will plenty of time to think. He thought too much most of the time lately, made himself crazy with thinking, in fact. The few hours that he slept each night were the only moments his thoughts didn't revolve around the work he needed to do and the problems that had been added to his load with Linnea McConaughy's arrival.

She had given him no reason to let her go. She'd done every bit of work she'd been assigned, and had even taken on more tasks that weren't required.

Apparently she was healthy and at no risk. The thought eased and disturbed at the same time. The closer she got to her time, the more impossible it would be to send her away.

He had to face it: she would be here until her baby was born.

For now she was more of an asset to the operation of the ranch than a detriment, he grudgingly admitted. But in a few months, after the baby came, when she had an infant to care for, then it would be time for her to leave.

He talked to the stallion before ending the lesson, getting the animal used to his voice, as well as his nearness.

Standing in the corral, he had missed the noon meal, and Linnea's cinnamon rolls only carried him over for so long. By supper time he was ravenous. After washing he entered the kitchen where the men were settling onto their seats.

A huge platter of fried chicken sent steaming waves of mouthwatering aroma into the air. Bowls of mashed potatoes, baked beans, and cooked carrots made his stomach growl. Will tucked into the meal with gusto.

Linnea didn't look at him, not even when she poured cold glasses of buttermilk and set one in front of him. She sat at the opposite end of the table with Aggie and ate in silence. Roy finished eating and immediately filled a tub with sudsy hot water and washed pans and utensils. Will's foreman often lent Linnea a hand with the cleanup, a familiar chore since he and Will had always taken turns with kitchen tasks before her arrival.

Will overheard Linnea speaking to Roy. "When you're finished, would you mind setting up the tub in the pantry for me?"

The large pantry doubled as a bathing chamber.

"I'll carry water for you, too, ma'am," Roy replied.

"Thank you, Mr. Jonjack."

"Glad to do it," he replied.

Linnea took Will's empty plate and replaced it with a smaller one that held a slice of dried-apple pie. Still, she didn't look at him. Why hadn't she asked him to help with the tub? Come to think of it, she'd never asked him. All this time, she'd either hauled the tub and the water herself or asked one of his men for help.

And he hadn't thought to offer.

Will drove away that weak thought. What the doggoned damned hell did he care? Just less work for him, and he had enough to do.

Glancing up, he caught Aggie piling on the agony with a taunting little pleased-all-to-blazes smile, and his hide warmed in irritation. All women were more bother than they were worth. He left his slice of pie unfinished and pushed away from the table.

She didn't talk to him for a week, not that he gave a good damn.

On Sundays the men looked out for themselves after breakfast. Linnea prepared their morning meal, but after that, they were on their own. Early evening arrived, and the steel triangle Clem had some time ago devised as a way for Linnea to call the men to dinner rang out.

Curious men appeared from the bunkhouse and various activities, speculating among themselves as to what was wrong. Will had been working with the stallion, so he was one of the last to straggle in.

Linnea had prepared lemonade, and she filled metal cups from a bucket and passed them around, surprising the hands with a tray of sugar cookies.

Will accepted a cup and tasted the cold sweetened drink.

"I only just discovered where the ice was stored," she told Cimarron.

Last winter Will and Roy had spent days cutting ice and storing it between thick layers of straw in a holding cave they'd dug into the side of a hill, in anticipation of a day such as this.

Ben and Nash sat on the porch steps beside Linnea; other men situated themselves on the railing, and a couple of them stood. Will marveled at the unlikely sight of the grizzled cowboys sipping lemonade on his back porch.

Will let his gaze settle on Linnea in the shade, her cheeks pink from her exertions in the warm kitchen. A curl of rich mahogany hair escaped her braid to lie against her slender neck. She took a drink, and her delicate throat moved.

The sun felt good on his shoulders; the lemonade was sweet and cold. Even in her mousy brown dress, Linnea made a becoming feminine picture, and it occurred to Will that subtle changes had evolved since her arrival. A Sunday afternoon refreshment was a new and obviously welcome diversion.

A bee hung in the air behind her head and flitted forward.

Nash raised his hand to swat the insect away.

Linnea's expression blanched. She jerked back instinctively, raising her arm to shield her face and scooting away at the same time. Her cup of lemonade hit her skirt, then clattered on the wooden porch floor and rolled.

"It was just a bee, Miz McConaughy," Nash said in apology.

Linnea lowered her arm, her face blazing, and glanced up at the air nearby.

The other men's stunned silence told Will he hadn't been imagining her defensive reaction. She'd had a purely elemental gut reaction to what she must have assumed was Nash raising his hand to her. It was glaringly obvious that she had fully expected him to wallop her good.

The lemonade in Will's stomach turned sour. He tossed the remainder out on the ground and stepped forward.

"Go back to the bunkhouse," he ordered the men.

"Thanks for the lemonade, ma'am." Subdued thanks filtered back as the men set down their cups and left.

"I didn't mean no harm," Nash said defensively to Will.

"I know," Will replied.

"I'm awful sorry, Miz McConaughy," he said.

"It's all right," she said. "I—I'm just afraid of bees. It wasn't your fault."

Nash sauntered off, glancing back over his shoulder.

Will set about picking up the tin cups and stacking them on the empty cookie plate. "Go change your clothes."

Seeing her recoil had made him feel sick. He knew now that he wasn't the only man Linnea flinched from, but that didn't make him feel any better.

She got to her feet. She hadn't met his eyes in a week, and she sure wasn't ready to now, he figured, so he ignored her, and she went inside.

When he carried the tray in, she was nowhere in sight, and neither was Aggie. He found hot water, poured it in a basin and scraped in soap shavings, then washed the cups and a few bowls and the cookie pans.

"I was going to do those." Linnea had changed dresses and carried the wet one into the kitchen. She set it aside in a wad.

"They're done now," he said.

She picked up a towel. "I didn't intend more work for you."

He pulled the towel out of her hand, and she

looked up at his face. Finally. There was so much unreadable emotion behind her brown eyes that they were shiny with it.

"If I hadn't wanted to do them, I wouldn't have," he said.

He wanted to tell her that she had nothing to fear from anyone on his ranch. Especially not from him. But she wouldn't believe him. Why should she? He would have to show her. Just like he showed that whiskey-colored stallion day after day by standing in the corral and letting the animal learn that nothing bad was going to befall it while he was there.

"I'm sorry about what happened," she said.

"It's okay."

"It's just that I'm afraid of bees."

"Everybody's afraid of something."

She just looked at him, as though gauging his sincerity. She hadn't met his gaze for days and now when she did, her expression pained him so, he wished he could look away and stop it. But he didn't. He let her golden-brown gaze find the chink in his armor and slide in a knife blade.

She blinked and her lips parted. "What are you afraid of?" she asked.

Chapter Eleven

What was he afraid of.

You. The reply that had jumped into his head rocked him to the core. Her! Why would he be afraid of a mousy wisp of a girl, and why would he even think it? He wasn't afraid of her. "I don't particularly cotton to small spaces."

The admission tripped off his tongue. Why on God's green earth had he said that? He'd never even admitted the fact to himself consciously, just knew he got uncomfortable when confined. Mad at himself, he picked up the metal basin and carried it toward the back door. "Soap's about gone," he said, changing the subject. "Plannin' to make more soon?"

"I was going to do it after the laundry is finished."

He dumped the dishwater and returned. "Get some rest now. Tomorrow starts a new week."

He turned his back and left the kitchen.

Linnea glanced after him, then picked up the wet dress. She was tired, and he had taken care of the dishes. She would simply hang this dress to dry and launder it with the rest of the clothing the following morning. She would have time to practice her letters before she met Cimarron.

They had taken off the past two Saturdays, the night that most of the men went into town. But fortunately for her, her young teacher was willing to pursue her lessons on Sundays, too, and she looked forward to learning more each evening.

Her reaction to Nash raising his arm to strike at the bee had humiliated her, but Will Tucker had allowed her to explain it away and had somehow even assured her it was okay. When everything she did made him angry, his lack of reaction to that had come as a surprise.

But avoiding his wrath was a consuming task, and she had no false illusions that tonight was a onetime respite. Every hour of every day required her utmost vigilance and her best effort. A niggle of apprehension worried her now.

She hadn't the vaguest notion how to make soap.

Cimarron was waiting for her by the stream, and her lesson proceeded. They had gone through the entire alphabet now, and she was memorizing the letters and sounds with ease. She recited them to herself the following morning as she scrubbed clothes and hung them on the line to dry. Practicing made the work go faster and gave her an even greater sense of accomplishment.

"Aggie," she said hesitantly, approaching the old woman in her rocker. "Do you know how to make soap?"

Aggie peered up from her needlework, her faded blue eyes enlarged by the spectacles. "Yup. You want to do it over a fire outside. Smells somethin' fierce."

"I plan to attempt it tomorrow with your guidance."

"You won't be makin' soap tomorrow, girl."

"Why not?"

"Takes three or four days of soakin' the ashes to make lye. You'll need five or six bushels of 'em. I have a recipe somewhere."

"I should start right away if it takes that long. Where do I get ashes? Whenever I clean the stove or the fireplace, I set the bucket outside and someone always empties it."

"Ask Roy where the barrel of ashes is kept."

Linnea knelt in front of her chair. "Please don't tell Mr. Tucker I didn't know how."

"Honey, I don't offer that man information." Aggie patted Linnea's shoulder.

At noon, Linnea asked Roy about the ashes, and he offered to start the lye for her. She watched as he carried a barrel with holes in the bottom behind the house and placed it beneath the hang of the eave, standing it upon a small stack of bricks. He then pushed a shallow tub underneath. Into the barrel he dumped several bushel baskets of ashes and poured a bucket of water onto them.

"That'll get ya started," he said.

"Thank you, Roy."

Inside she said to Aggie, "Now what do I do?"

"Just wait a few days while the ashes set, and then you pour water through to make the lye drip out the bottom."

And so she went about the next days with her usual cooking chores, as well as a thorough cleaning of the house.

Linnea loved Will Tucker's home. The rooms were not large, but adequate and filled with sturdy furniture and thick rugs. She took pride in polishing the varnished wood floors until they gleamed and washing the windows until they sparkled. No curtains hung on the downstairs windows, but there were shades on the two in the room she used.

The room beside the kitchen held a table and

chairs and a marble-topped sideboard, which Aggie said belonged to her. Meals were all taken in the enormous kitchen and Linnea had never seen the dining room used.

As a child, Linnea's home had been a crowded two-room cabin. During her marriage to Pratt, she'd stayed in cabins, tents, barns and an occasional seedy hotel, but had often slept under the stars in all types of weather. She'd never owned more than a few pieces of clothing and as many cooking utensils as would fit in a saddlebag.

Until meeting Will Tucker's sister, she had never known people who lived in homes and had nice things. This place was as fine as any place she could have dreamed for her baby. If only she could be assured of staying, then the worry that plagued her every day and night would be lessened.

"Never seen this place so clean since it was new," Aggie remarked one afternoon. Sitting in her rocker with a pan on her lap, she helped Linnea peel potatoes.

"I've never had such a nice place to take care of," Linnea replied.

"It's pretty simple," Aggie replied. "Not like my house, I assure you. My husband built a fine house and all the furnishings to go with it."

"It sounds lovely."

Aggie sighed. "It was."

Linnea let a peel drop and studied her. "Who lives in the house now?"

"Banker fella bought it for his family."

Linnea dumped all the peeled potatoes into a kettle and pumped water over them, before coming back for the scraps and the knives.

"He left it to Will, he did."

Linnea paused. "Who left what?"

"Jack left the house to Will."

She wouldn't have imagined that.

"And all his railroad stock and investments to Corinne."

That explained why the young widow and her children could afford to live as well as they did, Linnea thought. "Didn't he own a business, too?"

Aggie brushed her palms together. "He left the mill to a son nobody even knew about. Seems he had this boy while he was married to his first wife."

Linnea didn't know what to say. She could only imagine the shock that Aggie must have experienced, finding out a stepson she hadn't known about had inherited her husband's business. It must have been difficult for Will Tucker to learn the fact as well.

"What did you do?" She couldn't imagine Aggie

being as poor as Linnea had been when her husband died. Aggie's man had been wealthy.

"Will signed the deed to the house over to me and went back to Texas. Didn't see hide nor hair of him for ten years."

Will Tucker's generosity toward Aggie wasn't that difficult to absorb. Ever since Linnea had met him, he'd been concerned over the old woman's welfare. For all Aggie's taunting and their obvious distaste for each other, the two had come to some sort of unspoken truce in order to live in the same house.

"What happened then?" Linnea asked.

Aggie straightened in her chair, placed her bony hands on the arms, and rocked. "He came to Indiana on his way out here. He'd bought this land a few years before and was ready to start building."

Listening, Linnea wiped her hands on her apron and sat on a bench across from Aggie.

"I was there by myself," she said. "Took a bad fall a month or so before he came by."

Linnea imagined Will Tucker going into his late father's home and finding Aggie in her degenerated condition. "Did he invite you to come here?"

Aggie cackled. "He barked, 'You're comin' with

me and I won't stand for any argument.' Not exactly an invitation."

Linnea could hear him saying the words and just the way he would have said them. Like an order. "But you came."

Aggie nodded sadly. "Never had any children of my own. I was on the shelf when Jack and I married, and thought I was lucky just to have him look twice, let alone marry me and set me up in a fine house."

"Too bad you and Mr. Tucker couldn't..."

"Couldn't what?"

"Get along better."

"That's on my head, but it suits us fine now," she replied with a snort. "Neither one of us would know what to do if the other got soft."

Their relationship was an odd one, but Linnea was far from knowing anything about how families should get along. At least Will Tucker hadn't left Aggie alone or pawned her off on someone else. She admired him for that.

Over the next days, Linnea's lessons progressed. She had learned most of the alphabet, except for a few she mixed up. Most evenings she joined the men around their fire for an hour or so before stealing away to meet Cimarron.

In time she returned to the soap-making task,

pouring water into the barrel every hour for two days. With Aggie giving her instructions, she drew off part of the lye, mixed the lime with boiling water and poured it back through. She had never in the past appreciated a bar of soap as she would for the rest of her life, she was sure.

Finally Aggie judged the lye strong enough, so Linnea built a fire in the pit the hands used at night, set up an enormous kettle and boiled the lye with grease and a bit of quicklime. When the mixture became thick and ropy, Aggie pronounced it ready.

Dipping the hot liquid out into pails, Linnea carried it to the root cellar and poured it into a clean barrel.

Back aching and arms exhausted as she poured the last pail, she lost her grip. The bucket hit a stone on the side of the fire and the hot mixture splashed up onto her hand.

Linnea yelped and let go of the pail. It overturned, allowing an entire bucket of her hard work to pour over the flames and sizzle. The smell burned her eyes.

Pain shot up her arm.

"Let me see," Aggie said, rising from her stool with jerky movements.

Linnea showed her the mixture still burning

her first finger, thumb and the back of her hand. It stung so frightfully, tears welled in her eyes.

"Stick it in the rain barrel quick-like," the old woman told her.

Linnea did as Aggie said, swishing her hand to remove the grease and lye concoction. The cold water barely eased the discomfort.

"We'll get some ointment on that and bandage it."

Her hand throbbed. "This can't stop me from working."

"Girl, you're gonna have to let that hand heal."

"It will, but I have to fix supper and do dishes."

Aggie gave her a skeptical glance over the top of the spectacles. "You're not gonna be doin' dishes with that hand."

Linnea felt frantic over the thought of being unable to perform her duties. What would Will Tucker do? Tears dropped onto the surface of the water. "Don't tell him!" she said quickly. "Promise me you won't tell him."

Aggie hobbled a step closer with her cane and took Linnea's elbow, turning Linnea to face her. "Granted, he ain't the sweetest pickle in the barrel, but the man isn't going to send you packing over this."

"He's just waiting for a reason to send me away,"

Linnea replied. "This is just the excuse he needs." She gave Aggie an imploring look. "Please don't let on. I'll get by, I swear I will."

"Come on. Let's get to the house and take care of that hand. I won't tell him. Just don't let me catch you doin' any harm to yerself. You let Roy handle the dishes for a time."

"I will, I promise."

Aggie applied salve and wrapped Linnea's hand and finger in clean soft cloth. Linnea hid it in the folds of her skirts and sought help for the cleanup near the bunkhouse. Nash took care of the kettle and supplies, while she doused the fire.

She prepared supper, biting her lip and holding back a groan each time she used the wrapped hand. When the men came in, she hid her bandage with a towel, using it as a hot pad as she served food and coffee.

She ate with her left hand, and no one seemed to notice. Will cast her a glance from time to time, and she cringed under each look, no matter how scarce.

Finally the meal ended. Will strode out with the rest of the hands and Roy stayed behind, stacking plates.

"Linnea'll let you do those tonight, won't you, girl?" Aggie said.

"Yes," she replied. "Thank you, Roy."

With his shirtsleeves pushed to his elbows, he poured water, scraped soap and washed the dishes efficiently, whistling all the while. "I'm pleased to help, but I am a wonderin' if you're feelin' poorly, Miz McConaughy," he said while drying a pan.

"Just a little tired," she replied, which was true. The soap making combined with the pain had left her exhausted. "In fact, I won't be joining the men tonight. Mention it to Cimarron for me, will you, please?"

"Surely." He finished the task and wiped the table. "You ring the dinner bell if you need anything later."

She thanked him, praying she wouldn't need anything and that her hand would feel better the next day.

She slept in starts and fits for two nights, waking to the throbbing pain and trying uselessly to find a comfortable place to lay her hand. On the third day, she got up earlier than usual because she couldn't sleep, started the fire, heated water and prepared biscuits and gravy ahead of time.

As had become her habit, she carried a pail of

hot water up the stairs and set it on the floor outside her boss's door.

As she straightened, the door opened, catching her by surprise.

Chapter Twelve

"Something wrong?" he asked. He wore only a pair of trousers, which left his broad chest and wide shoulders bare to her startled gaze. The night she'd helped him tend the injured colt, she hadn't allowed herself to look, but her self-restraint had fled between then and now, and she stared.

Tanned skin sculpted his muscled upper body. Curly black hair matted the area in the shape of a T and narrowed into the waistband of his pants. The lantern she carried created shadows on each ridge and hollow and gave his body a warm golden glow. If she reached out and touched him, she knew his skin would be warm and smooth. Her fingertips tingled at the thought, and the sensation made her remember her burns and feel them afresh.

"Nothing's wrong," she managed to say. "Just

up a little early today." She had the presence of mind to keep her injured hand at her side.

She'd seen only a few men without their shirts, and this one looked nothing like any of those. Her husband had been spare and lean. Will Tucker would have made two of him.

He glanced down. "You don't have to bring me water every morning. I have cold from the night before."

"Hot is better for shaving," she said.

His gaze wandered, taking in her hair and face, his expression softer with his hair tousled and the hint of sleep still on his face. His equanimity was almost more frightening than his anger, and a tremor rippled through her body.

"Yes, it is," he agreed. "Thank you."

Breathing had become more difficult, which was surprising because the stairs had never winded her before. Her heart was racing and she fought the urge to reach up and make sure her hair was not straggling around her face, but she held the lantern in her good hand and kept the other hidden.

"You sure something's not wrong?" he asked.

"I—I'm sure." Quickly, she turned away.

Behind her the door closed with a soft click.

Shortly she had breakfast on the table and coffee poured. Will Tucker came into the kitchen, his face freshly shaven, and tossed water out the back door. The men entered and the meal was underway. She avoided her employer's gaze and saw to Aggie's food as well as her own.

By noon, she didn't feel well. Her skin felt feverish and her head hurt, but she stoically pretended nothing was amiss and went about her chores.

Only half the men were there to eat; the others were riding fences and had packed a cold meal. Her employer had been studying her with a critical eye, and Linnea did her best to avoid him. She stood with her back to the table, slicing a loaf of bread.

"What's wrong with your hand?" Will Tucker's voice sent a start of apprehension up her spine.

She stilled the knife, her heart hammering. "Nothing."

"Turn around and show me."

Desperate to avoid him learning the truth, she doubled her effort to slice the bread neatly. Silence had fallen over the room.

Wood scraped. Boot heels thudded across the wooden floor. "I said show me your hand."

His voice was so authoritative, she would have obeyed if she'd been able to move. Instead she stood there, her knees starting to shake, her heart thumping wildly in her chest, her bandaged hand still clutching the knife.

His enormous hand came into her line of vision, took the knife from her and laid it down. Capturing her wrist, he raised her hand for his inspection and frowned at the wrapping. "What did you do?"

"It's nothing. I'm fine."

Without hesitation, he began to peel away the white bandages. He continued gently unwinding, and as more fabric fell away, the last layer of material stuck to a portion of the wound. He stopped, but she couldn't hold back a cry.

He sucked in air through his teeth and bore his stormy gaze into hers. "This is a burn."

She nodded mutely.

"What happened?"

She looked down. "I splashed a little of the boiling lye mixture when I was making soap."

"Day before yesterday?"

"Yes."

"Why didn't you tell me?"

Benches scraped and the back door squeaked open and shut a couple of times. The ranch hands had all made a speedy exit by the sound of it.

"I didn't want you to be mad." She didn't look

up. "I didn't want you to send me away because of my clumsy mistake."

"You should have asked someone to help you." The anger lacing his voice was a direct contrast to the gentle way he held her hand cupped in his. She stared at the sight of his enormous fingers on her pale skin, and warmth crept into her cheeks. Her breathing constricted as it had while looking at his unclad body earlier.

With the other hand, he reached up, and she stoically kept herself from flinching. He tucked a knuckle under her chin and forced her head up until she had no choice but to look at him. "You're the damned stubbornedest woman I ever knew."

Linnea's heart hammered from his closeness, the warmth of his hand and the fervent look in his storm-gray eyes.

"Lets me off the hook," Aggie said from behind him.

He cast the old woman a sidelong glance. "You're still the crotchetiest." Turning back to Linnea, he said, "Let's pour a little water over that and loosen the bandage."

Letting go of her chin, he kept hold of her wrist, and they moved a few feet to the basin. Will Tucker dipped a ladle of warm water from the well on the stove, tested the temperature with a finger, then drizzled it over the bandage. After a few seconds, the fabric loosened enough that he could pull it cleanly away.

"I'm turnin' in," Aggie said. She had stood and turned toward the back hall.

"Call out if you need anything," Linnea told her.

The woman waved off her suggestion and shuffled away.

"What did you use on this?" he asked.

"The salve in the green tin, I think."

He touched the backs of his fingers to her cheek and startled, she stiffened and pulled away. "You have a fever," he said gruffly.

"I'm just hot from the stove."

"I don't think so. You shouldn't have been using this hand, cooking and lifting. Not giving it time to heal was damned foolish."

An ache grew in her chest at his admonishment, and overwhelming feelings of loneliness and discouragement swept over her. She'd been doing the best she could, surviving the only way she knew how, living with the constant worry of failing and having nowhere to go and no way to provide for her baby.

"Sit in the rocker," he said.

Resigned, she did as he ordered.

He bent over Aggie's sewing basket and found

a needle, then struck a match and ran it through the flame. Taking a tin of salve from a cupboard, he asked her if there were clean bandages.

"In the crate there," she said, gesturing.

He tore the strips narrower, then carried them and the tin to where she sat and knelt.

He extended his large palm in a gesture ordering her to give him her hand again. She meekly did so.

Will studied the red blistered skin. The burn must pain her something fierce, but Linnea had kept on with her work for two days without so much as a word to him, as though he was some sort of tyrant.

Her hand was small and delicate in his, the bones of her wrist so fragile, he took care not to bruise her.

With steady, sure movements, he pierced half a dozen blisters with the needle and used a clean rag to dry them. Mindful of her injury, he spread a thick layer of salve to seal the wounds.

Throughout his doctoring, she hadn't made a sound. He looked up at the same time she did, and their gazes locked. Tendrils of hair had come loose around her face and curled becomingly near her temples and ears. Her cheeks were flushed, and her eyes were wide and luminous in the lantern light.

She had a clean feminine smell all her own, a delicate combination of her crisply starched apron, her lustrous hair and some mysterious woman scent that captivated him as no perfume ever could.

His gaze slid to her lips, parted and moist looking, and he had a crazy fleeting image of kissing her. He imagined the sweet softness and taste of her mouth and his body reacted.

Will turned his attention to wrapping her hand. "You're not to use this hand again until I say you may."

"But there's water to heat in the morning, and breakfast to cook, and—"

He looked up again. "I'll get water. Roy will put on breakfast."

"But it's my job," she protested, her voice weak. "I get paid to do those things."

Her burns were not severe, but they would heal more quickly if she cared for them and rested the hand. He knew she was hurting and wished he could take the pain for her. "Your job for now is to rest and heal. Understood?"

She nodded resignedly, her expression so crestfallen, he couldn't comprehend. He finished the bandage, tied the end in a small secure knot and sat back on his heels to look at her.

The memory of her soft crying across the camp-fire that first night came to him again as he studied her. He'd wondered then if she missed her husband; it hadn't been that long since his death. She was alone and carrying a child—he hadn't known that at the time. But never in all the days and hours since then had he seen her cry. And he hadn't actually seen her that time—she had thought he was sleeping and had hidden her weeping beneath a blanket.

She'd been completely inappropriate for the job he'd wanted done—or so he'd thought at first. He'd been expecting a woman later in years, a woman with experience and a married life behind her, someone who could handle the hardships of ranch life.

He'd seen Linnea McConaughy as a frail little mouse of a girl, certainly not looking old enough to be a widow, and definitely not having the appearance of a sturdy capable worker.

Had he been so stubbornly narrow-minded that he hadn't wanted to give her a chance because of her tender age and her diminutive size? Had he imagined some weakness in her that was…perhaps a weakness in himself?

Will didn't like feeling out of control and he didn't like it when things didn't go as he planned. Linnea wasn't in his plans. And he definitely felt a progressive weakness toward her.

A weakness that created the sense of being trapped in a small suffocating space. That weakness frightened him, but the other sensations she prompted blotted out reason and logic and simply had him *feeling.*

There was nothing erotic or romantic about Linnea standing at the stove or pouring him coffee or leaving clean laundry on the foot of his bed. But there was something familiar and reassuring about having her here, bustling about his house and sharing meals. Her voice was a silver bell in the midst of the men's clanging banter, and Will had come to listen for it.

He didn't necessarily like the surprising jumble of thoughts and feelings, because he hadn't planned on having them—hadn't planned on Linnea. But at that moment he couldn't resist reveling in the sensory pleasure of her feminine scent and softness, in the lure of her liquid brown eyes and soft-looking lips.

Her size, her vulnerability, the hesitant way she looked at him, made him feel protective toward her.

"Linnea…" he said simply.

Her luminous gaze fluttered over his hair and face to fasten on his mouth. That was his undoing.

He leaned toward her, raised his face and pressed his lips to hers.

Chapter Thirteen

She didn't move a muscle, didn't breathe beneath the tentative kiss.

Her mouth was as soft and warm as he'd imagined, and she smelled like starch and vanilla and the ointment on their fingers. With only their lips touching in a sweet warm persuasion of the senses, he prolonged the contact, waiting patiently until she relaxed and began to breathe, and then he changed the angle of their lips and deepened the kiss.

His fingers ached to reach for her, to delve into her hair and experience yet another sublime sensation, but he held himself in check, not wanting to frighten or rush her. He didn't want her to pull away and end the pleasure of this sweet discovery.

To bring about the dream of his ranch, he'd learned to shut out physical needs and loneliness.

His determination and anger had kept him from losing focus. Until now.

It was Linnea who broke the contact finally, easing away and pressing the fingertips of her good hand against her lips. Her brown eyes were wide with surprise and confusion as she stared at him.

She was no longer the tired mousy-looking girl who'd arrived that first day. Her clothes hadn't changed; they were still brown and dull, but her eyes no longer had that weary-to-the-bone look, and her face and form had filled out. Her hair now had a shine and her skin glowed pink in the lantern light. Looking at her made his throat feel thick and his chest ache.

"What are you thinking?" he asked, wondering if he'd ever given her reason to think kindly of him.

Linnea shook her head and glanced away, unable to collect her thoughts enough to voice them—unwilling to reveal her confusion. But she looked back—she couldn't help it—and studied his handsome face in the glow of the lantern. Moisture from the kiss glistened on his lower lip. Her own lips felt thick and hot.

Want and fear spiraled through her chest and left her achingly incomplete. That touch of lips, and the way Will looked at her right then, made her feel more womanly than she had at any other time in her life—even more womanly than carrying this baby had ever felt.

He stood then, his dark hair brushing across wide shoulders with the movement, and reached for the supplies on the table. She was intently aware of the length of his arm, the size of his hand, the play of muscle beneath his shirt. He moved efficiently, swiftly, carrying the tin and bandages to their proper places and returning. The trembling which had begun inside her earlier intensified.

"You're shaking," he said, and knelt before her once again. "Is it—are you—did I scare you?"

"Yes—no," she amended quickly. She turned her knees to the side to move away from him and stood, her legs trembling.

"Are you feeling sick?" he asked.

She shook her head. "I'm all right."

"I'll help you to your room." He took her elbow, the warmth of his touch burning through her cotton sleeve, picked up a lantern and walked beside her until they reached the hallway. Its narrow space forced him to fall behind, and she was acutely aware of his presence.

He walked her into her room. After placing

the oil lamp on the chest of drawers, he glanced around, and she could only imagine what he was thinking. Nothing had changed in the time she'd been here. Her few garments were neatly stacked inside two of the five drawers on the bureau, and her hairbrush, combs, pins and the daisy hat in a third.

"A person would never know at a glance that I've been staying here," she said, speaking her thoughts aloud.

"They would if they'd seen the house before you came," he replied, and she understood he referred to the dishes and dirty laundry that had piled up.

But she could pack her belongings in one bag and be gone without leaving a trace. She felt small and empty at the thought that her presence was so insignificant that she could vanish and no one would know she'd ever been there.

"You've made a difference since you've been here," he said, his voice rough. "Things are better."

She turned to face him. "Things are easier for you? That's what you wanted."

He nodded. "And for the men. We never ate so well."

She experienced a small satisfaction at his admission. She had agonized over making herself so indispensable that he wouldn't send her away. But that small measure of relief was overshadowed by the magnitude of what had happened only moments ago.

Will Tucker had never shown any fondness toward her. She wasn't ignorant to the fact that a man would take his pleasure with any woman, even one he didn't like or find attractive. What would she do if he expected to come to her bed? She had no delusions about what he would want. But she wasn't married to him and he didn't own her.

"I won't take you into this bed," she stated baldly. "You're not my husband and you don't have any claim on me, other than the working arrangement we made."

Silence descended on the room in a deafening wave.

Will Tucker's mouth dropped open and back shut. He drew himself up and the muscles in his jaw tightened. "Of all the doggoned damned—" He slapped his hand against the doorjamb and she jumped. Running both hands through his hair, he drew it back and held his head as though it might fly off.

At his furious outburst, Linnea took several steps away. Toward the bed. The gun was tucked under the edge of the mattress, and she could reach it in a minute if she needed it.

As though righteously insulted, his face hardened into the mask of anger she knew so well. He stopped gripping his head and pointed a long finger at her. "You!"

She took another backward step.

"I gave you a chance. I let you talk me into keeping you when it was against my better judgment. I gave you full rein over the kitchen and the supplies. You tricked me by keeping your baby a secret. You hid this accident from me. And now—now you accuse me of planning to use you as part of your job?"

His eyes were as dark as thunderclouds. He was big and angry and maybe he had a right to be.

"What have I done to earn your mistrust?" he asked. "Have *I* lied? Have I kept anything from *you?* I may not be the best-tempered man you could run up against, but at least I'm honest about what I want. I'm a fair man, and I don't pretend to be anything else! And I am *not* an abuser of women!"

Linnea's entire body was trembling now. She tried to stop the quaking by stiffening her knees and pressing a hand to her breast. "I—I'm sorry, I didn't know."

He leaned his spine against the doorframe and laid his head back against the wood. Several leaden minutes past as he stood there. Collecting himself maybe. Thinking what to do with her.

"I'm truly sorry I offended you," she said, her voice too weak. "You did give me a chance and I did keep something important from you. Everything you say is true."

Several minutes passed that way, the hiss of the oil burning in the lamp the only sound save the thump of her heart.

Finally he raised his head. The anger was gone from his face and his voice when he spoke. "You let me kiss you, thinking that if you didn't, you might be sent away."

There was an edge of hurt in his tone now.

She hadn't thought that, however. She hadn't even questioned his motives until he'd walked back here with her and the insidious worry had invaded her mind. But she couldn't bring herself to admit that fear had nothing to do with letting him kiss her.

She'd never been kissed before. Not since her wedding day, anyway, when Pratt had sealed their marriage vows with a peck, according to the preacher's directions.

How could she voice thoughts or feelings as chaotic as those Will Tucker had raised? She didn't have words for them. But she had to say something—or he'd think he was right. And he wasn't.

"It just happened," she denied. "I didn't think anything at the moment."

He met her gaze, studied her expression. "If it happened again…would you think it was something you had to do? Or would it be something you'd like to happen?"

She'd seen how offended he'd been at her insinuation. How hurt. It amazed her to think she had the power in just a few words to hurt a man as large and as strong as this one. And in her heart—heaven help her—she believed him when he said he had no unseemly intentions. "If it happened again…" she said slowly, choosing her words with care "…it would just happen. That's all."

His mouth quirked up at the corner, a half a smile she'd never seen before, and it set her at ease. She couldn't believe she'd had the crazy thought of using her gun against him. He had no intention of hurting her.

She wondered then if he'd cross the distance that separated them and make that kiss happen again. Her heart even fluttered in anticipation. But he simply studied her from his place in the doorway, then straightened and said, "Sleep well."

It couldn't have been disappointment that dropped a weight in her chest, because she hadn't been hoping for anything. She wished him a good-night and closed the door, then turned the wooden block that served as a lock. Though her rational mind told her she was safe from him, a lifetime of experience told her she was never safe, so she shoved the bureau in front of the door, a task that was growing more difficult with every week that passed.

Will paused at the end of the hallway near the kitchen and listened to the sound of Linnea moving the bureau. After turning down the wicks until the lamps were extinguished, he carried the last one to his room.

Midmorning the following day, Will Tucker carried boards and tools through the kitchen and down the hall. At the sound of hammering, Linnea and Aggie exchanged a look. Half an hour later, he stopped for a cup of coffee and a slice of warm applesauce cake, wished the women a good day and disappeared out-of-doors.

Linnea hurried back to the end of the hall and peered around. Nothing looked out of the ordinary in Aggie's room, and hers appeared untouched, but the scent of fresh wood kept her searching.

Puzzled, she had turned to leave when she spotted the board affixed to the wall beside the door.

He had installed a wooden bar that, once the door was closed, could be dropped into place in two brackets on either side and thus prevent the door from opening. He'd provided her with a sturdy barrier against an intruder.

She experienced a thread of embarrassment. He knew her nightly practice of barricading her door. What had he thought? Slowly a glowing warmth spread through her at the realization that her safety and her peace of mind were important to him. Because he knew she would feel safer with a lock, he had provided one.

It was the nicest thing anyone had ever done for her. As kind and meaningful as Cimarron teaching her to read. As helpful as Aggie giving her aprons and recipes. As generous as Corinne Dumont giving her a bed in her lovely home while arrangements for Linnea's trip were made.

Linnea made her way back to the kitchen with a euphoric lift to her step. Ever since she'd responded to that ad in the Saint Louis newspaper, people had done nice things for her. That had been a turning point in her life.

"What did he do back there?" Aggie asked.

"Fixed the lock on my door," she replied. *My*

door. The door certainly didn't belong to her, and neither did the room, but she felt a certain possessiveness toward that long narrow sleeping space now.

"'Bout time," Aggie commented.

As the following weeks passed, Linnea sensed the change that had occurred. Will Tucker didn't seem quite so angry, and she wasn't nearly as skittish in his presence. There was still a tension in the air whenever they were in the same room, but it had taken on a different essence—more of an expectancy…a feeling of anticipation.

Each time she saw him, she remembered his question about the kiss: *If it happened again... would you think it was something you had to do? Or would it be something you'd like to happen?*

If it happened again. Would it happen again? She'd taken to wondering a dozen times a day. And a dawning realization crept up on her—and scared her witless. She would like for it to happen again.

"Miz McConaughy, are you paying attention?"

She and Cimarron were settled on a blanket on the bank near the stream in the dim perimeter of light provided by the lantern. Linnea's thoughts had once again drifted, and she returned her focus to the slate on her lap. Her backside was aching from sitting on the ground and her leg cramped. Mosquitoes buzzed around their heads and a splash sounded in the stream as something, a frog or a muskrat perhaps, jumped to safety.

"Sorry," she said, and read the words he had chalked. *"It was a hot day."*

The day had been uncomfortably warm, and the air still hadn't cooled off much.

Cimarron grinned at her. "I have a surprise for you."

"What is it?"

"Tomorrow I'm bringin' a book for you to read."

"A real book? Oh!" She dropped the slate and leaned over to hug him impulsively.

He returned the hug awkwardly and, chuckling, pulled away to gather his chalk and slate, and stuff them in the saddlebag.

"What is it?" she asked. "What book will I be reading?"

"That's the rest of the surprise," he said teasingly.

"You mean to keep me waiting until tomorrow night?"

"Yup." He bent and assisted her to her feet. After folding and packing away the blanket, he picked up the lantern and turned down the wick.

They started up the slope, and he took her hand to lead her.

"I may not sleep tonight, I'm so excited," she said. "You could give me a hint."

"Nope. You'll have to wait."

"Am I going to like it? Of course I'll like it. Will I be able to read it? What if I can't read it? I've only read the words you've written on the slate, not all the words in the book!"

"You'll figure out the sounds. I'll help you."

"I read the flour sack today," she told him. "And yesterday the brass plate on the wringer."

"And you figured those out, did you?"

"It was nothing I've ever felt before. It made me feel…not smart, but almost as good as other people."

"Miz McConaughy, you're as good any anybody else and better'n probably half."

She had grown to appreciate Cimarron's friendship. He was a kindhearted, fun-loving young fellow with views and opinions she respected and stories that made her laugh. She enjoyed sitting by the fire at night and listening to the yarns he and Roy spun for her amusement.

The Double T felt like home; Linnea experienced an unfamiliar and heady sense of importance and respectability, and it was a joy she meant to cherish while it lasted. Sometimes she let herself pretend that it was her home, that she truly belonged and that she'd never have to leave.

A tall figure loomed in the darkness ahead of them, stepping directly into their path. Moonlight shone down on a black Stetson and the hair lying against broad shoulders.

Will Tucker.

Chapter Fourteen

"Mighty warm night," Will said, not knowing what to think of finding the two of them together.

"Cooler down by the stream," Cimarron replied. "We took a walk."

"Thank you for escorting me," Linnea said politely to Cimarron. Nervously, she rubbed her palms together, and Will noted she no longer wore bandages on the freshly healed skin.

"My pleasure, ma'am. Evenin'." The hand walked toward the bunkhouse, a saddlebag conspicuous on his shoulder.

Will stepped into place beside Linnea and they approached the house. He'd noticed her behavior around Cimarron more than once. She seemed more at ease with him than with anyone else, especially more than with Will himself. He supposed it was only natural, what with Cimarron being the one who'd brought her from Denver—

the first person from the Double T that she'd met. And he was a likeable fellow. Friendly. Handsome. Young.

Those thoughts ate at him. Worked up his ire.

Why? Because Will was attracted to her, in some off-kilter inappropriate way. He felt a tenderness toward her that was as unfamiliar as a stiff new pair of boots.

And because he also felt a fierce protectiveness, he was going to keep an eye on the two of them.

The next morning, he studied the ground beside the stream, noting the matted grass near a towering oak. A rusty lantern hung on a limb, hidden by leaves and discovered only because he was looking.

He observed her that day, noting nothing unusual. She served their meals and ate at the end of the table with Aggie as always. Whenever their eyes met, she gave Will a shy smile.

She and Cimarron exchanged no secret glances that he was aware of.

Ever since her burn injury, he'd assigned one of the men to her each week. That cowboy was responsible for carrying wood and water, and any other chores too heavy for her. She accepted the help and the men seemed glad to assist. To them she was the best thing that had happened to the

ranch since their bunks were built and topped
with feather mattresses.

Nearly every evening, she sat around their fire
with them, the dancing embers illuminating her
soft features, a smile on her face. The more the
child grew within her, the gentler the curves of
her face and body became, and the more he worried about what would happen when it was time
for the birthing.

Corinne had written, saying she would be arriving, but that there were matters she had to attend
to first.

That night from the corner of the barn, Will observed Linnea with the men around the fire, her
soft laughter creating a hollow place inside him,
and he didn't know why. She seemed especially
fascinated when the men spoke of places they'd
been and where they'd come from, but she never
offered insight into her own past.

Cimarron left the gathering and sometime later,
Linnea excused herself. Was it possible they met
secretly at the same place often?

His mind didn't want to grasp the concept, but
he couldn't let go of the possibility. He stopped
near the corral and spoke softly to the whiskey-
colored stallion. The animal was more uneasy
than usual at his presence, and Will suspected
it sensed the tension he radiated, so he checked

on the foals and mares in the barn and raked hay into feeders.

When he couldn't stand not knowing any longer, he threw down the rake and stomped out into the night. Along the stream grew thickets of shrubs: chokecherry, buffaloberry and box elder. A family of deer mice skittered beneath them at his passing.

The halo of light beneath the tree could be seen from afar, and it surprised him that he hadn't noticed it before. But the stream was set down in the landscape and quite possibly couldn't be seen from the yard or the ranch buildings.

They were there, Linnea and Cimarron, their heads together, and her soft voice was stumbling over something she was saying. His heart felt as though a strip of rawhide had been lashed around it and squeezed tight.

"'You only just tell a boy you won't ever have any—any...'"

"Anybody."

"'Anybody but him, ever ever ever, and then you kiss and that's all. Anybody can do it.'" Linnea's words were spoken haltingly.

Will crept closer.

"'Kiss? What do you kiss for?'" Linnea was saying.

"That's good," Cimarron said.

Will moved into the circle of light and confronted the two who sat close, absorbed in each other and unaware of his approach.

Cimarron heard the movement, jumped to his feet, and instinctively drew his revolver. Recognizing Will, he lowered the gun and his face took on a mask of guilt. He holstered the gun. "Evenin', boss."

Will took a few more steps toward him. "This is a cozy scene."

Linnea struggled to her feet and moved protectively in front of her companion. She stood clutching a book to her protruding belly, her brown eyes wide, staring at Will in fear.

Her gesture was laughable, really. If he wanted to do harm to Cimarron, there was nothing she could do about it. Will could toss her aside in a heartbeat.

"It's not what you're thinkin'," Cimarron said, and tried to step around her, but she prevented it by staying in front of him. "Miz McConaughy, I can handle this."

"No, you won't, I'll handle this." The lift of her chin and the frightened yet defiant look on her face gave Will pause.

"This was all my idea," she explained rapidly. "I asked Mr. Northcoat to help me read the lists you gave me and not to tell you. He wanted to tell, but I asked him not to. And when he said he would teach me to read, I made him promise to keep it a secret. He was just helping me. We're reading *Tom Sawyer*."

Taken aback, Will absorbed her words. She hadn't been able to read the lists he gave her? Why hadn't she said something? "You couldn't read?" he asked, his minding rolling over the confusing information.

Linnea gripped the book with both hands and held his gaze.

Why hadn't she told him she couldn't read the first time he'd handed her a list for supplies?

In the glow of the lantern, he thought her cheeks were flushed.

She hadn't wanted him to know. She'd been afraid that if she couldn't perform the tasks he'd assigned to her, her position would be at risk. And it had been. But not for the reasons she thought. He wouldn't have let her go because she couldn't read.

"My father never let me go to school." Years of yearning and shame edged her words. "My husband forbid me to learn. He agreed with my father that it only gave women foolish ideas and made them uppity."

That admission added a whole passel of insight

to her past and to her marriage. It also said something about her character. Even though she'd assumed that Will would feel the same as her husband, she wanted to read so badly that she had risked his anger.

It also said something about Will's character. He was so angry and closed-minded that she'd been afraid to let him know her perceived shortcomings.

The spark of admiration he already felt for her blazed into a steady flame.

"I don't give a fig if you want to learn to read and that Cimarron is willing to teach you," he said gruffly. It pained him that she wasn't able to share these elemental, crucial facts with him in the first place.

Surprise crossed her features.

"Just don't be sneakin' around like you're doing something wrong. What will the others think of the two of you meeting in secret out here in the bushes?"

His insinuation obviously embarrassed both of them, and they didn't look at each other.

"Then it's okay with you?" Linnea asked in a hopeful voice.

"It's okay with me if you sit in the kitchen where the gallinippers won't eat you alive, and where anyone looking in can see you're simply readin'."

Linnea's whole posture relaxed. The hand with the book dropped to her side and she turned to cast Cimarron a joyful smile. "And you're not angry with Mr. Northcoat?"

She watched Will for confirmation.

Will looked at his young hand. "I think it's commendable that you're helpin' Mrs. McConaughy learn to read," he said.

"She's a quick learner," Cimarron stated proudly. "Learned the whole alphabet in just a couple o' weeks."

"You can head back now," Will told him. "I'll see that she gets to the house safely."

Having been dismissed, Cimarron picked up his saddlebag, wished Linnea a good night, and ambled into the dark toward the ranch yard.

Will watched him go, then turned toward Linnea.

She took a few steps away from him and bent to pick up the blanket and shake it out.

Moving closer, he placed his hand on her wrist, preventing her from her task.

She raised round brown eyes to his face in question.

"What happened to make you so afraid of me?" he asked.

She looked down at the wool clutched in her fingers. "I—I don't know what you mean."

"You know what I mean. You shy away from me, you're afraid to tell me truths, you barricade your door at night...you walk out of your way to not step close to me. And you look at me as though I'm the very devil. What is it you're afraid of?"

She swallowed, but didn't move her hand. "You have the power to send me away. And I have nowhere to go. You know that."

"I'm not going to send you away before your baby is born, Linnea." Ashamed of himself for allowing her to remain so insecure and fearful of her near future, he clumsily tried to assure her now. "You're safe here. You have a place to stay until after the baby comes. I wouldn't send you off without a place to go. I'm a cranky son of a bitch, but I'm not coldhearted. When it's time for you to leave, I'll make sure you and the baby will be okay. You have my word."

She looked up again, and he thought tears glistened in her eyes. "You're word is good enough for me, Mr. Tucker."

"Will," he corrected.

With that promise, and what had transpired just now, Linnea began to see Will Tucker in a whole new light. His approval of her reading lessons was like a weight lifted from her shoulders.

He was cranky, as he admitted, but he had never once raised a fist to her. He was loud and he wore fierce expressions, but his wrath always passed quickly, and she'd never seen him strike a person or an animal to get them to do his bidding.

He unconditionally provided a home for his stepmother, who had never treated him well. He barked at the old woman and at his men, but none of them had actually shown any fear.

Perhaps his bark was worse than his bite.

Linnea had no doubt he meant what he said, and he had assured her she could stay until after the baby came. She would worry about that when the time came—day-to-day life was enough to handle right now. As he helped her gather things, fold the blanket, and walked beside her, a profound relief settled over her like a soft wrap on a blustery day.

For at least a few more weeks she didn't have to worry over her fate. She could take care of herself and her baby, and enjoy a brief peaceful respite. The temporary lifting of that burden made her feel as though her feet barely touched the ground as they approached the house.

She climbed the back stairs ahead of him and entered the kitchen. He placed the blanket and lantern on the table. Linnea pressed the book to her breast.

"Do you like the story so far?" he asked.

"Oh, yes! It's wonderfully exciting. I can't wait to go on."

The sparkle in her eyes and the joy in her voice touched Will. He would have offered to listen to her read, to help her with the words, but she and Cimarron shared a teacher-student relationship that he didn't want to intrude upon.

"I'm sorry I didn't trust you," she said in a soft voice. "With the truth about not being able to read. And before that about the baby."

"A person has to show themselves worthy of trust, I reckon," he said. Added to that, he had the impression that she'd never met a man she could trust before. Or one that wasn't threatened by her learning to read.

Things had changed since he'd kissed her. Until that moment he hadn't known he wanted to. Or that she would have allowed it. But he had. And she had. Now he thought about it all the time. Thought about the way she smelled and how soft her lips had been. Thought about doing it again.

Right now, he was looking at her standing in his kitchen, and instead of saying good-night and going up the stairs, or pouring a cup of coffee and settling down at the table, he was thinking about kissing her—this brown little mouse with the liquid eyes and the belly swollen with another man's child.

How was it he could even imagine taking intimacies with her? How was it he would lay awake tonight wondering how her hair would feel in his hands, what the skin of her ivory throat would feel like against his lips?

He'd predicted that having a woman on the ranch would spell trouble, but he'd never dreamed the trouble would be his.

"I do trust you," she said.

"What?"

"You said a person needed to be worthy of trust, and I do trust you. I won't worry about my place here until the time comes. Until the baby's here."

"Okay." He struggled to bring his thoughts back into order. Apparently she wasn't worrying about the actual event of the birth like he was. "Maybe we should talk about that."

"About what?"

"About when the baby comes."

"We have weeks yet."

"We have to be prepared."

"All right. Say what you want."

"I sent for Corinne, but I don't know if she'll be here in time."

"There's Aggie—"

"Aggie is an old woman. She won't be much help."

"I'll manage," she said. "I don't know what you're worrying about."

"I'm worrying because the doctor is a half day's ride away."

"I think babies take longer than that," she assured him. "There will be time."

Considering her aversion to the last time he'd summoned the doctor, he took it as a good sign that she didn't argue with him, and instead assured him. The fact that she wasn't worried amazed him. "All right then."

She took a lantern from the table. "Good night."

"Night."

Her skirts rustled as she turned and disappeared down the hallway.

Each night Linnea joined the men at their fire, and after about an hour, she and Cimarron left the group to enter the kitchen and read. No one seemed to think much of it, but once, Ben asked what book they were reading.

Occasionally Will passed through for a cup of

coffee on his way to his room, and when he did, he greeted them as he normally would, with a nod. But as a rule they were left alone for her studies.

The following week Will rode out one morning after breakfast and when he returned after the noon meal, he placed a large brown-paper–wrapped bundle on the end of the table where she and Aggie usually sat. Linnea eyed the package curiously, but set out a cup and a fork and brought him the plate of chicken and potato salad she had saved.

Aggie was sitting on the porch in the shade, so they were alone. Linnea poured him a cup of coffee.

He pointed at the package. "That's for you."

For her? She set the coffeepot back on the stove. "What is it?"

"Look and see."

Pressing one hand to her breast, she stepped to where the mysterious bundle sat. Hesitantly, she untied the string and peeled back the paper.

Chapter Fifteen

Peeling back the stiff paper revealed a folded stack of fabric, topped with thread and needles. One of the lengths of cloth was a deep vivid green with tiny sprigs of white-and-yellow flowers, the other a soft cornflower blue. In between were layers of plain white cotton, along with eyelet trim. And lastly, she discovered a length of soft white flannel.

"Can you sew?" he asked. "I know you can mend, but can you make clothing?"

She glanced up. "I can do a fair job."

"Mrs. Carmichael helped me pick 'em out and buy the right amounts," he said. "Should be enough for two dresses and some under—other things. There's a pattern in there somewhere, too."

Linnea's cheeks had grown uncomfortably warm. "I don't understand."

He concentrated on eating his chicken a few

moments before replying. "The Independence Day celebration is comin' up, and you'll need something that fits properly."

He carefully hadn't said something prettier than her plain brown skirts and overshirts, but the implication was clear in her mind.

"I didn't know about the celebration, but I don't think I'll be going."

"We'll all go," he said. "It's a chance to meet neighbors and bargain crops and stock. Last year I arranged to get a hog in the fall in trade for cutting ice last winter."

She understood how important it was for him to be part of the community and to barter services, but was it necessary for her to go?

"The men enjoyed the food and the dancing," he added.

Dancing? Her child chose that moment to move, creating an uncomfortable pressure on her innards and a rolling kick across her belly. "Mr. Tucker—"

He sipped his coffee. "Will."

"Will," she managed uncomfortably. "Do you think it would be proper for me to attend? In my condition? And without a husband?"

"You're a widow, Linnea." He set the cup down. "It's not a shame to have lost a husband."

It felt shameful. But she'd been ashamed with the husband she'd been forced to marry when he was alive, too.

"People out here don't live by the same standards as the prigs in the East," he said. "They aim for practical and sensible."

"I don't know anyone."

"You'll meet other women from nearby ranches, and I guarantee you'll see a few in your same condition."

"I don't know..."

"You need to meet other women." It was an order.

She stared at him. Back to his worry about the baby, she guessed. "If you insist."

"I do."

"And I suppose you insist that I make myself a dress, too?"

"Yes."

If she didn't look upon the dressmaking material as a gift, she could accept it. He didn't want his fellow ranchers and their wives to think he didn't pay his help enough to buy decent clothing. At that moment, she felt terribly plain and dowdy in her brown dress, and only now because he had noticed.

"The flannel is for the baby. Mrs. Carmichael

said you'll need flannel for changes as well as for gowns and such. I think there's enough."

For the baby. Linnea stared at the fabrics until her vision blurred. He'd thought to inquire and purchase something she would need—something she hadn't even considered in her ignorance and her frantic worry over her day-to-day existence. Her throat constricted on the rising swell of emotion.

"If it's not enough, you can pick up more when you're in town again."

She nodded, wordlessly, afraid to speak for fear she'd burst into foolish tears. She swallowed back a confusing jumble of appreciation, embarrassment and caution, pursed her lips, and raised her head. She dared look toward him then. "Thank you."

If she hadn't known better, she would have sworn that relief crossed his stoic features, that his shoulders eased somewhat and that he released a breath. Probably glad to be finished arguing with her and get on with his day's work.

His plate was empty, except for chicken bones, and he picked up it and his cup and set them beside the basin.

"Appreciate you savin' me a meal." He grabbed his hat and headed out the back door.

Aggie said something to him that Linnea couldn't hear and her cackle followed.

Linnea stepped out onto the back porch and let the breeze cool her flushed face. She watched Will cross the yard toward the corrals. One of the cow dogs ran to greet him and Will stopped to stroke the mutt's head before moving on, the canine at his heels.

She rubbed a spot on her abdomen where vigorous kicking continued. So far her baby was safe and protected inside her. But soon, as her employer kept reminding her, the little one was going to be ready to come out into the world. "Do you know anything about birthing a baby, Aggie?" she asked.

"Nary a thing."

Linnea nodded that she'd assumed as much. Maybe Will was right. Maybe she did need to meet some womenfolk so she'd have advice handy. She would not call for that doctor if it was the last thing she ever did. If she never had to let a man poke or pry her body again she'd be happy. Just the thought of it shamed her to no end.

After several minutes she went in to prepare sausage and stuffing for supper.

Linnea explained her need for time to sew to Cimarron, and for the next two weeks, she sewed in the evenings. Every moment she could spare, she cut and basted and stitched until her fingertips were sore, but she had two sets of the prettiest undergarments she'd ever owned and a green calico wrapper with a ruffled yoke and hem. Even though the dress was loose-fitting and unadorned, it was the nicest dress she could remember owning. After the baby came, she would take out the seams and alter the garment into a close-fitting bodice and skirt.

When the first of July arrived, she had finished the ensemble she would wear on the Fourth and started on the baby garments and flannel nappies.

"How about you?" she said to Will one evening as he sat going over his ledgers and she finished a hem on a tiny gown. "Do you have proper clothing to wear for this occasion?"

"I do," he replied simply.

"Does anything need to be ironed?"

"I'll bring down a shirt if that makes you happy."

After he'd finished working and put away his book and ink pen, he climbed the stairs and returned with a white shirt, which he draped over the back of her chair. "I'm turnin' in. You need your sleep, too."

She stood awkwardly and placed her sewing on the seat of the rocker. "Good night."

Once he'd ascended the stairs, she picked up his shirt. It was made of fine linen, tailored to fit, and embroidered with white stitching on the collar and cuffs.

Since the evening was cool, she would perform the task tonight, rather than in the heat of the day, so she stoked the fire, adding cattail as tinder, and placed two irons on the stovetop.

As she pressed fabric he wore next to his skin, her thoughts drifted into imagination. Laundering and pressing a man's shirts was something a wife did. Along with cooking and cleaning and seeing to his everyday needs. She performed all the duties of a wife for Will Tucker.

Well, all but one.

The unwanted thought shocked her out of her reverie. She didn't mind the cooking or cleaning, ironing or weeding the garden, but she'd rather wrestle a bear than be a wife in that respect again.

Life with her husband had been miserable, and the memories brought it all back to keep her aversion fresh. Overhead a board creaked, making her acutely aware of the man upstairs. She pictured him undressing and climbing into his bed. She remembered how tender he'd been the evening he had doctored her burn and kissed her.

The iron grew cool as the image of kissing Will warmed her soul and confused her mind. Kissing him hadn't been unpleasant at all, and that had shocked her. It had been…nice. An eye-opening revelation, no less. She hadn't known an intimate encounter with a man could be so pleasant. And unthreatening. And *incomplete.*

Now, why had she thought that?

Linnea set the iron aside and ran her hand over the crisp white fabric and imagined his chest filling it out, his shoulders wide and strong, his back a column of flexing muscle.

She pulled her hand away as though she'd been burned and quickly folded the garment.

When had she become a raving lunatic, thinking of her employer in that manner? Such scorching imaginations had never been a part of her thinking before, and she'd be wise to snuff them out before they went any further.

Turning out the lamps, she hurried to her room and lowered the bar across the door. She stared at the lock. Aside from his scowls and his barked commands, Will had given her no true reason to fear him. In fact, when it came right down to it, the man was considerate of her needs, protective and respectful.

Never had she thought of Will's presence upstairs in such a inciting manner, and the preoccupation was enough to keep her awake. That night and the next…

The morning of the holiday, Roy helped Linnea fry chickens and grate cabbage and pack them into crates for the trip. Linnea had baked and iced spice cakes and sliced a mountain of cucumbers and tomatoes. When the food was loaded into a wagon, Roy took the seat and urged the team of horses forward.

Linnea rushed back inside to help Aggie dress. Cimarron carried water to the stove to heat, then to the tub in the side room, and quickly disappeared so she could bathe.

The task of bathing was becoming more and more difficult, and she felt like the stuck cows she heard the men talk about, the ones that wandered into mud on the riverbank and couldn't get themselves out. The pretty new chemise and drawers and the green dress made her feel better about herself, even though donning her stockings winded her.

There was nothing she could do about her boots, which were worn and scuffed, but she had polished them and her skirt hem was long enough to hide their unsightly appearance.

Will, having mentioned he would bathe in the stream, had donned his clothing and found her drying her hair in front of the stove.

She turned at the sound of his boots on the wooden floor, and the sight of him took her breath away.

He wore the white shirt she had ironed—and fondled…her cheeks warmed…with a string tie and black trousers with stiff creases. A matching suit jacket emphasized his height and the breadth of his shoulders. His dark hair had been brushed back from his face, though it still fell to his shoulders in waves. In his strong dark hand he held the black Stetson.

He was looking at her strangely, and she realized he'd never seen her with her hair down and loose as it was now. It was improper for a woman to have her hair unbound in front of a man who wasn't her husband, but she'd been trying to dry it quickly, so she could arrange it and be ready to leave.

The fingers of his other hand, the one not holding the hat, flexed open and shut a few times. Knots ran along his jaw. His gray eyes held a thunderstorm of unreadable emotion. Was he angry?

"I'll be ready in just a moment," she told him. "I wanted my hair dry and it's taken a while."

"No rush," he replied, his deep voice sounding as though it rumbled up from his toes. But he continued to watch her as she leaned sideways and ran the comb through her hair.

It was impolite of him to stare as she performed this personal task, but his attention didn't seem rude. More like fascination, if she wasn't dreaming.

At last, deciding the strands were dry enough, she hurried to her room, plaited a thick braid to wind around her head and pin in place. She didn't want to muss what she'd just accomplished by wearing the daisy hat, but neither did she want the sun scorching her skin all day, so she grabbed it and met him where he still waited.

He was looking at her as though he'd never seen her before, and the study made her uncomfortable. She sensed he wanted to say something.

"Is anything wrong?" She checked the yoke of her dress, smoothed the fabric over her belly self-consciously and raised a hand to the wisps of hair she'd tugged in front of her ears.

He caught her hand and pulled it away. "Don't. It's perfect."

"Why are you staring at me?"

"You look so pretty," he said.

A gentle mountain breeze could have blown her over with the astonishment she experienced at those words. The way her skin flushed all the way from her midsection, up her chest and into her cheeks, anyone would have thought the man had written a love sonnet and whispered it in her ear. "Oh—well, you look quite handsome yourself."

That brought him around, with what she thought was a dusky red stain on his tanned cheeks. He quickly led her out the door, stuffing his hat on his head and escorting her to a wagon where Aggie waited, ensconced on quilts in the bed, a perky yellow bonnet shading her wrinkled face. Her rocker lay on its side at the rear.

"Don't you look like a spring flower!" Aggie said as Will helped Linnea onto the seat above.

"A rather *large* spring flower," Linnea replied, adjusting her hat.

Will laughed.

Aggie chuckled.

And Linnea realized she'd make a joke at her own expense. She laughed, too, and smiling, Will joined her on the seat and picked up the reins and clucked to the horses.

She'd never seen that smile before. It bared his even white teeth and creased his lean cheek and made butterflies swoop and dip in her stomach. She would have jumped off the wagon and run all the way to Rock Creek to see that smile again. And at that ludicrous picture, she laughed again.

And he turned to her and smiled.

Chapter Sixteen

The festivities were held in a flat pasture that had been freshly mowed and raked. The fresh green summer smells and the warm sun assaulted Linnea's senses. Will pulled the team and wagon up beside a dozen others, and Linnea's heart fluttered nervously at the bustle of congregating townspeople and ranchers. Many were unloading wagons, others were setting up kegs and tables.

A wooden platform for musicians and dancers had been constructed and posts for lanterns placed at each corner. A group of men were hanging red-white-and-blue banners between the posts. From a pole with fresh-turned dirt at the base, an American flag rippled in the breeze.

A few open-sided tents were being raised for those who wanted protection from the sun.

Will assisted Linnea to the ground, then went back for Aggie and her chair. Carrying the rocker, he led the way, and Linnea followed slowly with Aggie on her arm.

Oh, my goodness, there was food. Makeshift tables were already laden with bowls of custard, pickled peaches and molasses-sweetened beans, jars of preserved cucumbers and oysters, platters of chicken and ham and turkey, baskets of rolls, apples and sliced breads, rows of johnnycakes and waffle cakes. Linnea spotted her own offerings among them, so she knew the men had handed the food into the capable hands of the dozen ladies who bustled and sliced and tasted.

And there were people. Young and old, some dressed in silk taffeta, others in faded broadcloth, and Linnea realized she fit comfortably somewhere in between. Children shouted and laughed, playing games of tag and hide-and-seek.

Keeping track of Will as he moved through the throng and found a spot in the shade for Aggie's chair, Linnea observed a cluster of men gathered beside the kegs of beer, another in the shade of a nearby willow grove.

"You'll be comfortable here," Will said to Aggie. He'd placed her chair beneath the cover of one of the tents, where she'd be out of the burning sun, but able to see the activity. Then he turned to Linnea. "There were a few folding stools packed on the other wagon. I'll see that you have one to use when you get tired."

Was he leaving her here now? "All right."

"Have a good time," he said, confirming her mental question. "Mingle."

She nodded. Mingle.

The bustle of activity held her interest after he left to join a group of men. She observed the women putting the finishing touches to the tables of food. And then, at Aggie's insistence, Linnea walked into their midst to offer help.

A tall brown-haired woman in a calico dress and yellow apron gave Linnea a warm smile that created charming dimples. "I'm Mavis Pruitt," she said, glancing at Linnea's protruding stomach. "Me and my husband, Piper, have a spread on the other side of Sweetbriar Canyon. What's your name, dear?"

"Linnea McConaughy," she replied, and then knowing she needed to add some identification as the other woman had, she added, "I'm the cook at the Double T. Will Tucker's ranch."

"You're the widow woman I heard was working for him?" Mavis asked with raised brows.

Linnea nodded.

"You aren't quite what I imagined."

"I don't think I was what he imagined either," she replied.

Mavis chuckled. Linnea liked her right off. "I don't suppose," she said. "You're so young to be a widow, dear, and a baby on the way, too? You poor thing!"

Mavis had a sprinkling of freckles across her cheeks from the sun, and her hands were tanned, telling Linnea she did a good share of ranch work, unlike some of the other, more fancifully dressed ladies whose hands were soft and white.

Linnea wasn't good at guessing ages, but she would guess that the woman was ten years older than herself.

"Well, I'm looking forward to whatever you brought," Mavis said and glanced at the tables.

"Nothing fancy," Linnea replied. "I cook for cowboys, and all they care about is quantity."

"I cook for our hands, too," Mavis replied with a knowing rise of one brow. "They get breakfast and a big meal at noon, then they're on their own for their supper. They take turns with that at the bunkhouse. Gives us one meal a day with our family. So what did you bring?"

"Fried chicken and pickled eggs, coleslaw—that one—and spice cakes. Those." She pointed.

Mavis hurried over and broke off a piece of the

cake with her fingers. She grinned at Linnea and bit into the dessert. "Mmm, the texture is perfect." She licked frosting from her fingers. "I love these shindigs, because I can eat someone else's cooking all day." With a little shrug she added, "And I do."

Linnea smiled at her friendly chatter and affable manner. She had expected to feel out of place and inadequate among the women, but the first one she'd met had put her at ease.

A boy of about eight or nine ran up to Mavis and, out of breath, said, "When are we gonna eat? Me'n Petey are hungry!"

"Won't be long now," Mavis told him, smoothing his wavy brown hair with a loving hand. "Mind your manners now and greet Mrs. McConaughy."

The boy turned wide hazel eyes toward Linnea. "How'd do, ma'am. I'm John Pruitt."

"Pleased to meet you, John."

He turned back to his mother. "Papa said for me to ask you where the quilts are that I'm to spread out."

"Still in the back of the wagon," she replied. "See that you don't drag the ends through the dust."

"Yes'm." He ran off.

Linnea admired Mavis's easy way with her

son, and his polite introduction indicated she'd coached him with his manners. Was she as smiling and friendly with her family as she was with Linnea? What a lucky husband and son she had.

Mavis turned back to the tables and soon had Linnea slicing the latest arrived cakes and pies. She introduced her to a few others, including Mrs. Carmichael, the mercantile owner's wife.

"What a delightful job you did making your dress," the woman said appreciatively. "I had to guess on the amount of the material. Will said you were on the smallish side, but you know men. I didn't want to short you on fabric."

"I had a little material left," she replied. "Enough for an apron or a bonnet, perhaps."

"Will was amusing," Mrs. Carmichael confided to Linnea and Mavis. "He didn't want to come right out and say you were carryin' a babe, so he said—" the woman lowered her voice and frowned in imitation "—'she's a mite bigger around the middle than she'll be in a month or two.'"

Linnea could just hear Will describing her in that way, and she and Mavis giggled.

"Think everyone is here?" Mavis asked Mrs. Carmichael a few minutes later.

"Looks about right. Latecomers can always eat when they get here," she replied. "Let's call 'em."

Soon lines had formed on both sides of the tables. Uncertain what to do, Linnea went back to stand by Aggie, and Will approached, carrying saddle blankets. John Pruitt ran up to Will. "My mama says you're to come join us over there."

Will glanced to where the Pruitts had spread their quilts. "Thanks, son, we'll be pleased to eat with your family."

John ran back and Will carried Aggie's chair while Linnea assisted her over the uneven ground. They must have made quite a pair, Aggie with her cane and Linnea waddling beside her. But the Pruitts had nothing but smiles at their ponderous approach.

"This is Piper," Will said, introducing Linnea and Aggie to the stocky, bearded man with round hazel eyes like his son's. "Mrs. Pruitt," Will said.

"Uh-uh, Mavis," she corrected.

Four children surrounded the couple, and Mavis proudly identified each one as Rachel, John, whom Linnea had already met but Aggie hadn't, Petey and Sarah. Rachel was the oldest and carried Sarah, the youngest, on her hip. Mavis took the little girl from Rachel and instructed her children on politely waiting their turns and not helping themselves to the last of anything on the tables.

Linnea followed the example set by Mavis's children, appreciating the instruction Mavis had unknowingly provided for her as well. It took quite a while to move through the lines, select food and settle themselves on the blankets. Linnea had prepared a plate for Aggie first, then gone back and filled her own, so she sat down after the others.

Will handed her a tin cup filled with lemonade.

"Thank you," she said in surprise.

Since the sun was high and hot, everyone kept their hats on throughout the meal, and Will studied her from beneath the brim of his. "Met a few people, did you?"

She nodded. He'd been right. She'd had no way of knowing, but it was good to meet other women.

"Linnea's spice cake would win a ribbon at the county fair," Mavis declared.

"It would if I was a judge," Piper agreed.

Linnea warmed under their praise for her baking.

"Can me'n Petey play mumblety-peg with the other boys after we eat?" John asked his father.

"Use your common sense, John Robert," his father said. "Watch how you set up, so that the throwing circle is a safe distance from where all the boys stand."

He referred to the game where boys threw knives and tried to make the blade stick in the ground. Linnea had seen her brothers do it on many occasion.

"I remember," the boy replied earnestly.

"Does he have to pull the pegs out of the ground with his teeth?" Mavis asked.

"Not if he doesn't miss," Piper replied with a grin.

"I sat up and rocked him nights when he was cutting those teeth," she added.

"That's the way it's played," Piper said. "I pulled a good many pegs from the ground as a boy and I still have a charming smile. Don't I?" He gave her a wide smile.

Mavis couldn't help laughing at her husband.

"You might offer the ladies more lemonade before you hurry off, though," Piper said to his boys.

John and Petey immediately scrambled to their feet and hurried to take the women's cups and returned them filled with fresh drinks. "How 'bout you, Mr. Tucker?" Petey said to Will. He stood before Will, his expression solemn. "Can I get you some more, too?"

"Mine's beer, young fella, and I'd be much obliged for a refill."

Petey ran off with Will's cup and returned more slowly, concentrating on not spilling. "Here ya go, Mr. Tucker."

"Thanks, Pete." He accepted the cup and sat with his wrist propped on his knee. "You know, I suspect you and John will be prime ranch hands one of these days. Maybe when you're a little bigger, you'd be willing to help me cut hay in the fall."

"Sure thing," Petey replied proudly.

"Me, too," John offered.

The boys ran off to play.

Mavis wiped Sarah's chin with a napkin. The child was about two perhaps, with fine silky hair that hung to her shoulders.

"Shall I take Sarah with me?" Rachel asked, helping her mother pick up plates and cups.

"No, you run along and visit with your friends. It's time for Sarah to take a nap."

Rachel hugged her mother before turning away.

"I'll move a quilt into the shade for Sarah," Piper offered.

Mavis shooed him away by waving a napkin. "You go join the men. I'll take care of it."

"You heard her," Piper said to Will.

"Tell me where you're moving, and I'll take Aggie's chair," Will offered.

"That willow grove over there," Mavis replied. "It'll be cooler than the tents."

Once the ladies and Sarah were settled, Will took his leave.

Linnea had never seen a family interact as the Pruitts did. They spoke respectfully to each other, and their love was obvious. The brief interaction she'd witnessed between the married couple spoke volumes. She tried to imagine how they'd met and married, and as she glanced around at other couples and families, she wondered the same thing about them, too.

And seeing Mavis and Piper with their children, she knew none of them would be considered a waste of food and shoved out the door. It did her heart good to know there were children who were loved and appreciated. On the other hand, it hurt deeply to know, with growing hurt and anger, that she hadn't been one of them. She would love her child and make him or her feel loved.

She prayed she would be able to provide a home, clothing and food. As well as all the other unforeseen things needed. How would she know what a baby needed? Will had made her aware of flannels and gowns. If she had a son, what would she say if he wanted to play mumblety-peg?

"How do you know?" she asked Mavis. "How to do for your children? What do you do if they get sick, for example?"

"They're just little people," Mavis replied. She used a napkin to fan herself. "You love 'em, that you can't help, and you figure it out as you go. The good thing is they start out as babies, so they don't know if you're makin' a mistake." Her soft smile helped to ease Linnea's worries. "You should have seen me when Rachel was a baby. I was the youngest in my family, so I didn't know how to do for younger ones, not like Rachel does. Now, she'll make a good mother. I have to stop her from helpin' so much and see that she acts like a child sometimes."

"I was the youngest, too," Linnea said. She thought a few moments and then asked, "What about when Rachel was born?"

Mavis leaned over and patted Linnea's hand. "It's perfectly natural to worry some with the first one. Truth is, once the time comes, it all pretty much happens and you can't control any of it. But then I had my mother. My folks came west same time as we did. And of course there's always my Piper standin' by me. He's a good man."

"I can see that."

"Don't you worry, dear," Mavis said. "You send for me. I'll come."

"You would?"

"Well, sure, I will. Womenfolk got to stick together. Else, what would become of this world?"

Tears of relief smarted behind Linnea's eyes, and she gave Mavis a watery smile.

"When do you 'spect that baby's due?"

"I'm not certain. A few weeks probably."

"You're still carryin' pretty high, so that's probably a good guess. Baby'll drop down lower, once it's closer to your time."

"Lower? I'll be in the outhouse half the night!"

Mavis laughed. "Stop *that* nonsense and use the chamber pot, dear."

Aggie had been silent through their entire conversation, but she piped in with, "Is it safe for her to hang the laundry with her arms over her head? My mother always said that wrapped the cord around the baby's neck."

Linnea gasped, but Mavis was quick to reply. "That's one of those old wives' tales that gets passed around," she assured her. "I didn't have any choice but to hang laundry and every other chore that needed doin' and my children all came out just fine."

After another half hour of conversation and Linnea asking a hundred questions, both Aggie and little Sarah napped.

"I'll sit here with her," Linnea told Mavis. "You can go visit with the other ladies if you like."

"You sure you don't mind?"

"Not at all. I might just lie down there beside her and rest my eyes."

"You're a gem," Mavis said and got to her feet.

After she'd gone, Linnea reclined on the soft quilt, glad to be off her feet and out of the hot sun. Studying the patterns of the willow leaves and the fluffy clouds in the vivid blue sky, her mind absorbed all that she'd learned and seen that day. She most appreciated the nurturing advice of another woman, and Mavis Pruitt was one of the kindest, warmest human beings she'd ever met. What would it have been like to have parents like the Pruitts? How would her life have been different?

Within minutes she slept, and when she woke it was to Will Tucker's husky whisper near her ear.

Chapter Seventeen

"Games are startin', Linnea," he said.

Her eyes fluttered open. Little Sarah no longer slept on the quilt beside her, and Will had knelt to wake Linnea. His breath on her cheek was warm and yeasty smelling.

She pushed upward to sit and discovered her hips ached from lying on the ground. "Oh, my."

"What's the matter?" Will lowered his eyebrows with the question.

"Just stiff from lying here. I'll be all right in a few minutes."

"Let me help you."

Grateful for his assistance, she let him take her arm and steady her as she rose. "Oh, my," she said again.

"What?"

"I—um…I need to…"

He pointed to an outhouse a short distance away.

A woman and two girls were walking away from it. "There."

"Aggie, do you want to join me?" Linnea asked, turning to discover the old woman watching them.

"I want to, but it'd take me till midnight to walk that far," she grumbled.

Will turned from Linnea to his stepmother and leaned down. "Put your arm around my neck."

Effortlessly, he picked up Aggie and carried her toward the outhouse. Linnea fell in step behind him, thinking of the night of her arrival when he had carried her into the house and to her room while she slept. She couldn't help wondering what it was like to be held in those strong arms.

By the time the games started, he had left Aggie seated with a group of older women and escorted Linnea to the sidelines of the first event. Cimarron and Roy set up the folding stools, and invited Linnea to sit. Ben, Clem and Nash greeted her with nods and grins. Glad to see the familiar faces of the Double T hands, she took a seat among them. Will stood close by.

There were three-legged races and sack races, barrel races, a knife-throwing contest, which Roy and Cimarron entered, and even a spitting contest. Linnea refused to watch that one; neither did she want to know who had joined in.

When the arm-wrestling competition was announced, Nash and Ben clapped Will on the back and pushed him forward, shouting, "The champ!"

"The boss won last year," Cimarron told her, "so he'll wrestle the final winner after the preliminaries."

Linnea watched with mild interest. The sport was friendly and the contestants good-natured. Only now and then did anyone grumble or throw down their hat in frustration. All the contestants were paired off. The winner from each pairing was matched with another, until only one remained.

That remaining competitor was a huge Swede, dressed in baggy trousers, a brown vest and cap, and Cimarron informed her that he ran the livery. The man was tall and broad-shouldered with a thick neck and hands even larger than Will's.

He removed his hat and vest, as well as the front-laced shirt, revealing acres of bulky muscles. Murmurs rippled through the crowd, and Linnea recognized the show of intimidating brawn as part of the sport.

When he moved to sit at the small square table at the center of attention, Linnea noted that he didn't move as gracefully as Will.

A cheer rose from the crowd as Will stepped

forward to take his place across from the Swede. He removed the white shirt Linnea had so carefully ironed, and one of the bystanders took it from him. He turned the chair backward and straddled it, his left hand on the wood, his right flexing. Sunshine glowed on his wide, muscled shoulders.

Realizing she was openly admiring his unclothed back and shoulders, she glanced around in embarrassment, hoping no one had noticed her looking.

Will planted his elbow solidly on the table.

The Swede did the same.

Excitement buzzed through the crowd, and the tension was infectious. Linnea watched expectantly.

A silver-haired gentleman dressed in a white shirt with the sleeves rolled back circled the table, eyeing their positions and the arrangement of Will's arm.

"That's Enoch Brimley," Cimarron told her. "He's the officiator of the contests and the owner of the bank. There's a cash prize for this contest."

Glowering at his competition, Will waited until the other man raised his hand, then clasped it firmly.

A hush fell over the spectators.

The bank owner shouted, "Begin!" and the contest was underway.

The men stared daggers at one another. Knowing firsthand the full effect of Will's disturbing glare, Linnea suspected he held the advantage in that department. With her fingers laced against her lips, she watched the match with tingling anticipation.

It became apparent right away that this event would not be over in a matter of seconds as some of them had been. There was no wavering this way and that in the pose of their locked arms. Both men held fast with a show of strength that had the crowd leaning forward in awe.

Will's sledgehammer biceps bulged with the effort it took to give the other man no leeway. From her position, she could see even the contracting muscles in his back. Linnea held her breath and her heart fluttered nervously.

The liveryman's face contorted with the exertion.

Will's expression remained stoic.

Drops of perspiration broke out across the Swede's upper lip and rivulets ran down his temples.

Will showed no sign of strain, save the impressive bulge of muscles in his arm, shoulder and neck.

Minutes passed with no sign of change. Their arms trembled with strain, tendons stood out in their necks.

Linnea began to wonder how long the two men could hold the other in the same position without tiring. She found herself gripping Cimarron's arm and let go self-consciously.

At last there was a change in the angle of their locked fists: Will had inched the other man's arm back.

The Swede bared his teeth and straightened their locked grip again, but now their hands shook with tension. The bystanders cheered and shouted encouragement.

Will gained the inches again. Sweat dripped off the other man's forehead, and now Will's face was beaded with perspiration as well, but the thunderous gaze that bored into his opponent's remained unchanged.

A tiny smile lifted Linnea's lips. By all appearances, the Swede stood a better chance of winning: he was marginally larger, rippled with muscle and honed by swinging a hammer all day before a glowing forge. Will was no featherweight in comparison, but she suspected that his unshakable countenance—that glare he had perfected—was his ace in the hole.

The tension drained from Linnea's body at the reassuring thought. Glancing at the men around her, she noted the pride and excitement on the faces of Will's men as they cheered him on. At the ranch, he hung back and never participated in their nightly gatherings around the fire, but here, for this event, he was in the limelight.

Even Aggie watched with a fierce expression, her eyes bright and one gnarled fist raised in the air as if she were helping him.

A shout went up and Linnea turned her attention back to the contest.

Sure enough, inch by inch, the Swede's arm gave way, twisting backward toward the table. He emitted a growl in his frustration, and the crowd yelled above him.

With a final, mighty shove, Will pinned the back of the man's hand to the tabletop and held it there for a moment. Then he released his hold and jumped from the chair to stand.

The crowd was wild with shouts and applause.

Linnea and Cimarron exchanged grins and the other hands whooped with excitement over their boss's win.

Will was accepting congratulations and wearing a lopsided grin. He approached the Swede and they shook hands good-naturedly. The crowd surrounded them and Linnea lost sight of Will.

People dispersed, and Linnea observed the women setting out and uncovering food again. She was considering going to help when Will sought her out. His face and hair were damp, as though he'd washed, and he was once again wearing his shirt.

"Congratulations," she said to him.

He ducked his head, almost boyishly.

"Too bad some of that muscle ain't between your ears, boy," Aggie said from beside Linnea.

He ignored her comment to ask, "Are you ladies hungry?"

"I believe I am," Linnea replied.

"Why don't you both go back to our shady spot and I'll get your food."

"You don't have to—" she began.

"This is your day to relax," he interrupted. "Stop arguing."

Without further argument, she led Aggie to their blankets.

By the time the sun set and the fireflies came out, a band had organized and tuned up. Will and the men arranged blankets and stools near the wooden floor that had been constructed.

The town's mayor made a speech and the schoolchildren, led by their teacher, sang patriotic songs. Linnea spotted the Pruitt children right away. The crowd clapped and cheered when the pupils finished.

The smells of beer and watermelon drifted on the night air. Conversation and laughter were a constant drone, and lanterns hung from posts illuminated a wide area.

Linnea's nap had refreshed her, and she enjoyed talking to the ladies who sat nearby and then watching the musicians perform and eventually the dancers move out onto the wooden planks.

Mavis and Piper were among the first couples to step out, and others joined them. Sarah and Petey slept on their nearby quilts. Linnea observed the Pruitts as they danced, marveling over how smoothly they moved and the smiles wreathing their faces: Mavis's was beaming, her husband's enamored. Their relationship was a marvel to Linnea. Mavis adored her husband and it was obvious he felt the same way toward her.

Respect and love were apparent in their speech and actions and in their interaction with their children.

An intense yearning came over her and she hoped the yawning ache inside wasn't jealousy.

She didn't begrudge the Pruitts a moment of their happiness.

Linnea experienced a slice of pain at her own situation. Her child would not have a father, would not know security the way the Pruitt children did. She would love her child, of course, but that was the only thing she was prepared to give. It was more than she'd ever received as a child, but it wasn't as much as her child needed and deserved. At the thought, she got weepy and swiped at her eyes.

The music stopped then. Popping sounds echoed across the pasture and bright lights burst in the sky overhead. Fireworks!

Linnea watched in awe, silent while others clapped and ahhed. She'd seen fireworks in the distance a time or two, but never this close. The colorful show went on for nearly half an hour, then dwindled to a few sporadic bursts, and the band began playing again.

"You ready to give it a whirl?" Will knelt beside her on the blanket, one wrist dangling over his upraised knee. The lantern light glowed on his dark hair.

She blinked self-consciously. "You mean—" she glanced uncertainly at the dancers who resumed their steps "—dance?"

Chapter Eighteen

"I mean dance." He took her elbow. "Come on. I won't let you say no."

"But I *can't* dance," she objected.

"You never have?"

"No."

"There's nothin' to it, really, I'll show you. Come on."

He had urged her to her feet, but she still resisted his tug on her arm. "I don't think so. I'm—I'm—"

"You're what?"

"I'm clumsy," she finished.

"You're not clumsy," he argued, gently pushing her forward.

Linnea planted her feet firmly and refused to move any farther. "I'm as big as a barn, Will Tucker, and I am not going to make a spectacle of myself!"

Her objection was spoken in a loud whisper above the music.

"I'm not askin' you to do a reel, just something easy. Nobody's lookin'."

"Everybody's looking, what do you think all these people on the sides are doing?"

"Well, they're not havin' as much fun as the dancers, I know that." But he released her arm.

Fun? Had he just spoken of fun? She blinked at him again. A burst of color lit the night sky above. Will glanced up. How much beer had the man consumed?

Slowly she slid her gaze to the Pruitts and the other couples, dancing just for the simple enjoyment of it.

"You work as hard as anybody here," Will told her. "You deserve a good time." He held out his hand.

She wanted to join in and know what dancing was like. She didn't want to feel awkward and out of place. She wanted to have fun. She regarded Will's extended hand.

Hesitantly she reached for it, and his large warm fingers swallowed hers. He led her forward.

"What will people think of us dancing together?" she asked.

"That we like to dance. No harm in that," he

replied. "Look, there's a father and daughter, the Homers are sister and brother, I even see in-laws together. Enoch Brimley danced with Rachel Pruitt a while ago, did you miss that?"

She must have, she'd been so fascinated by Rachel's parents.

He guided her onto the wooden planking and between the dancers, where he stepped before her, kept her hand in his and wrapped his other arm around her waist. "Put your hand on my shoulder."

She did so. Thank goodness, he had long arms, but her belly still reached him waist level. "Follow me," he said as though he didn't notice, and counted, "one, two, three, four…one, two, three, four…"

Linnea wasn't as clumsy as she feared, and she caught on quickly. Beside Will she didn't feel as enormous as she thought she was most of the time, and as she'd noticed before, he made her feel more womanlike than she'd ever known.

She'd spent so many of her years feeling like a worthless girl that the concept of being a woman and having someone desire her company was difficult to grasp. The fact that others chose to visit with her, ask her questions about herself, simply *notice* her had been a revelation since she'd been on the Double T.

Will *wanting* her as a dance partner didn't even register on her scale of possibilities. "Do you feel sorry for me?" she asked out of nowhere.

He drew his brows down. "Why, is somethin' wrong?"

"In general. Do you feel sorry for me?"

Thinking, he glanced aside, then back at her face. "I know you've had some hardships, what with losin' your husband and needing work and all. I sympathize with your situation."

She thought over his words.

His expression had relaxed. "Have I ever treated you as though I felt sorry for you?"

He had shouted at her, piled on the work, assigned her chores and responsibilities, ordered her about, chased her down under a bush to rave at her… "No, I don't believe you have."

"There's your answer, then."

The fireworks had ended. The night smelled of sulfur and beer. The music changed, the rhythm becoming a little slower, and he drew her closer, firming his hold at the small of her back. Her belly pressed against his belt.

"That uncomfortable?" he asked.

"No."

The baby inside her chose that moment to shift, the thump reaching Will's shirt above his belt. The roll and kick came again.

Linnea dared a glance up at his face.

He was studying her. "That happen all the time?"

She nodded.

"Does it hurt?"

"Not there. Under my ribs, it's painful sometimes."

"That's amazin'."

She couldn't hold back a smile. She had never shared the miracle of her unborn child with anyone. "It is, isn't it?"

It seemed Will was moving slower, just so he could feel the baby when it kicked. It happened again and they shared a private grin.

For Will, feeling the life inside Linnea was an incredible revelation. He'd felt the bellies of mares with foals and of cows with calves, had witnessed the births of a hundred animals, but he'd never been this close to a woman carrying a child before. There was no real comparison.

There was something entirely unique and intimate about such a feminine condition, and its very mystery enticed him.

Since Linnea's arrival in the spring—and since

his discovery of her secret—he'd watched her expand with the growth of her child. Thinking herself unobserved, she sometimes placed a hand at the small of her back as though it ached; occasionally she flattened her palm over a place on her belly, as though something had drawn attention, and he'd wondered.

With her close like this, the scent of her freshly washed hair teased his senses, and the image of her brushing it out before the stove that morning rose in his mind's eye. A dozen times he'd pictured her hair as it had been that first night she'd brushed it out before the campfire. And the sight had been breathtakingly erotic. He studied the highlights now in the glow of the lanterns and wondered how the texture would feel in his hands.

The more he saw, the more he knew, the more he wondered. A mere taste of Linnea provoked a man to want more.

And now he'd kissed her. That memory was confusing and provocative at the same time. He'd thought of her as a mouse, a frail, frightened creature that scurried at the sound of a footstep. Initially, she had run from him.

But not so lately. She stood up to him more and more, even voicing her thoughts and opinions. She didn't seem like the same person who had arrived on the wagon that first day.

Her former life was still a mystery. He didn't know where she'd lived, what her life had been like or anything about her relationship with her husband. She had revealed only that he hadn't wanted her to read. If she'd been grieving for the man, would she have allowed Will's kiss that night in the kitchen? Or was she lonely, confused and hungry for comfort? Maybe she still feared Will.

He didn't think so. She had at one time, but that wasn't the case now. He'd spent a foolish amount of time thinking over these things—things he wouldn't have given two seconds' thought a year ago—six months ago.

She was looking up at him, and she had eyes so dark and full of mystery, Will could fall right into their depths. Her innocent reaction to his kiss still flustered and aroused him, and he wanted to kiss her again right then and there.

• Shocking himself, he drew his attention from the delicate bow of her upper lip to the other couples. No one was paying attention, thank goodness. His body had become uncomfortably aroused and heat and humidity dampened his skin.

When Cimarron interrupted, requesting a dance

with Miz McConaughy, Linnea's eyes showed her surprise at Will's easy acquiescence. Will released her and backed away from the dance floor to stand in the cooler air…catch his thoughts… compose his physical reaction.

She and Cimarron began the dance a little stiffly, as she adjusted to the younger man's steps, but within minutes they blended in with the other dancers. Will studied them together.

She probably needed a young husband like Cimarron, someone affable and outgoing, though Will had never seen any indication that she regarded Cimarron in a romantic way. Had Cimarron had any fanciful thoughts toward Linnea? Probably.

"Boss!" Roy called.

Will turned and followed the voice, which led him toward the wagons.

Roy and Ben were unceremoniously dragging Clem toward Will's wagon. The older man's head flopped to the side and his heels dragged along the ground. They reached the wagon and Will helped them lift Clem into the bed, climbing in so they didn't drop him or bang his head on the side.

Clem lay where they placed him, snoring.

Ben staggered when he stood up, out of breath and chuckling, then attempted to climb down.

Roy helped him, and both nearly fell in a heap at Will's feet. Will couldn't help a laugh.

"I'm goin' into Rock Creek," Ben told them. "Don't look for me back tonight."

"You plannin' to service that pretty filly, Gussie, again?" Roy asked, referring to one of the sporting women at the Big Horse Tavern. "Hope she has a coffeepot in her room or you'll look just like him." He jerked a thumb over his shoulder toward the drunk in the wagon bed.

Ben punched Roy's upper arm good-naturedly. "I guess you wouldn't know what Gussie has in her room, would you?"

They ambled away, and Will returned to the festivities.

Cimarron was leading Linnea from the dance floor. Several of the others were leaving as well, gathering their families and belongings.

Linnea's face was flushed, and her dark eyes twinkled. He'd never seen her looking so carefree and happy.

"Ready to head home?" Will asked.

She nodded.

He woke Aggie, who dozed in her chair, and carried the rocker while Linnea waited with her. He came back to carry Aggie, and Linnea walked beside him in the dark, holding his arm for guidance.

"Sorry, Aggie, but you'll have to sit back here with Clem. He won't bother you."

"Clem tied on a good one, eh?" Aggie asked with a cackle.

Will helped Linnea up onto the seat and guided the team home.

It took him half an hour to assist Aggie in, carry Clem to the bunkhouse over his shoulder, and put up his horses for the night. When he returned from the barn, Linnea had lit a lantern on the kitchen table, and made a pot of coffee.

"Want a cup?" she asked.

He did, and he thanked her. "I'll drink it outside, want to join me?"

She followed him out the door to the porch and settled on the top step.

Will stood leaning against a post and sipped his coffee. "I set the crates with the dishes on the porch there, covered with the toweling. I'll help you wash them tomorrow."

"I'd appreciate that."

After a few moments of silently enjoying the bright stars and the crickets' night melody, she said, "You were right."

He glanced down at her. "What?"

"About meeting other women. I really liked Mavis. It was good to talk to her."

He didn't want to know the details of their talk; it was enough that she'd had someone to question about female things.

"She said she'd come if I sent for her. You know, when it was time."

"That's good."

"If Mavis comes, you won't have to send for the doctor, will you?"

He didn't know why she was opposed to the doctor, but she had made her aversion plain on more than one occasion. "It's just wise to have a doctor attend you," he replied.

She pressed her lips in a line and looked the other way.

He was going to make sure she had the best care possible; she didn't have to be happy about it.

In the distance a coyote howled, a sad lonely sound that always made Will feel comfortably isolated from the noise and confusion of the populated regions. He would check the horses in the corrals before turning in. Their calm or restlessness was his key to nearby danger, and he relied on their senses.

The approach of a single rider snagged his attention, and he studied the dark outline as Roy rode near.

"Who is it?" Linnea asked.

"Roy."

"How can you tell?"

"The sorrel, the way Roy sits the saddle."

Roy spotted them on the porch and reined to a halt several feet away.

"The rest of 'em go into town?" Will asked. The men probably wouldn't return until the early hours of the morning.

"Yep. Clem in the bunkhouse?"

"You might want to take your bedroll outside tonight," Will replied.

"That bad? You should have left *him* outside," Roy answered good-naturedly.

"Considered it, but he wouldn't wake up if a grizzly stood on his chest."

Roy chuckled. "Night, ma'am," he said to Linnea. "I'll help you with those pans in the morning."

"Will said he'd do it," she answered. Thanks anyway, and good night."

Roy urged his horse toward the barn and dismounted to open one of the double doors and lead the animal inside. A moment later, light spilled out of the opening, and the door closed.

Will had unexplainably liked the sound of his name coming so conversationally from Linnea's lips. *Will said he'd do it.* He lashed the simple words and the sound of her saying them into his memory with unfamiliar pleasure.

"Roy's a nice man," Linnea said softly.

"Couldn't ask for a better partner on a trail drive or a better foreman for this spread," he replied.

"You've known him a long time?"

Will thought back. "'Bout eighteen years, I recollect."

"I wonder…" Her words trailed off.

"What?"

"Nothing. None of my business."

"Were you wondering why he'd want to work for me?"

She turned her head quickly to look at Will over her shoulder. "Of course not. Why would I wonder that?"

He shrugged.

"This is a good place to work and to live," she said. Then a minute later she confessed, "I was wondering why he didn't have a wife and family."

Will didn't have a wife and family either, but she hadn't asked *him*. Maybe she thought she knew why—because he was too cantankerous. "Can't answer that one," he replied.

Roy had fallen in love with a woman years ago, but had backed away in order for her to marry someone with more money and position. Will had been acutely aware of the situation, but it had never been discussed between them again. Roy had seemed to shrug it off and move on.

"I guess you were busy working and saving to start this ranch," she said as though thinking aloud.

The conversation was getting around to him.

She glanced up again. "I know there aren't many single women in these parts, but did you ever think about a mail-order bride? Maybe some-one your sister knows?"

Will placed his coffee on the rail before moving down a few steps to sit beside her. He propped both arms on his knees. "I thought about it."

"Didn't appeal to you?"

"Think I would have appealed to one of them?" he asked in a self-derisive tone.

She shrugged noncommittally. "There's worse places, worse people to be married to."

She had started asking questions, so she couldn't say he'd begun the prying. He had a dozen things he'd like to know. "And you would know about them?"

"Some of them."

"Like your husband?"

She nodded silently, not offering any information.

"Why did you marry him?"

She looked away so he couldn't see her face. "I didn't have any choice."

As desperate for a place to live and a job as she'd been when she came here? Pregnant? Not this baby, but another one perhaps… No, she was too young, too ignorant of childbearing. A bargain of some sort maybe.

Will thought back over her reactions to him and her reaction to Nash the day he'd swatted at the bee. "Did he hit you?"

Still looking away, she nodded.

The thought of a man, so much bigger and stronger than this tiny woman, abusing her in such a way, sickened him. The coffee settling in his stomach burned.

"Did you love him?" Will couldn't believe he'd asked that question! Even his ears burned with embarrassment. He opened his mouth to tell her not to mind him, but she replied first.

"No," she said, turning to look at him finally.

Why had he cared? Why was he immeasurably relieved to hear her say that simple word? He should have left well enough alone.

She wasn't grieving for a beloved husband.

A dozen more questions whirled in his head. Why had she married him? What had happened to him? Why had she been forced to seek work here? Where was her family?

"The closest thing I know to love is what I feel for my baby," she said softly, placing her hand on her round belly. "I love him even though I've never seen him. And he's..." Her voice broke and she swallowed. "He's going to love me, too."

Helpless to comment, Will nodded dumbly.

Crickets chirped from their hiding places at the corner of the house and the nearby bushes. A horse in the corral nickered and another neighed in reply. Farther away, an owl hooted.

"Would you like to feel him again?" she asked.

Her offer surprised Will. He had been fascinated by the feel of her belly against his midsection as they danced. "You wouldn't mind?"

"No. Put your hands here." She placed her own on the left side of her stomach.

Will started to move in front of her on the steps, and then changed his mind and instead sat behind her, placing one leg on either side of her so her back was against him, and wrapped his arms around her to reach where she indicated.

She took his hands and placed them on the hard mound of her belly, and the firmness amazed him. An infant so large and solid inside her was incredible. Her skin through the fabric of her dress was

warm and her hair still smelled fresh and feminine. He could have wrapped his arms around her
twice, she was so small.

A tiny fluttering grazed his palm. Another. A
moment later a series of kicks were aimed at his
wrist and he moved his hand over them. Linnea's
baby thrived, safe and nourished by her body for
the time being. What would happen after he was
born? When she would need to spend her time
taking care of him and be unable to work?

Will had promised she could stay until then, but
warned her she would have to leave. He'd been
eager to be rid of her since the moment he'd laid
eyes on her. He'd deemed her inappropriate for
the job, but she'd proved him wrong. He'd thought
she'd fold under the workload, but she had held
her own.

Maybe he was wrong about her being able to
care for a baby and stay here, too. He'd never been
so uncertain of himself and his judgment until
she'd shown up, and he didn't like the feeling.

But the other feelings…the ones that caught
him unexpectedly when she was near…when he
touched her…when she looked at him or said his
name…those feelings he regretfully liked.

Her hands still covered the backs of his, her
arms rested along the length of his, and she had

leaned her shoulders back to relax against him. The way he sat straddling her brought her back into contact with his groin and her hips against his thighs. He grew more aware of her body against his than the movement beneath his hands.

Her apparent ease with the intimate contact pleased him, adding to his rising ardor, and he struggled with guilt over holding and desiring a woman he planned to send away.

She turned her face up toward his, an innocent invitation if ever there was one, and smiled hesitantly.

Will surrendered to the temptation and the desire, lowering his head, and kissing her full on the lips.

Chapter Nineteen

William savored every moment of kissing Linnea's warm moist lips, plying them with firm gentle pressure. He took his hands from her belly so he could move to her left side and better align their mouths. With one hand he held her shoulder, and with the other he cupped her fragile jaw, slowly ran a finger along the silky skin to her chin…her cheek.

Her breathing was shallow and warm, and she raised a hand to grasp the front of his shirt, as though holding him in place.

After caressing her cheek, then her jawbone, he fingered a silky curl at her ear and dared to slip his forefinger inside the collar of her dress and draw a line along her collarbone. Lord, she tempted him to touch her, to hold her close and feel her soft body against his. Because he sensed her timid reactions, he used all the restraint he could muster to keep his caresses sweet and unthreatening.

He nibbled on her top lip, then the bottom one, then darted his tongue along the crevice. With utmost delicacy, he traced a line of kisses across her chin and to her jaw, then gently nibbled on her earlobe.

Linnea sucked in a quick breath as though startled, but her grasp on his shirt held fast. "What are you doing?" she asked in a weak whisper.

He kissed the silken skin behind her ear, inhaled the heady fragrance of her, nuzzled his nose to her neck and opened his mouth to sample her flesh. "Tasting you," he said between kisses.

A shiver ran through her body.

Linnea raised her hand to the side of his head, threading her fingers into his hair. His scalp prickled with the delightful sensation her touch created. The fact that she hadn't pulled away, but rather touched him in return filled him with exultation.

He raised his head, and she pressed her cheek to his, her breath catching against his ear and sending fire through his veins.

Will pulled back to look into her eyes and run his thumb over her moist velvety lips. From her naive reactions of surprised pleasure, he could think she'd never been kissed before. Her dazed expression was illuminated in the light from the doorway, and her expression was one of discovery. "Did you like it?"

She nodded.

With the pads of his thumb and forefinger he rubbed her earlobe, then moved in to kiss and taste it again.

"What do I taste like?" she asked.

He plucked kisses against her neck, her jaw, up to her temple. There weren't words to describe the delicacy that was Linnea. He brought his nose to hers and replied simply, "More."

"How much more could there be?" she asked.

Her question confounded him. There was plenty more that he could think of. She wasn't one to tease, so was she asking a sincere question? "How much more would you like there to be?" he asked.

She shook her head slightly, which rubbed her nose against his. "I don't know. But I don't want to stop feeling this way."

"I want to touch your hair," he said, daring to hope.

"You do?"

"I really do."

"Okay." She reached upward.

"No," he said, stopping her hand. "I want to do it."

"Okay," she said again.

To prolong the anticipation, he slowly and deliberately searched along her thick braid for the pins that held it in place. After he'd removed them one by one, her braid loosened and dropped to her back.

Will found the end and unbound the strip of cloth that held the rope in place, then began threading his fingers through the ends, higher and higher, loosening strands until her hair fell in luxurious ripples across her back and shoulders.

Her head had dropped back and her eyes were closed in an expression of sheer ecstasy. Will delved his hands into the cool silken mass of hair and massaged her scalp.

A throaty moan escaped her, fueling his lusty desires. He pressed a kiss to her exposed neck. "You're hair is beautiful," he said, his voice hoarse with desire.

She raised her head to look at him. "It is?"

"And it feels like silk."

"It's just…hair."

"No. It's shining mahogany that catches firelight and glows from within."

A nervous laugh escaped her. "You're talking about my hair."

"Yes."

She shook her head as though dazed. She looked so different with it loose, so natural, so...sensual. Every muscle in his lower body tensed.

He stroked her shoulder through the mass of hair. "I noticed right off. That first night when I was taking you back to Denver, and you brushed out your hair beside the fire."

"You did?"

He nodded, wondering if he'd revealed too much about himself with that confession. But a woman should know she had beautiful hair—and how it affected a man. Where had playing his cards close to his chest gotten him until now, anyway? "I heard you crying," he blurted.

She grew very still.

Obviously his arousal had dulled his brain and loosened his tongue.

"So you *did* feel sorry for me," she said softly.

"More likely I felt like a heel for barking at you. I mean, you didn't exactly deceive me about your age and your... Well, the fact that you're small. I just assumed that bein' a widow, you'd be older."

She faced forward, leaving him to study her

profile, and said nothing. A ball of anxiety knotted in his belly.

"I figured you'd lost your husband and were hurting, that's all."

"It's late," was all she said.

"You're probably tired."

She stood, escaping his touch. "Yes."

He watched her in the moonlight, self-consciously pushing her hair over her shoulder. Whatever he'd said wrong had made her uncomfortable and torn down the bridge he'd so patiently constructed between them.

"I had a wonderful time today," she said, then added, "…and tonight. Thank you for everything. The dancing."

"My pleasure," he replied, and nothing had ever been so true. The time they'd spent together had been indescribable pleasure.

Standing, he wanted to ask her if the kissing had been wonderful, too, an idiotic male urge for validation, but he held his tongue for the first time that night. "Good night, Linnea."

"Good night." She climbed the steps and pulled open the screen door with a squeak.

The euphoria of kissing her mixed with the reality of their situation, her glaring misgivings and the knowledge that she would inevitably be leaving in a month or so. A feeling of emptiness and yearning gaped in his chest.

After walking away from the house, Will turned and studied the light behind the curtains at her window. He'd drunk enough to loosen him up and enough to loosen his tongue, maybe, but not so much that he wasn't thinking clearly. Linnea had changed everything. His life was not the same since she'd arrived at the Double T.

Driving himself and his men from sunup to sundown hadn't been all that satisfying, now that he looked back. Staying angry hadn't provided a whole hell of a lot of comfort. There had been more missing in his life than he'd ever wanted to admit.

A shadow moved behind the illuminated shade. Will caught himself staring and looked away. He couldn't watch her window and imagine her undressing or washing or going to bed, or he'd work himself into a state and would never sleep. He turned away and sauntered to the corral, where he leaned on the fence and clucked to the whiskey-colored stallion.

The animal lifted its head and whinnied in reply.

Will smiled to himself. Two months ago, the horse would have reared and run to the far side of the corral, but tonight the magnificent animal stood with its nostrils flaring in the moonlight to catch Will's scent. The horse didn't trot over to greet him and have his poll rubbed…but Will had confidence that eventually it would. Trust. Familiarity.

A glance at the window showed him she'd gone to bed.

He'd ridden herds and worked cows for ten years to afford this spread. It had been his dream, his ambition, his destination. He'd been so driven he hadn't taken time for anything else, and now he recognized the things that were missing.

Family had never been a priority. Getting free of the mill and his father's demands had been his initial goal. He wouldn't feel guilty for not wanting the life his father demanded of him, nor would he feel bad about hightailing it out when he could.

If his father had been more understanding, they might have held on to some kind of relationship.

Will vowed again he would never place a son of his in that position. As much as he loved this ranch, if his son wanted to be a city banker or a goat herder on a mountaintop, he would give him his blessing.

At the same time he had those thoughts—and

he'd had them plenty—the nagging question arose: Where would that son come from?

There'd be time, he'd told himself. Time to find a woman who didn't drive him crazy and time to have children.

He'd been on the ranch only over a year now, and just as there'd never been time before, there seemed to never be time now. And even if there was time, where would he meet a woman? Would he be desperate enough to advertise for a wife? He'd seen how well that had worked out with a cook.

The stallion took a few steps toward him. Will spoke softly to let the animal know he was paying attention.

Well, hell, the cook hadn't worked out all that badly. Not bad at all, except for the fact that she would be leaving after the baby came. The thought gnawed an ache in his chest.

A soft nicker and a few more steps brought the horse within six yards of the fence where Will stood.

Days weren't suddenly going to multiply. Hell would freeze over before suitable women threw themselves at his feet, begging to be his wife. If change was going to come about, he was going to have to make it happen.

Linnea. This insane thinking was all about Linnea. His mind was skirting around the fact that the woman had broken down his barriers and made him think about something other than the day's chores, the coming year, the carefully laid plans for his ranch....

She'd made him think about her.

About them together.

About a life that included more than day-to-day existence and proving to himself that his dreams were important.

But she was a widow about to give birth to another man's baby, his logical mind argued.

Somehow that didn't matter to his heart. He wondered like hell about the man to whom she'd been married, the man who didn't want her to read and had most likely scared her off men. He had a feeling that if he'd ever met McConaughy before he'd died, he'd have had to pound him into the ground.

And the baby? The baby was a part of Linnea, a sweet innocent bonus thrown into the mix. At first he'd thought she wouldn't be able to survive on the ranch, as incapable and delicate as she appeared, but she'd fooled him there. He'd been sure that this was no life for a baby, either, but maybe he'd been wrong about that, too.

The Pruitts had babies who thrived. Mavis managed motherhood as well as cooking for ranch hands. He'd seen children running all over that day, babies on hips and napping in the shade. Just because life was difficult out here didn't mean people didn't get on with their lives.

So where were his thoughts leading? He'd just argued himself out of sending Linnea away.

The stallion bobbed his magnificent head, tossing his mane, then took several more steps forward.

"I think I'll call you Whiskey," Will said.

The horse wheeled on his hind legs and galloped to the opposite side of the corral.

Turning to lean back against the fence, Will stared at the darkened window at the corner of the house. So what was he thinking? About taking Linnea as his wife?

What would happen if he walked into the house, knocked on her locked door, waited for her to open it and suggested they marry?

Terrified as she was of someone coming into her room, she probably wouldn't even open the door.

But she'd know it was him; she'd open it to him. And what would he say? *Say, I was standing down by the corral thinking, and I figured, as a wife, you wouldn't make me too crazy. How about staying on and making a family here with me?* That would sweep her off her feet.

Did she want to be swept? Was he capable?

Will snorted, mentally chiding himself. He'd had too many beers and his thinking was muddled. Tomorrow he'd wake up and wonder why the doggoned damned hell he'd even let such wild thoughts bounce around in his mind.

Heading back to the house, he discovered his half-empty cup sitting on the top step. He tossed the cold coffee into the dirt and went inside. After placing the cup near the basin, he picked up the single lamp left burning and stared at the darkened hallway.

Linnea, with that thick silky hair and the sweetest lips he'd ever tasted, lay in the dark on a bed down that hall. His lusty desire was to tap on the door, find it not quite latched—as though she'd been hoping he'd come—push it open and discover her lying in the moonlight slanting through the curtains. Her hair would be draped across her bare shoulders…and breasts….

The coffee hadn't helped, he must still be drunk to be thinking like that. The door was barred with a sturdy device he'd installed himself, and Linnea was sound asleep, resting after an exhausting day.

She'd braided her hair and donned a prim night-dress and would be terrified if he woke her.

Will turned away and took the stairs up to his room.

Linnea lay in the darkness, listening to Will's footsteps on the stairs. Her heart hadn't found a natural rhythm since he'd looked at her in her new dress that morning. Her mind whirled with the events of the day and evening. She thought over every word spoken between her and her new friend, Mavis, and delighted at the knowledge that she could count on Mavis to assist her if she needed help when the baby came.

But always her thoughts came back to Will. Dancing with her. Smiling at her. Kissing her for the second time.

Kissing. Her mind rolled it over. She slid her fingertips across her lips in wonderment. Who'd have known kissing could be such sweet pleasure? That a man as big and fierce-looking as Will could be so tender and bring her senses to life so abundantly? That a man's touch would bring anything other than resigned grim submission?

The fear he created was a different fear than she knew. This new fear was over what he could make her feel, rather than what he could do to her.

Feeling something—anything—for him was dangerous. With all her heart she wanted to learn the secrets of Will Tucker's arousing touches, but she could not let herself be used and hurt, no matter how tempting the temporary pleasure.

The fact that she could associate pleasure with a man was astounding. And foreign. Deliciously alluring. Impossible.

Will was her employer. *Temporarily.* She splayed her hands over her belly and faced reality. After her baby arrived she would be leaving the Double T, and she would never see Will Tucker again.

Chapter Twenty

He wasn't drunk the next day. He wasn't even hungover. And the same thoughts still plagued him.

Linnea still didn't seem comfortable around him, but she no longer jumped when he spoke or watched him warily as though he was going to overturn the table and roar at any moment.

Throughout the morning and noon meals, she would meet his eyes and look away shyly. Embarrassed about what they'd shared? Sorry? Will had never given this much thought to anything except the price of a good horse or which stallion would cover his best mare, and now here he was thinking about Linnea and how he wanted her to stay.

He wasn't the most agreeable fellow, but he could work on that. He wasn't rich, by any means, but he owned land and good horses. He'd built and furnished an adequate home, and he could provide for her. A wife had never been a priority before. None of the women he'd met had made him think about marriage—want a wife. Until Linnea. And he wanted her.

For several days he thought and considered the words he would choose. He observed her and tried to read her mood, gauged how receptive she would be to his proposal and the arguments he would use if she hesitated—or refused.

On Thursday he made up his mind he would ask her that evening. She usually spent at least an hour reading in the kitchen with Cimarron. After their lesson, he would ask her to sit on the porch with him...or take a walk down by the stream. The walk would offer more privacy.

Darkness fell over the countryside. He bathed in the stream, dressed in clean denims and a freshly pressed shirt, and let his hair dry in the warm night air. As he approached the house, he noticed that the light was not glowing as bright as it usually did when she and Cimarron read at the table.

Will opened the back door and stepped inside. Aggie sat in her rocker by the cold fireplace, dozing with an embroidery hoop on her lap. At his arrival, she raised her head and blinked.

"Where are Cimarron and Linnea?" he asked.

Aggie slipped her spectacles from her face and squinted at him. "They didn't read tonight. I was mighty disappointed not to hear the story."

"That's unusual," he commented, thinking aloud.

"Said she was tired. Told me to tell the lad when he came around, so I did."

"Is she all right?"

"I asked her, she said she was fine."

Will stood for a moment, his plan interrupted by the change of routine. Linnea had retired this early? He should check on her. "I'll help you to bed, Aggie," he told his stepmother.

"I have to go out back first."

"I'll walk with you."

"Won't that be a treat?" She chuckled and got up with an audible creak of her bones.

Will got the lantern and accompanied the old woman out of doors, waited for her, then walked her back to the house.

He carried the lantern down the hall for her. She took it from him and entered her room. Will turned and tapped lightly on Linnea's door.

There was no response.

"Linnea, are you all right?"

"I'm fine," she replied, her voice weak. "Did you need something?"

"Open the door so I can see you," he insisted.

A moment later, he heard a shuffle and the scraping sound of the bar being raised. Linnea squinted out at the light. Behind her the room was dark. Her braid lay over her shoulder, locks of hair were loose at her face, and she had draped her shawl over her nightdress. Her sleepy gaze flicked over him in mild recognition. "Going somewhere?"

"No. Aggie said you were tired."

"So you woke me up to see?"

Putting it that way made him feel foolish. "Are you sick?"

"No."

Something didn't feel quite right, but he didn't have anything to go on other than the fact that she'd never gone to bed early before. "Sorry to bother you. Night."

"Good night."

She pushed the door shut, the bar came down on the other side, and Will stared at the wooden barrier, disappointment chugging through his veins. Of all the scenarios he had imagined, as well as their possible outcomes, this had never been one of the possibilities. In his imaginings, he'd always had a chance to ask her.

Returning to the kitchen, he stared out the back door for a length of time, then finally closed it and climbed the stairs to bed. He didn't sleep much that night.

The following morning, Linnea took longer than usual to carry platters to the table and to make the rounds pouring coffee. Once, she paused and leaned on the corner of the table. Will studied her exhaustion, noting lines at the corners of her mouth and across her forehead. Fatigue? Some sort of illness?

"Roy, you and the men head to the east range, and I'll catch up with you later," he told his foreman when the meal was nearly finished. "I'll pack food for a cold lunch."

"Okay, boss," Roy replied.

"Cimarron, fetch a rocker from the porch and wipe the dust off. Then bring a wagon around."

Cimarron did as asked.

After the men headed out, Will added wood to the stove and pumped water to heat, then filled the enamelware basin, scraped soap, and plunged the plates in. "Sit down before you drop," he told Linnea.

"I'm okay."

"You're not okay. Sit."

She sat in the rocker beside Aggie and the two women exchanged a look.

Will scrubbed and dried the dishes, then stacked

them on the table. "I want you to rest today," he told Linnea. "I'll fix our noon meal, so you won't have to handle that."

She nodded wordlessly.

He assembled the food in crates and carried it out to a wagon. Coming back to stand just inside the door, he gave her a scrutinizing glance. "You sure you're not sick?"

"I'm not sick." She waved him away with a flick of her wrist.

He hesitated a moment longer, then turned and left the house.

Linnea listened as the sound of the horse and wagon dwindled. Turning, she discovered Aggie staring at her.

"My back hurts," she explained.

"Maybe you should lie down," Aggie suggested.

"Maybe I should."

Linnea got to her feet and struggled to keep her balance as a pain shot through her back, wrapping around her sides like a vise. Her back had started hurting the day before, and lying down had helped somewhat. She'd awakened several times during the night with an agonizing, twisting knot in her back muscles. She couldn't imagine what she had done to cause so much discomfort. Maybe it was just because of her advanced pregnancy and the burden of the baby she carried.

Lying down didn't help a bit this time. She dozed, and awoke each time the pain increased. By late afternoon, the pain had moved around to the front, and with dawning realization, she admitted what she already knew: this was not a backache.

Her baby was ready to be born.

After long minutes of panic and tears, she collected herself and firmed her determination. She'd suspected the night before, but she'd refused to jump to conclusions. This morning, she'd realized that she might be ready to have her baby, and there would be no one around to call on for help.

But if she'd let on about her suspicions, Will would have wanted to go for the doctor, and she wouldn't allow that to happen. Given her own choices, no man would ever have been allowed to touch her, even if he was a doctor. If she waited long enough, she could escape that and send someone for Mavis.

When dusk came, she roused herself from the bed, her belly seizing with cramping pain, and shuffled to the kitchen. The men had eaten a cold noon meal, so she couldn't let them fend for themselves for supper.

With Aggie studying her, she quickly peeled potatoes and sliced ham to fry. She had to stop every few minutes and lean on the counter or the table and wait for the cramping to pass.

With the smells of food in the air and the kitchen hot from the stove, the familiar sounds of the men and wagons drifted through the open door.

She could make it a while longer.

Moving from the stove to the table, a pain seized her. She paused and let the kettle hit the table with a whack. Something low inside her seemed to burst and warm liquid ran down her legs. The pain grew so intense, she couldn't breathe.

Panic claimed her, and she let out a cry of alarm.

Leaving everything as it was, she turned, holding the wall for balance, and stumbled to her room.

In agony now, she lowered herself to the bed and laid on her side in a ball, squeezing her eyes shut. Everything in her lower body pushed downward, and she groaned.

She had no way of knowing how long she lay there like that, the tide of agony ebbing and flowing. Sometime later, Will appeared, his freshly washed face a familiar anchor in the sea of torture. "Will," she said.

"Linnea, what in God's name is going on?"

She didn't reply, just bit down on her lip as a pain gripped her in its teeth.

"Holy shit, woman!" he shouted. He sprang away from her momentarily, gripped his head with white knuckles, and then seemed to come out of his initial shock to spring to action. He leaned over her. "How long has this been going on?"

"All day," she ground out.

"Why the hell didn't you tell me?"

She shook her head.

"I'll send for the doctor." He started to move away, but her hand whipped out and gripped his wrist.

"No," she said through clenched teeth. "That's why I didn't tell you. I don't want the doctor." Her nails bit into his skin like talons, and her strength astonished him.

"You damned fool woman."

"I *don't* want the doctor," she insisted.

"Linnea, you need a doctor."

"Send for Mavis." A pain clenched her abdomen, and she bore down with it.

He ran out of the room long enough to shout orders to the men in the kitchen. A clatter of chairs scraping and doors slamming followed. The kitchen pump squeaked as someone drew water.

Back at her side, Will studied Linnea's sweat-soaked hair and clothing. Her face was red with exertion and from the looks and sounds of it, she had started pushing that baby out. This process was supposed to take hours—days sometimes—how had she gotten this far without him knowing? He fought back a stab of panic to think clearly.

His suspicion the night before had been his hunch, and he'd missed the truth. He could castigate himself later. It appeared he had no choice right now but to deliver a baby.

Chapter Twenty-One

"We're going to have to get you out of these clothes," he told her.

She shook her head.

"Yes. You're soaked. I'll get a dry nightdress." Turning, he pawed through the bureau drawers and found a cotton garment.

She pushed his hands away to unbutton her own shirt, but she allowed him to help her out of it. She wore a cotton chemise which was damp as well, and he turned his head while she untied and removed it and pulled the nightdress over her head.

"Now this skirt is coming off—and whatever else is under here." He picked her up and placed her on the opposite side of the bed. After stripping the wet bedding away, he placed layers of papers and blankets under her, then moved her back and used a scissors to cut off her skirt and drawers.

She didn't complain at that point, but drew a

sheet over her lower body and gripped the hem with white-knuckled fingers. Her face was white, her lips dry and her breathing ragged.

"I'm going to look," he said, after another contraction drew a cry from her.

Beyond modesty, desperate for help and relief from the pain, she allowed him to spread her thighs and assess the progress.

As he did, she bore down and made a tortured sound in her throat. To his amazement, the top of the baby's glistening head was crowning. He cursed in surprise, caught himself and fought for composure.

She laid her head back and panted. Tendrils of hair lay plastered to her pale cheeks.

He was sweating as much as Linnea, his face perspiring, a trickle running down the center of his back. He'd soothed a hundred mares through this process with his voice, but Linnea was no horse. She was a fragile young woman, and he had only a rough idea of what to do to help her. Aggie would be of no help, being feeble and never having gone through this herself.

This was beyond Will's experience, too, but her labor had progressed so far that help would never arrive in time. He was all she had.

"You're doing just fine, Linnea," he said as

assuringly as he could and stroked her damp hair away from her face. "Your baby is almost out. A few more contractions like that should do it."

"I can't," she said, her voice weak. She cried openly, tears running down her cheeks.

With one hand on her thigh, he took her hand in the other and squeezed it. "Yes, you can. I'm sorry I didn't listen to you about the doctor. You should have had Mavis here with you, but you were afraid I wouldn't listen. It's my fault, but I'm going to help you."

She nodded her understanding, but continued to cry anyway. Hell, he probably would, too, if he had something the size of that coming out of his body. He swallowed hard, felt her frantic grip on his hand tighten and looked again.

Linnea held her breath and groaned. A head covered with wet dark hair emerged from her body. Will's heart hammered. "There you go," he told her. "His head's out. Just a little while longer and it'll be over."

She was concentrating now, and maybe his words were helping her to focus, so he continued to talk, speaking softly and assuring her the ordeal was almost finished.

Within minutes, he guided a slippery little body into the world. Though her face was scrunched, the infant was amazingly perfect; her scrawny legs were drawn up like a frog's until she squirmed and stretched one out. Her tiny foot trembled and Will closed his huge hand over it gently, amazed at the sight. His hand swallowed the baby's entire spindly leg.

"It's a girl," he told Linnea, his voice thick. "You have a daughter."

After wiping blood and moisture from the infant, he tied the umbilical cord with a piece of string and cut it. The baby's first cries reached a place in his heart he hadn't known was there until that moment. He wrapped the baby in one of Linnea's clean aprons and held her to his chest to keep her warm.

The one small doubt he'd had—that he would be able to accept this child as his own—fled in that instant.

"Let me see her," Linnea said.

Will placed the child in her arms. Linnea examined every finger and toe and gave the squalling red infant a watery smile.

Will delivered the afterbirth and cleared away the soiled papers and blankets, making Linnea comfortable and seeing to her needs. She wanted a drink, and he brought her a cup of water.

The baby's cries grew increasingly pathetic.

"She probably wants to suckle," he said over the noise. "That's the first thing most animals do."

"Oh." Linnea looked at the baby. Then at Will with raised brows. He hadn't the vaguest idea what to do and didn't like being helpless.

Voices carried down the hall. A feminine voice. Mavis.

Thank God.

"Have I missed all the excitement?" Mavis asked, sweeping into the room and hurrying to Linnea's side. "Oh, what a darling baby! What do you have there, Linnea?"

"A girl," Linnea replied with a smile.

"She's as pretty and delicate as her mama," Mavis said.

"I'll let you two get on with it," Will said, feeling quite out of place and gratefully backing toward the door.

"Looks like you both did a fine job bringing this little girl into the world," Mavis said, casting a smile from one adult to the other.

"I had no idea," Will said.

"Most men don't," Mavis replied.

Starting to shake, Will left the room. He found Aggie and Roy in the kitchen. Roy was putting away pans and starting a meal for the next day.

"Everything okay, boss?" he asked.

"She's fine. The baby's fine."

Roy placed a cup of steaming coffee on the table. "There you go. What did she have?"

Will picked up the cup and took a sip. "A girl."

"What's her name?" Aggie asked.

Will shook his head. "Don't know."

He went outside where the air was cooler and took a deep breath. The scent of pines and horses was a welcome relief.

Cimarron sat on the top step. At the corner of the bunkhouse, Will could see the flicker of the fire where the others would be gathered.

"She's fine," Will told him. "So's the baby. A girl."

Cimarron grinned, jumped up and pumped Will's hand. "I'll go tell the men."

He sprinted away.

After finishing the coffee, Will removed his shirt, hung it on the porch rail and walked out into the yard where he pumped water, dunked his head and splashed water on his upper body.

Pausing while bent over the trough, he stared at his hands. They were shaking. He flexed his fingers, grabbed the soap and scrubbed his face, hands and arms. By the time he'd dried himself and walked toward the corral the trembling in his body had subsided.

The yawning ache in his heart, however, was still there.

* * *

Linnea was so grateful for Mavis's help and attention that she cried when she woke that night and found the woman sleeping beside her, fully clothed.

Mavis raised on one elbow. "What's wrong?"

"Your family needs you, and here you are."

"They'll get by for a day or two," she replied. "Do you need the chamber pot? Something to drink?"

Linnea nodded and Mavis assisted her. Afterward they both fell back to sleep. When dawn crept around the edges of the curtains, Mavis woke Linnea and handed her the baby she had just changed.

Linnea roused and took the infant to her breast.

"She caught on just fine." Mavis watched with approval. "I'm going to light a fire in the stove and get water."

"Roy will probably do it," Linnea told her.

"He's a right handy cowboy, isn't he?" Mavis asked with a grin.

Linnea nodded. "He and Will did the cooking and laundry before I arrived."

"I'd like to have seen that," Mavis replied.

"According to the other hands, they cooked

well enough to not starve anyone to death, but the wash was another story."

With her hand on the doorknob, Mavis glanced over her shoulder. "Either one of them would make a fine husband."

Linnea looked down at the baby.

A second later Mavis hurried out of the room.

Sleepily Linnea closed her eyes, but was immediately visited by memories of the ordeal the night before. She hadn't been prepared for childbirth. But then, she hadn't been prepared for a child, period.

Thinking back over her life, she couldn't recall anything she ever *had* been prepared for... not for being evicted from the only home and family she'd ever known, certainly not for being married to a man who considered her a possession, not for the life she'd been forced to lead with him. Even her widowhood had been a shock, and neither had she been ready to work and support herself and a baby.

Now she definitely wasn't prepared to leave the comfort and security of the Double T, or the friends she'd made. How she would get by with a baby to care for she wasn't sure. She would have to find a position where she could work and take care of her daughter at the same time. How likely was that? Perhaps she could find a well-off family, one like Will's sister's, who needed a housekeeper and cook. She didn't know any fancy recipes, but now that she could read, she could learn. The thought gave her slim satisfaction.

The baby had fallen asleep nursing, and Linnea held her to her shoulder and patted her back as Mavis had showed her.

Mavis entered the room with a tray of food. The aroma of hot coffee and bacon made Linnea's stomach growl. "Oh, that smells good."

"Good, you're hungry." Mavis arranged the tray on Linnea's lap and took the infant from her.

Linnea eagerly picked up her fork and ate.

Mavis settled back into a rocker that had been moved into Linnea's room and held the baby on her lap where she could look at her. "She has delicate features like you."

"She isn't as red as last night. And her ears and nose aren't so smashed."

"No, I'd say she's about perfect."

Linnea smiled and sipped her coffee. It was rich and strong and tasted wonderful. The familiar everyday sounds of the ranch reached the open window—horses, men's voices, hammering. Ordinarily she would be hanging wash on the line about now, the morning sun warming her back.

"What are you gonna name her?" Mavis asked.

Linnea cradled the hot cup between her palms. She hadn't even thought about a name, she realized with a pang of guilt. There'd been so much else to worry about, she had completely ignored something that considerable. "I don't know."

"She needs a feminine name, don't you think? Nothing like *Mavis*." The woman shook her head as though scornful.

"How did you name your girls?"

"Our little ones all have Bible names," Mavis told her. "The girls were easy, because Rachel and Sarah were our mothers' names."

"That's lovely."

"What was your mother's name?" Mavis asked.

Linnea had jaded memories of a meek woman, bent and broken to the will of an abusive, demanding man. She wouldn't burden a child of hers with that legacy. "I think she needs a strong name," she replied.

Mavis stood and tucked the baby into the blanket-lined drawer she had prepared for her bed during the night. "You know best."

Linnea was thoughtful for several minutes. "Have you ever read *Tom Sawyer?*"

"I have."

"So have I. Do you think Becky is a good name? A strong name?"

Mavis appeared to think for a moment. "I believe so. It's short for Rebecca, and Rebecca is a Bible name. A fine one."

"Rebecca it is, then," Linnea decided, admiring the way the name sounded and imagining calling to her little girl a few years from now. She couldn't really imagine it though, because their future was so uncertain.

Mavis stayed another night, and on the following morning, Linnea insisted she go home to her family.

"You've been so much help," she told her. "And a comfort. I wouldn't have known what to do without you. Thank you so much."

"You'll still have questions," Mavis warned her, "so you have someone bring you to my place for visits now and then."

"I'll try. But I'm not sure how much longer I'll be at the Double T. My agreement with Mr. Tucker was that I'd leave after the baby came."

"Whatever for? It's obvious you run an efficient kitchen and have the household in order. The hands ask about you every meal, and Aggie thinks you're an angel. Will couldn't have any complaints about your work, so why are you thinking to leave?"

Linnea lowered her gaze to the faded quilt. "I deceived Will," she confessed.

"Deceived him how?"

"When I arrived, I didn't let on that I was going to have a baby. I wanted to prove myself and show I could do the job."

"And you have."

She shrugged and met Mavis's concerned eyes. "A baby wasn't part of the bargain when he hired me. It was a mistake not to tell him."

Mavis placed a stack of clean folded flannels on the bureau, then picked up Linnea's hairbrush. Linnea moved to the edge of the bed and Mavis sat behind her. "You did the best you could for both of you," she said firmly, and began to stroke the bristles through Linnea's hair. "Why, you'd just lost your husband and had to fend for yourself. You were carryin' a babe, to boot. I think you were very brave to come out here and take on such a hard job."

"You do?"

"I certainly do. I'm guessing that once you and Will have a chance to talk things through, you'll both see that for you to stay is the best thing." She continued brushing Linnea's hair, then began to gather strands from the front to the back for a braid. "Besides, I've seen the two of you together...the way he looks at you." She chuckled. "I'll bet he has ideas that don't include you leaving."

Linnea turned her head. "What do you mean?"

Mavis nudged Linnea's head forward again so she could work with her hair. "You know what I mean. Romantic ideas."

Heat flooded Linnea's neck and face. "No," she said softly.

"Don't tell me you're not aware. He danced with you on Independence Day—"

"A lot of people danced together, that doesn't mean anything."

"He's never looked at you in a certain way, a way that let you know he thinks you're...special?" She leaned over Linnea's shoulder and asked, "Perhaps *kissed* you?"

Linnea couldn't reply. Her heartbeat skittered crazily.

"Uh-huh, I thought so." Mavis chuckled and finished the braid. "The man has rocks in his head if he doesn't make you his wife."

"It's not like that," Linnea replied uneasily.

"Whatever you say."

Linnea knew Mavis thought Will had only to

say a few sweet words and she'd fall into his arms and marry him. Even if Will knew any sweet words, Linnea wouldn't be staying. She had pressed her luck long enough.

"Thank you, Mavis. Thank you for everything."

Mavis packed the small bag she'd brought, gave Rebecca a last loving look and touched Linnea's cheek. "You come visit me now."

With a false smile, Linnea nodded. It would never be.

Chapter Twenty-Two

Linnea introduced Rebecca to Aggie that afternoon. Aggie blinked through her spectacles. "Tiny, ain't she?"

Linnea nodded and asked if Aggie wanted to hold her.

The old woman settled the snugly wrapped infant in the crook of her arm and rocked her while Linnea set about peeling potatoes and scraping carrots while sitting in the other rocker. A savory-smelling roast was cooking in the oven, and she added the vegetables.

The screen door creaked and Roy entered, removing his hat and hurrying forward. "What are you doin' out of bed? The boss'll skin me alive for lettin' you in here."

"You didn't let me in, I came on my own," she replied.

"If you're stayin', then you're sittin'," he told her firmly. "Go."

Linnea sat beside Aggie.

Roy's attention wavered to the baby Aggie held. "Is that her?" He walked forward and bent over the sleeping infant. The expression on his weathered face changed to one of awe. As she'd noticed before, Roy Jonjack was a nice-looking man. "She's a pretty little thing, Miz McConaughy. What's her name?"

"Her name's Rebecca." She took the baby back from Aggie.

He finished the preparations, set the table, made coffee and poured milk into pitchers. By the time the vegetables were cooked, the men started arriving. One by one, they quietly admired Linnea's daughter, then conspicuously departed and returned with gifts.

Clem had carved a pair of horses, Nash had found a pastel crocheted blanket somewhere and Ben a tiny pair of booties—Linnea suspected Mavis had helped with both of those items. Roy presented Rebecca with a fabric-covered box containing colorful silk ribbons. "Little girls need ribbons for their hair," he said.

"And Rebecca will be using them before long." Linnea smiled and fluffed the dark hair on her baby's head.

Cimarron moved forward last, carrying a large bundle covered with a wool blanket. He set the armload before Linnea, then swept away the covering to reveal a large, sturdy cradle.

The wood had been sanded and stained, polished to a lustrous sheen. Adorning the headpiece was a carving of running horses, manes and tails flying. "It's from all of us."

The interior was padded with blankets and a silver rattle lay atop them. "The rattle's from me," Cimarron added.

Linnea blinked back tears to raise her gaze to each man who stood in a semicircle before her. "Thank you, all of you," she managed to say in a choked voice.

Ben cleared his throat, and the men broke up their gathering and took seats at the table.

Linnea's gaze discovered Will, standing beside the table where'd he'd been observing the scene as a bystander, like always. She hadn't seen him since the night Rebecca had been born. He moved toward her now. "You up to this?" he asked.

She nodded. "Yes."

There was so much she wanted to say to him, but the room was filled with activity and Aggie sat right beside her.

Will's gaze fell to the baby in her arms. "Rebecca, huh?"

"It's a strong name."

"Mavis said she's healthy."

"She is."

He nodded. "Good."

He turned then and took his seat.

Linnea placed the baby in the cradle. The kitchen was warm, so she placed the soft blanket beside the baby. She and Aggie moved to sit at their places at the end of the table.

The hands smiled and Roy stood beside the women to hold the platters and bowls while Linnea dished out their servings.

Conversation swelled around Linnea, and her heart felt full as it had never been before. She looked from one face to the other. She knew much of these men's history from their tales of trail drives and family memories. She'd seen them work and play, had watched them react in emergencies and heard their teasing.

She didn't think it was only because of their fear of Will that they treated her with respect and concern. Will had chosen his "family" of ranch hands well. They were good, decent, hardworking men, the kind of men Linnea had never before encountered, and knowing them—*knowing Will*—had gradually turned her opinion of males inside out.

The Double T was more than a place to work.

It had become of haven of sorts, a place where she felt needed and safe. The feeling was wonderful, because she'd never experienced such security; the feeling was terrible, because it was only a false security: she had to leave.

That evening, after Aggie had gone to bed and Linnea had fed Rebecca, she carried the baby to the porch to rock. The night sounds were comforting and the refreshing mountain breeze cooled the air. She hummed and enjoyed the opportunity to relax and hold her baby.

A tall broad figure approached the house and Linnea made out Will's familiar form. He climbed the stairs and removed his hat, hanging it on the branch of a box elder bush that had grown over the edge of the porch rail.

"Don't push yourself to do more than you're ready for," he told her.

Always in charge, always giving orders, but she'd come to trust his judgment for the most part, and now suspected that some of the bossiness was just blustering. "I won't."

"Nash and I started the springhouse today," he told her.

"I heard the men's talk about moving stones last week," she replied.

"Complaining, more likely."

She tipped her head noncommittally. Ben and Clem *had* been jawing about their aching backs and arms. "So it's to be a stone structure nearby?"

"Built over the spring where we've been storing milk and butter in crocks and jars all this time. The water running down from the mountains is ice-cold year round. We'll be able to store meat and perishables and keep animals out."

"Rebecca and I will walk over and see it in a day or so."

Silence lapsed between them, and she sensed there was something more he wanted to say. He didn't speak however, so she said, "I want to thank you. For helping with the baby, you know…"

He crossed his arms over his chest and leaned his hips against the rail. "In case you don't recall, I said it was my fault that you didn't send for help sooner. I don't understand why you didn't want Dr. Hutchinson, but you'd told me so, and I was too pigheaded to let it go. If you'd trusted me, you could have told me and I would have sent for Mavis a lot sooner."

"It has nothing to do with not trusting you," she argued, feeling terrible that he'd think so. "It has nothing to do with you."

"Well…"

"No need to be sorry," she said quickly. "Everything turned out just fine."

"Well, I'm sorry anyway. About other things, too."

She didn't know what he meant and he didn't say.

"When you're rested, Linnea, we'll talk more."

When she was rested, she'd be able to leave. That was what he wasn't saying.

Chest aching, she nodded.

"I'll take the cradle to your room. Do you need anything else?" he asked. "Can I carry water for you?"

"That would be nice." She got up and he followed her into the house.

After taking the cradle down the hall, Will returned. He dipped a pail of hot water from the well on the stove and carried it and a lamp to her room, where he poured water into the pitcher on the night table. Turning, he looked at her where she stood just inside the door. His gaze fell to the baby in her arms. He took a few steps closer.

"Would you like to hold her?" Linnea asked.

Without reply, he reached to take the baby from her. Rebecca's head fit in the palm of his enormous hand, and the rest of her body in the other. The baby's mouth formed an O and she stretched.

Cradling her against the front of his shirt, he held her securely in one arm. With a long finger, he touched her cheek and ear, then her tiny fingers. "So much more helpless than other creatures," he said. "Even a colt or a calf gets up and walks to its mother's teat right off. Babies can't do anything for themselves."

He glanced up and found Linnea looking at him. Turning, he placed the baby in the cradle. "Night."

"Good night. Will."

A week passed. Will finished the springhouse and Linnea and Rebecca visited the site. The small stone structure was charming, with four walls, a roof and a wooden door with a latch. Will had to bend over to pass through the opening, but Linnea passed under the doorway with the frame barely grazing her head.

Inside, it was as cool and crisp as a December morning in Kansas. Linnea breathed the air in surprise, snuggled Rebecca to her breast and covered her with the hem of her apron. "Oh, my!"

Water gurgled in through an opening on one side, caressed the crocks and pails in the trough down the center, and flowed out through the hole in the opposite wall. The trough was built with

sides to hold containers and keep jars from float-
ing away.

"I've never seen anything like this," she
breathed. "Or felt it! It's like winter in here."

Will grinned. "I 'spect I'll be chasin' cowboys
out on scorching August afternoons from here
on out."

The thought that this would be a good place to
cool off on a hot day had already crossed Linnea's
mind, and she laughed.

By the time another week passed, Linnea had
worked caring for the baby into her daily routine. Rebecca slept an amazing amount of time, as
Mavis had assured her she would, giving Linnea
sufficient time to cook and serve meals, though
Roy and Will often helped.

When she tackled the laundry for the first time,
the baby wailed, so she tucked her into a sling she
fashioned from dish towels, tied it at her shoulder
and waist and carried her daughter as she worked.

Will laughed and called Rebecca a little pa-
poose.

The days passed and Rebecca opened her eyes
and stayed awake for longer periods of time. In
the middle of the third week, Will got a telegram
from his sister and sent Cimarron to escort her
and her children to the ranch. Linnea prepared

an upstairs bedroom and baked extra bread and a cake.

The baby woke Linnea before dawn the next day. Linnea nursed her, then settled on the porch to enjoy the sunrise and the first signs of activity. In the dense green vegetation to the west of the house, away from the corrals and bunkhouse, a pair of elk fed on rootstocks and new shoots. Linnea watched them until Will strode from the barn toward the house and the animals bounded up the forested incline out of sight.

He built a fire in the stove and started coffee. Linnea settled Rebecca in her cradle while she prepared johnnycakes and sausage.

The men had settled in to their breakfast when the sound of a wagon alerted them to someone approaching.

Will laid down his fork, stood, and moved to the doorway. With one hand raised to the doorframe, he said over his shoulder, "It's Cimarron with Corinne and the kids."

He pushed open the screen door and went to meet them.

Conversation resumed around the table. The men ate and drank their coffee, and eventually headed out. All but Roy, who scraped plates and poured hot water into the enamel basin.

"I can finish those, Roy, if you'd like to get on with your chores," Linnea told him.

He scrubbed plates and dipped them in rinse water. "I'm goin' full chisel now, ma'am. I'll have these done in a shake."

Linnea wiped the table and placed Will's un-eaten breakfast on the stove to warm. She itched to go look out the door and see what was happening, but Corinne was Will's family and she was the hired help, so she kept to her work.

Finally the door opened and a dark-haired boy wearing a shirt and vest bounded into the kitchen. He glanced around, spotted Linnea and Aggie and greeted them both. "Morning, Mrs. McConaughy, ma'am."

Linnea had met Corinne's children when she'd stayed two nights with them in Saint Louis. This young fellow was Corinne's son. "Hello, Zach. Did you have a good trip?"

"The train ride was great fun, and sleeping out-of-doors last night was a splendid adventure. Cimarron showed me bear tracks! That's why we headed out so early this morning. He was afeared there was a bear close."

"That was wise of him. Are you hungry?"

"Sure am." He slid off his cap and stretched

to hang it on a lower peg before approaching the table.

Linnea prepared him a plate and set it before him.

The door opened and Corinne entered, followed by Will, who carried five-year-old Margaret on one arm. The cherubic girl wore a frilly blue dress and matching bonnet, beneath which long dark curls hung over her shoulders.

Corinne was a tall woman with a curvaceous shape and lustrous dark hair in an elegant up-sweep, and Linnea couldn't help wondering how she achieved such an elegant appearance after sleeping on the ground and waking beside a campfire.

"Linnea!" she said, and swept forward. "Don't you look well!"

She greeted Linnea with a warm hug, surprising her.

Corinne then turned to Aggie and said politely, "Agnes, how are you faring?"

"Got no complaints today," Aggie replied.

Corinne turned to her daughter, whom Will had just set down. "Margaret, mind your manners and greet your nana."

"Ma'am," little Margaret said with a curtsey.

Linnea's head spun at hearing Aggie referred

to as Agnes, then nana. She glanced at Aggie and didn't note a disapproving reaction.

"Where's the baby?" Corinne asked.

Linnea stepped aside and gestured to the cradle.

Corinne swept forward. "Cimarron told us she was a beautiful little girl." She caressed the sleeping baby's tiny fist with one finger and smiled. "So sweet and innocent. I can hardly remember when my babies were this little. Matter of fact, I don't think they were ever this little." She grinned and looked up at Linnea. "Rotund, they were."

Corinne glanced toward Roy and straightened. The ranch hand was drying plates and stacking them, but at her notice he stopped and gave her an awkward nod. "Hello, Mrs. Dumont."

"Roy," she replied with high color in her cheeks, and Linnea wondered if it had been there all along and she hadn't noticed, but she didn't think so.

Roy averted his gaze.

Will glanced between the two of them, then at Linnea.

"Margaret, would you like to join Zach at the table for breakfast?" Linnea asked.

Margaret said she would and Will helped her onto a bench near his seat.

Linnea prepared plates for Margaret and Corinne and placed Will's unfinished meal before him, then poured coffee.

Quickly finishing the dishes, Roy grabbed his hat and left.

Corinne was talking to Will at the time, but her gaze slid briefly to the door.

The encounter puzzled Linnea, and she couldn't figure out why Corinne's reaction to Roy seemed odd.

"You sounded highly agitated in your telegrams," Corinne said to her brother. "I had business to attend to, but I came as soon as I could. Whatever had you in such a snit?"

Embarrassment heated Linnea's skin. As angry as he'd been upon her arrival, she could well imagine what Will had written to his sister. She had food to prepare for the noon meal, but it could wait while she left them alone to talk. She started toward Rebecca's cradle.

Will glanced at Linnea, then back at his sister. "I may have been a little hasty in my first reaction," he said. "I thought you'd hired someone completely wrong for the work."

"I had a feeling the two of you needed each other," Corinne replied with unabashed frankness. "Was I right?"

Chapter Twenty-Three

Needed each other?

Linnea had bent over Rebecca to check her flannel. Corinne's words caused her to pause and stare at Aggie.

A twinkle lit Aggie's eyes behind her spectacles but she said nothing.

An eternity passed as Linnea waited for Will's reply.

"Things have turned out better than I thought," he said finally.

Corinne laughed. "That's a pretty big admission for a mule-headed man like you! She must be a wonderful cook!"

"Linnea, come sit with us," Will called over. "I don't like talkin' about you like you're not here."

"I was just going to go out and pick beans for supper while it's still cool," she replied.

"The beans will still be there," he said. "Sit a minute." Then he added, "Please."

Linnea turned in time to see Corinne's eyebrows raise and a smile touch her lips. She poured herself a cup of coffee and sat with Zach between her and Will.

"So you've found your niche on the Double T rather nicely," Corinne said. "And from what Cimarron said, you're quite popular among the hands."

"They're good men," Linnea replied.

"My brother always made wise choices." Corinne glanced at her brother and back. She turned to Aggie then, "Agnes, will you join us for coffee?"

Linnea started to rise, but Corinne waved her back down. She assisted Aggie to the table and poured her a cup of coffee.

Eventually the children were finished and asked to go outdoors to play. "Uncle Will will bring our trunks in. You must change clothing first," their mother told them.

"May we play with our shoes off, Mama?" Zach asked.

Corinne smiled. "Yes. And you will remember everything that Uncle Will has taught you about safe places to play, and you will stay close by."

Will went out for the enormous trunks that had already been placed on the porch, and carried them up the stairs, one at a time.

Corinne said to Linnea, "This is their time to be carefree and have fun. They can't go barefoot in the city, you know."

Linnea had grown up in a family where shoes were a luxury and worn only in winter, so she didn't share the Dumont children's excitement in being able to go without. She merely nodded as if she understood.

"You've visited the ranch before?" Linnea asked.

"Just once last summer," she replied.

"I had the feeling that you and Roy already knew each other."

Corinne slid her gaze away and picked up plates and cups. "I've known Mr. Jonjack since we were...well, a lot younger. He's from Indiana, where Will and I grew up."

That explained a little more, but still left Linnea curious. Her life experiences were on the other side of the moon from this woman's. "Oh."

"I'd love a bath once the children go out," she said, "to wash off the grime from the train ride and hopefully ease the aches from sleeping on the ground."

Linnea knew exactly how she felt and told her so.

"Will you ask one of the men to set up the tub and heat water?" Corinne asked.

"Right away."

Corinne hurried upstairs to help the children change.

Will had come back downstairs and plucked his hat from a peg. "One of the men will help with the noon meal," he said, and left.

Nash arrived to help Linnea with both the noon meal and supper that day. Since Roy was always the one to assist with meals, Linnea found Nash's assignment odd. Nash wasn't nearly as efficient or helpful, and she ended up sending him away after dinner, so she could clear the dishes and set things straight herself.

The sounds of children's laughter floated in through the open door, and she paused in the doorway to watch Will playing with Zach and Margaret in the yard. The sky was beginning to turn dark and fireflies already danced across the landscape.

Margaret rode on Will's shoulders as Zach chased them around a clump of rabbit bush. The child's dark hair was a wild tangle of curls about her shoulders, her once-white apron grass-stained, and the soles of her feet dirty. She laughed joyously, jumped up and down on Will's shoulders and grasped his hair for balance. He grimaced in pain but didn't halt the frivolity.

Both uncle and niece laughed when Zach caught up to them, and Will let Zach tackle him, careful to cushion Margaret's fall. Immediately Will pounced upon Zach and tickled the boy mercilessly. The three romped on the grass like playful puppies.

As she observed, a hollow awareness crept over Linnea.

Zach jumped up and darted away, frightening a rabbit from beneath a bush. The lightning-fast creature bounded into the nearby woods.

"I didn't even see him there!" Zach shouted.

"That's why they call it rabbit bush," Will explained. "See the olive-green leaves and gray branches? The colors blend with the rabbit's fur so he can hide."

Although Corinne was a widow, her children had once known a father's love, and still had an uncle who adored them so much, he'd seemingly changed personalities when they'd arrived. Who, besides Linnea, would Rebecca have to play with her, teach her things…to love her?

"What are those bushes by the porch?" Zach asked.

"Sweetbriar roses," Will answered.

"I saved water for you to bathe," Corinne called to her children. "I'll add a kettle of hot to it now, so brush yourselves off. You first, Margaret."

"Oh, Mama, do we have to take a bath now?" Zach asked. "We're just going to play again tomorrow."

"Yes, you do," she replied. "Mrs. McConaughy keeps a fine house with freshly washed bedding, and you will not be placing your dirty feet under her sheets."

"Zach can bathe with me," Will suggested, brushing off his trousers.

"In that cold stream?" Corinne asked with a shudder.

"Feels great on a hot night," he replied. "Come on, boy, I'll get soap and toweling and you bring clean pants."

Linnea turned back to set a kettle to boiling. She poured it into the water in the tub just as Margaret and Corinne reached the bathing room.

"Thank you kindly, Linnea," Corinne said.

"There's more soap and towels," she told her, pointing to a shelf, then left them.

Down on the stream bank, Will stripped and plunged into the refreshing water, and Zach followed, squealing at the temperature. Will laughed and lathered the boy's hair.

"When I get big, will I have hair all over me like you, Uncle Will?" he asked with his nose inches from Will's chest.

"You can bet on it."

"I want to let my hair grow long like yours, but Mama says it's uncivilized."

Will chuckled. "You'll be old enough to wear your hair any way you like soon enough, until then you do as your Mama says. She knows what's best for you. Dunk your head and rinse now."

Zach dunked and sputtered and came up talking. "Mama says Mrs. McConaughy is just what you needed, do you think that's so? Do you know what she means by that?"

As they washed and dried and dressed, Will listened and answered questions, but his thoughts kept returning to Linnea and his sister's words. *I had a feeling the two of you needed each other. Was I right?*

Had he needed *Linnea*? He'd never questioned that she'd needed his help and security, but what about the other way around? Something about her had drawn him from the very start. He'd felt an overwhelming protectiveness and later an unmistakable attraction. Maybe he was the one who'd needed her all along, not the other way around.

He and Zach approached the house, their hair

already drying in the breeze. Will escorted his nephew to the house and wished him good-night, then sauntered to the corrals.

He'd already decided to ask Linnea to stay. Had been prepared to propose to her the night before Rebecca had been born. What good were fine horses, prime cattle or a sturdy house if he had no one with whom to share his dream and his life? No one to love and love him in return?

That foreign thought threw dirt on his fire. What could make a fragile china doll like Linnea fall for a coarse cranky man like him?

Perhaps he needed to rethink his plan—not rush headlong into asking her until he was sure she felt something for him. She should have more of a reason to stay than for only the security of a home for her baby.

A light in the upstairs bedroom revealed that his sister was busy with her children. He walked back to the house and found Linnea in a rocker on the porch. Rebecca slept on her lap. "Care to take a walk?"

Linnea stood, and he met her at the bottom of the stairs to take the baby from her. Cradling Rebecca in one arm, he offered the other to Linnea and led her away from the house.

They walked along the stream, where moonlight glistened off the bubbling water and gurgled along the banks.

"Is the water really cold to bathe in?" she asked.

"I only notice the cold in winter," he replied. "'Course, the ice is a clue."

She contemplated his teasing grin.

"Put your feet in and see for yourself," he suggested.

She regarded him. "Really?" she asked, her tone hopeful.

"Go ahead."

She sat and removed her shoes and stockings, rolled up the legs of her drawers, and while holding Will's hand for balance, took a step into the water. It was cold, but not uncomfortably so. The sensation felt wonderful on her feet and ankles, but the stones hurt her feet.

"Wade up here," he said. "There's a rock where you can sit."

She did so, and sat with her feet dangling in the cold water. After a few minutes it didn't feel so cold anymore. Will settled behind her, holding Rebecca.

Some time later she turned and placed her feet flat on the rock, which was still warm from the sun. Will regarded her in the moonlight, once again contemplating how he could win her affection.

With the baby safely nestled on his lap, he reached for Linnea's foot. The skin was damp and cool, the bones small and delicate to his touch. She seemed surprised, but she didn't pull away. He massaged the sole and stroked each toe, then gave her other foot the same attention. "Does that feel good?"

Her reply was a whispered "Yes."

"Move closer."

She scooted up beside him, her knees to the side, and he wrapped one arm around her, his other hand securely on the sleeping baby.

Will threaded his fingers into her hair, reaching to the back and bringing her braid over her shoulder to stroke it.

He touched her face with one finger, ran it across her lips and over her brow. His finger tingled, and his body responded. Her lips parted and she leaned forward.

Covering her mouth with his, Will let himself be absorbed by the explosive sensations her lips created against his. He wanted to kiss her more deeply, pull her against him and lose himself in her, but he held back, keeping their embrace light and the kiss gentle. He had frightened her in the past, with his curses and his angry outbursts. He was aware that a man, or men, had frightened her at some time in the past; her reactions had revealed that long ago. He didn't want to be another man who scared her.

A shiver went through her body. On his lap, the baby stirred.

Will drew away. "I think she's waking up."

Linnea observed Rebecca yawn and stretch. "It's time for her to nurse."

She donned her stockings and shoes and they strolled back to the house. By the time they reached the porch, Rebecca had begun to cry.

"Here's your mama, little one," Will told her, handing Linnea the baby.

Their hands grazed as Linnea accepted the bundle, and she glanced up at his face, lit by the light from the kitchen. She'd once thought his face so hard, his eyes dark and angry, but now she found him strikingly handsome, his eyes filled with stormy passion.

He backed away and she carried Rebecca to her room, where she nestled on the bed to feed her. By the time an hour had elapsed, the baby slept again, and Linnea had gone for water, washed, changed and slid into bed. Thinking of the delightful children in the bed upstairs, she smiled.

Minutes later a knock sounded on her door.

Linnea's heartbeat stumbled. She pushed off the light sheet and padded to the door. "Yes?"

"It's me." Will's voice.

She pressed a hand to her breast. He'd never come to her room except for something important. She raised the wooden bar and opened the door.

Will shot a glance toward Aggie's room, then took a step forward. Automatically, Linnea backed up for him to enter.

He pushed the door shut.

She took stock of him in the darkness. "Is something wrong?" she asked softly.

"We weren't finished...were we?"

She caught her breath.

"It's not proper for me to be here, I know, but we never have time alone." His voice, rough and low, stirred something to life inside her. "Tell me to go, and I will."

She said nothing. He smelled like a combination of the soap she'd made and fresh summer air. Her skin tingled all over at the sensory onslaught.

"I want to kiss you again."

Chapter Twenty-Four

Heaven help her, she wanted that, too. She wanted more of the sweet nerve-tingling sensations he created with his gentle kisses and reverent touches. He had never demanded or expected or forced himself on her, and she had begun to experience something altogether new and wonderful.

She took a small step that brought her breasts almost to his chest and looked up expectantly.

Will placed a hand on each shoulder and drew her closer. With an infinitely slow and purposeful movement, he lowered his head and covered her lips with his. He tasted like coffee and enchantment, his hands gentle on her shoulders, his hard chest grazing her breasts.

Linnea leaned into him, learning the length and masculine strength of his body against hers. She gave in to the need to touch him and flattened her palms against his chest, feeling the heat of his skin through his shirt. Moving one hand to his jaw, she hesitantly explored the rough exhilarating texture.

Will angled his mouth over hers, kissing her more deeply. Her entire body warmed and she returned the kiss.

His touch slid from her shoulders to her back, and one hand drew circles on her spine, the other held her waist. His touch made her light-headed and eager for more, and she moved against him, drawing a groan from his throat.

He lowered his hands to cup her buttocks, where only a thin layer of cotton separated him from her flesh. Her heated reaction to the intimacy was startling and unexpected. She loved his gifted hands on her, the gentle kneading, the measured stroking. Her body quivered with the potent pleasure he was creating.

Will rained kisses across her lips and chin, nipped her lower lip, drew a line across her lips with his tongue. Linnea hesitantly opened to his unspoken request and their tongues met in a deep erotic mating. In the cocooning darkness, they tasted and discovered, stroked and sighed, blindly caught up in the euphoria of new sensations.

Linnea's legs grew so weak, she clung to Will for support, but he didn't seem to mind. Eventually, without breaking the kiss, he moved her backward until her knees touched the mattress. She sat, and he knelt before her, his head now inches below hers, changing the slant and manner of their kiss.

Taking his mouth from hers, he pressed his lips against her neck, licked her collarbone and sent shivers skittering along her spine and across her scalp. These feelings were new and surprising... and wonderful. "I feel so strange," she said, her voice weak. "So—I don't know, not like myself."

"Is it a good feeling?" he asked.

"Oh, yes."

He cupped her face and smiled at her in the dim light that filtered through the curtains.

Linnea threaded her fingers into his heavy shoulder-length hair as she had always wanted to do, enjoying its cool texture. She understood then, as she hadn't before, his fascination with her hair. She untied her braid quickly, and in seconds the loosened tresses spread over her shoulder.

Will ran his fingers through the mass, drew it to his nose and inhaled. He kissed the end of her nose, her eyelids. "I want so much more, Linnea."

Something dropped like a lead weight in her belly.

Did she understand? A smothering sensation dimmed her pleasure as she remembered her husband's demanding physical attentions and the way the repulsive act made her feel. But then Pratt had never made her feel the way Will did—had never tried. Her husband had demanded and taken and hurt. Will stroked and inflamed and titillated. She had recognized the differences in a hundred other ways. This was different, too.

"Do you want me to lie on the bed?" she asked.

His hands stilled on her back. "Only if you want to."

Withdrawing from his embrace, she moved across the covers to lie down.

Will stood slowly, placed a knee on the mattress, causing her weight to shift, then crawled to where she lay. He stretched out beside her, braced on one elbow, and feathered her hair out over the pillow.

Linnea grasped his wrist and studied his face, wanting all those strange and delightful feelings to be there before anything more happened, and afraid they wouldn't be.

"What is it?" he asked. "What's wrong?"

She shook her head. "Nothing. I'd like you to kiss me again, if you wouldn't mind."

He chuckled before saying, "That's no great hardship, Linnea."

He lowered his head, and she met him eagerly, wrapping her arm around his neck and trembling with her need to recapture the incredible sensations she'd known only moments ago.

But Will was slow and tender and deliberate and didn't respond to her impatience. Instead, he plied her mouth with his, took her in his arms and held her so that she felt every inch of him along her barely clad body—the rough denim of his trousers, the hard metal of his belt buckle.…

He held her as though she was fragile and would break beneath his touch. Which only made her bolder, more eager to prove herself a worthy match. Her fear of losing those new feelings abated and she relaxed into him, under him, smiling against his kiss until he stopped and questioned her.

"What's so funny?"

"Nothing's funny. I'm just happy, that's all. I never knew what wanting was before."

"What do you want?"

"I'm not sure."

He brought his hand from her back and placed it beneath her breast. "Is it okay? To touch you here?"

She nodded. Her heart thumped crazily. Her breasts felt tight and tingly, an unfamiliar sensation.

He cupped her breast through her cotton night

dress, held it as though learning the weight and feel of her. Linnea's eyes drifted shut and she allowed herself to simply feel. This was the first time they'd been so close since Rebecca's birth, the first time the obstacle of her belly wasn't lodged between them, and she felt wonderfully free and unencumbered.

Will leaned over her, pressing her into the mattress, and his weight was sublime pleasure. "I don't want to hurt you," he said.

"Your belt buckle is a little uncomfortable," she admitted.

Will took his hands from her to rise and unfasten his belt. After a brief struggle, he slid it from the loops and dropped it to the floor beside the bed. Without pause, he lay beside her again. Linnea had expected him to remove his clothing, and her body had flushed with nervous heat. Instead, he had removed the offending belt and resumed his place and the sweet caresses.

In wonder and appreciation, she framed his face with her palms and kissed his lips. Moving her hands into his hair, she reveled in the contrast between this man and the one to whom she'd been married. Pratt had acted nice and sweet at first, but after she'd married him, he'd been mean and controlling.

Will, on the other hand, had appeared loud and angry, when in reality he was gentle and considerate. If he knew of her life before, of her marriage, would he still treat her so kindly? Would he still desire her this same electrifying way? She didn't think so.

But he didn't know, and his touches grew more inflaming, his kisses hotter, deeper. He rolled her sensitive nipple between his finger and thumb and an unfamiliar throbbing began at the juncture of her thighs. His hands stroked her breasts, her belly, his lips traveled a path along her jaw to beneath her ear. A shudder of exquisite sensation rippled through her body.

Linnea was caught up in the euphoria of the feelings and sensations. She clasped him firmly against her with one arm around his wide shoulders.

"Linnea," he said beneath her ear, his breath hot and moist. "I love you."

His words rang in her head. Her hands stilled on his back. "What did you say?"

He raised his head and spoke with his face inches from hers. "I said I love you. Marry me." And then he added with a grin she could see in the darkness, "Please."

The weight dropped inside her again, a spiraling downward sensation this time, followed by a chilling fear. He didn't know of her background or her experiences, or he would never have suggested such a thing.

She could never be a lady like Corinne. She bore stains that time wouldn't erase, and the fact that Will didn't know about them didn't mean they weren't there.

Studying her as though her stillness puzzled him, he raised himself on one elbow. "You don't have to answer right away," he said. "Take time to think about it."

Withdrawing from his embrace, Linnea scooted to a sitting position, drew her knees up and tucked her nightdress primly over her legs and feet.

Clearly puzzled, Will moved to a sitting position in the center of the bed. "I know I didn't make a very good impression when you arrived," he told her. "But I'm trying to make up for that. I'm ornery and quick to lose my temper. But I have a fine spread here, Linnea. Prime Texas beeves, horseflesh from good stock. The house isn't fancy, but it's solid. You can change anything you like. Buy nicer furniture. I'll be a good father to Rebecca, she'll be my own. If you'd like, I'd be proud for her to have my name—"

She shook her head and raised a hand to make

him stop. Her chest ached with the impossibility of it and his determination to convince her. He didn't understand.

He reached for her hand and drew it to his lips, where his warm breath skimmed her fingers. "Just say you'll think about it. For a week. How about a week?"

Leaning toward her, he pushed her upraised knees aside and kissed her swollen lips. A sob rose in her chest and she swallowed it down. He stared into her eyes. "Say you'll think about it."

She would do nothing else—for the rest of her life. "I'll think about it."

He kissed her then. Touched her hair and reluctantly got to his feet. "Good night, Linnea."

After bending to pick up his belt, he left and pulled the door shut behind him with a soft click.

She didn't bother to get up and drop the lock into place. Danger hadn't come barging through the door like an intruder; she had welcomed it in. She'd offered him everything she'd once been afraid he would take from her, but he'd wanted to give her something instead. A home. His name. A father for her baby.

Linnea pressed the heels of her palms against her burning eyes. She wasn't the woman he deserved, and it wasn't going to take her a week to figure that out. She was a poor uneducated girl that nobody had ever wanted. Coming here hadn't turned her into someone different.

As much as she had wanted to stay, she now knew she had to leave. It would be her decision this time. A decision she had to make.

Her heart was heavy the next morning. Nursing Rebecca hadn't raised her spirits, neither had Zach and Margaret's charming observations over breakfast. Though Will smiled and Corinne included her in the conversation, Linnea was an outsider, and pretending different wouldn't change anything.

Every hour Linnea mentally listed another reason, another difference, another way she didn't measure up. Corinne spoke in a cultured manner, dressed in expensively made clothing and dressed her hair in an elegant fashion. She was nothing but kind and friendly toward Linnea, and often asked to hold or change the baby.

But Corinne had a background and a life far from Linnea's. Linnea learned that Corinne's husband had been a banker from a well-to-do Saint Louis family. From Aggie, however, she'd learned that the bulk of her money had come as an inheritance from her father.

Aggie had resented Corinne for a good many years, but Corinne treated her as kindly as she did everyone else, and Aggie seemed to eventually warm to her and the children.

"Mama!" Margaret said, bursting into the house one afternoon. "Uncle Will says I must wear my boots around the horses! Roy is going to let me help with the saddle and we're going riding!"

With a flurry of skirts and the flounce of dark hair, the child ran to the other room and up the stairs. Moments later, she returned with stockings, boots and buttonhook in hand.

Corinne urged her daughter onto a bench and knelt before her. "Mind your uncle and Mr. Jonjack, Margaret May," she said. "Their lessons are to be taken seriously."

"Yes'm."

Corinne stood and watched her daughter run out the back door. Moving to the open doorway, she said, "Once or twice a year is not enough for them to receive fatherly attention and instruction," she said, her voice wistful. "Especially for Zach. He needs a man in his life."

"What about you?" Aggie asked from her chair at the other side of the room. "Do you need a man in your life?"

Linnea glanced up to see Corinne's reaction to the question.

"I'm beginning to think I do," Corinne replied. She slipped the buttonhook into her pocket. "I'm going outdoors to watch the children for a while."

Linnea hadn't missed the looks between Roy and Corinne at meal times, and apparently even old Aggie had observed.

By the middle of the week, Linnea knew she couldn't let Will go on thinking she might agree to marry him. If he truly had feelings for her, drawing out his hope wasn't fair. She waited until the men were gathered around their fire and Corinne had taken the children upstairs to find Will alone.

He was working in an open stall in the barn, wrapping the forelegs on one of his mares. "I knew it was you," he said, looking up.

She'd never come to him out here before. "How did you know?"

"The sound of your steps." He finished wrapping the leg and stood. The mare butted his chest with its nose, and he rubbed it distractedly. "I probably smell like a horse, I haven't washed up yet."

"I just wanted to say something to you," Linnea said.

"Okay."

"It's about what you asked me...."

"You said you'd think about it, Linnea," he said and drew his brows together in a frown. "A week, you said."

"I don't need a week." She gripped a wooden rail nervously. "No amount of time will change what I have to say."

His face changed to the unreadable mask she knew so well. "Say it then."

"I can't marry you, Will."

His disturbed gaze bore into her. "Can't or won't?"

She couldn't tell him all the reasons she couldn't stay. She never wanted him to know the truth about her marriage. Nothing would spare his feelings—or hers—anyway. "I can't. I'll be prepared to leave when it's time for Corinne to go, whenever that will be. That way you won't have to spare a hand twice."

The telltale muscle in his jaw twitched, and his lips were drawn into a firm straight line. "I can't change your mind, can I? You've made it up."

"I have to go."

"Then I won't try to convince you. You obviously know what you want and don't want."

"It's not like that, you don't understand."

"I understand well enough. What's not to understand?" He bent to pick up a pile of rags and a bucket, and she backed up to let him pass out of the stall. He pushed the gate shut and slid a lock into place.

Linnea followed him to the tack room, where he put supplies away as though she wasn't there.

"Will?" she said.

His hand stilled. He stood without moving for several seconds. Finally, he looked at her. His expression remained shuttered. "Say whatever it is you want to say, Linnea."

She could never say what she wanted to say. He'd told her he'd loved her, and that had made everything real. She didn't know what she'd been thinking before, playing with the fire of their kisses and touches, not imagining anything more than each moment of awakening passion.

I want to stay here with you more than anything I've ever wanted in my whole life. I wish I was worthy of your love. I wish my life could start over, and that I could be somebody like Corinne. I will wonder my whole life if you've found someone to marry and what she is like. If you danced with her and kissed her—gave her children of your own.

"I'm sorry," was all she said. Then she turned and fled the barn.

Chapter Twenty-Five

William stared at the empty doorway until his eyes burned. He had to respect her decision to leave. If he couldn't, he didn't respect her. He would not try to change her mind. She didn't want him in her life and that was the end of it.

Maybe he'd bullied her into those passionate encounters. Maybe he'd been the only one who felt the emotion and the desire, and she'd been appeasing a demanding employer. He hadn't thought so at the time, but everything was confusing now.

He'd thought from the first that this was no place for her. Maybe he'd been right all along. And the baby? Will's chest ached at the thought of Linnea taking her away and him never seeing either of them again. Would a city be a better place to raise a daughter? Granted, there would be schools. But there would also be saloons and gambling halls and unsavory characters on the streets.

He couldn't think about that. He couldn't protect them if they weren't here.

A crash of thunder startled him. He put away his supplies and hurried out to look at the sky.

Jagged lightning split the night sky. "Damn!" Where had this storm come from? The day had been clear. Will turned and ran to where the men had been sitting around their fire, and were now picking up their belongings.

"Two riders head east and bunch the cattle on higher ground—Nash and Ben."

The two men broke away and headed to saddle horses.

"Clem, you and Cimarron ride the stream bank, send any cows their way. Roy, come with me. We'll bring the horses into the barn and corrals."

From the porch, Linnea watched the flurry of activity. Men on horseback galloped through rain just beginning to fall.

"What are they doing?" Corinne asked, coming up beside her.

Linnea had been at the ranch long enough to know the workings. "Herding the cattle onto high ground in case the creeks and streams flood. Someone will bring the horses from the pastures into the corrals and stable the mares and colts."

A bright flash of lightning lit the sky and illuminated the ranch yard as though it was daytime. Something cracked and sizzled, and both women jumped. Darkness immediately settled again.

"What was that?" Corinne asked, her voice shaky.

"I don't know." Linnea shook her head.

A slim trail of smoke fingered toward the sky.

"You stay here with the children and Abby," she said. "Rebecca is in her cradle in my room. I'm going to have a look."

Linnea took a hat and jacket from a hook inside the door and donned them as she covered the yard with hurried steps. From the corner of the house, she could see smoke curling from the outhouse. On closer inspection, a corner of the roof was singed and still burning.

Linnea ran to the pump in the center of the yard, dipped a bucket into the trough and ran back, swinging the pail so that the contents flew upward and landed on the outhouse roof with a hiss. After a couple more trips and buckets of water the rain had begun to fall in sheets and any perceived danger was gone.

She returned the bucket and ran to the house.

Corinne was holding Rebecca on her shoulder. "So far mine are still sleeping. Do you think

I should bring them downstairs? The lightning is terrifying."

"Wouldn't hurt to have them all close and together, just in case," Linnea replied. "I'm going to get a towel for my hair."

Before she could do that, hoofbeats sounded, and Linnea turned to discover Will riding toward the house, another figure slumped in front of him.

Linnea ran down the stairs. "What's happened?"

"Lightning scared Roy's horse and it threw 'im. I can't see anything but a cut on his head, but he's not conscious."

"Bring him in."

Linnea cleared a few cups from the table and Will half carried, half dragged his foreman through the door, removed his slicker and stretched him out on the tabletop.

Roy's clothing was dry, except at his feet and ankles. His head and hair were wet, and a trickle of blood seeped down his temple.

Will stood and glanced from his friend to the door.

"Go take care of your horses," Linnea said. "I've got him."

Will backed away and hurried out.

Linnea grabbed rags, dipped water from the

stove, and proceeded to wash Roy's head and face, and examine him for injuries.

Corinne showed up, still carrying Rebecca and leading her two children, and hurried them through the kitchen and into Linnea's room. She returned alone, and her face was pale, her eyes wide. "What happened to Roy?"

"Horse threw him." Linnea had checked his arms and legs, not finding any breaks. "The only thing wrong with him seems to be this cut on his head. It's bleeding pretty bad."

"What should we do? Did Will send for a doctor?"

Linnea blinked. "I don't know." She examined the edges of the cut. "I can do it."

"Do what?"

"Sew it up."

"Linnea, are you sure?"

She nodded. "I've treated wounds worse than this before."

Aggie shuffled out of her room in her night dress and shawl, her wiry gray hair lose over her shoulder. "What's all the ruckus?"

Linnea explained while she gathered supplies.

"What can I do?" Corinne asked.

"If blood doesn't make you sick, dab the wound as much as possible, so I can see what I'm doing."

She nodded. "Okay."

Linnea fought back her own queasiness as she pieced Roy's flesh and stitched the cut high on his forehead.

His eyelids fluttered, he frowned, and his eyes opened. "Damn!" A flurry of curses followed.

"Be still," Linnea told him. "We're almost finished here and I'll have to charge you extra for your laundry if you get blood on this shirt." She smiled to let him know she was teasing. "And you're cursing in front of Mrs. Dumont."

Roy's attention wavered from Linnea to Corinne. "Sorry, ma'am."

"Apology accepted," she replied, and some color returned to her cheeks.

"One more stitch, Roy," Linnea told him.

"Go ahead."

"I'll hold your hand," Corinne said and proceeded to pick up Roy's hand and clasp it between both of hers.

"If you should have a little scar, your hair will cover it," Linnea told him.

Roy chuckled. "A little scar would get lost on this face, Miz McConaughy."

Finished at last, Linnea washed the area around her handiwork and Corinne blotted a little seepage away.

"Think you can sit up?" Linnea asked. "I'll get you a cup of coffee to warm you up.

Roy sat on the edge of the table. "I'd best get back to help Will. Where's my hat?"

Linnea brought him a steaming cup. "Drink this first. You weren't wearing your hat when Will brought you in. You took a nasty fall, I think you should rest."

Roy sipped the coffee and got to his feet and immediately favored one leg.

"Does your leg hurt?" Linnea asked.

"My knee, but I've done enough lollygaggin' for one night. Thanks for the doctorin', ladies."

"Roy, wait!" Corinne called to his back, but he had picked up his slicker and limped to the door.

Aggie chuckled.

Roy made it no farther. He swayed on his feet. Linnea and Corinne both ran and barely caught him before he knocked his head against the wood. Even with two of them, his weight bore them to the ground, where they eased his head to the floor.

Rebecca's cry reached them. "She's hungry," Linnea said.

"What are we going to do with him?" Corinne asked.

Linnea thought a moment. "Let's make a pallet on the floor in the parlor. There's barely any furniture in there, so if he wakes and thrashes around, he won't hurt himself."

Linnea ran to pick up Rebecca, changed her and handed her to Aggie while she and Corinne made a bed of blankets and comforters on the floor. Together they dragged him into the other room. "We should get his pants off and check that knee," Linnea said. "Wrap it probably."

Corinne looked flustered at the idea.

Linnea didn't particularly want to undress the man, either. "We could cut his pant leg."

"I'll get scissors," Corinne agreed quickly.

Together they sliced his pant leg and tightly wrapped his knee.

Rebecca was putting up a fuss in the other room.

"Poor Aggie. If you'll watch him for a while, I'll feed her."

Corinne nodded.

Sitting in her rocker in her room, Linnea nursed her daughter and let herself relax. Outside the thunder still rumbled, but sounded farther away. The lightning had dwindled to an occasional flicker.

Corinne showed up and sat beside her children on the bed. "Where's Aggie?" Linnea asked softly.

"I helped her back to bed."

"Roy's resting?"

Corinne nodded and touched each of her children with a brief caress.

"Lay down with them," Linnea offered. "I'll stay up and keep an eye on Roy. Later, I'll wake you so you can return to your room, or I'll go sleep up there."

"You sure?"

"I'm sure. Rest."

Corinne removed her shoes and lay down, wearing her dress.

The rain was a steady patter on the ground outside the window and a continuous splash in the water barrel at the corner of the house.

"I knew Roy back in Indiana, where we grew up, you know," Corinne said much later.

Linnea thought the other woman had fallen asleep. "Will told me they'd been friends for a long time," she replied.

"Roy was around quite a bit. My father didn't care for him, because he didn't come from money. And, like Will, he didn't have aspirations in business."

"What do you mean?"

"My father wanted Will to work in the mill. To take it over one day. Will didn't want any part of it. He and Roy worked there because the money was good, but they always talked about horses, about how one day they would have a ranch."

"And here they are."

"Yeah." She glanced at her soundly sleeping children. "I wanted to marry him."

"Roy?"

"Yes. He courted me, along with suitors my father arranged. He was the one I wanted, though, ever since I was old enough to think about things like that."

Her story held Linnea captive. Linnea had known there was more to the relationship, but she hadn't imagined. "What happened?"

"Edward Dumont asked me to marry him. I didn't reply because I was waiting—well, *hoping*—for Roy to ask. But when the time came that I thought he would, instead, he told me that I should marry Edward. I guess he didn't feel as strongly about me as I thought."

"What did you do?"

"I didn't have much choice. Soon after that, Will and Roy took off on a trail drive. My father was livid that Will had deserted him. He was in no mood for argument, and he wanted me to marry Edward."

"So you did."

"He was a good man. A good husband and provider. He gave me beautiful children."

"How did he die?"

"A carriage accident two years ago. I've had several men calling on me since, but I am financially sound and see no need. If I was ever to marry again, it would have to be…"

"What?"

"For love," she said. Corinne turned away.

Later, after placing Rebecca in her cradle, Linnea returned to the kitchen to clean away the bloodied rags and set things straight. She checked on Roy, finding him still asleep. Studying him, she imagined him younger, tried to picture him slicked up and calling on the beautiful young Corinne. Why hadn't he proposed and asked her to be his wife? What would have happened if he had, since Jack Tucker hadn't liked him?

Had he ever regretted not asking her? Of course he had. One had only to look at Corinne to see she was a woman any man would desire. Linnea covered Roy with a blanket and ignored the sadness Corinne's story made her feel.

Will entered the kitchen, lit by a single sputtering candle, and found Linnea, asleep with her head on her arms at the table.

He touched her shoulder. "Linnea?"

She raised her head quickly and blinked. "Is everything all right?"

"Everything's fine. How's Roy?"

She straightened. "He woke up once, while I was stitching his head, but—"

"You stitched him?"

"Yes. It wasn't a very big cut, but it was bleeding a lot. He passed out trying to leave, I think it was the pain in his knee. So Corinne and I got him settled in the parlor and wrapped it. He's been sleeping ever since."

Concern etching his face, Will hurried out of the kitchen and Linnea followed.

"Roy?" Will said, leaning over his foreman. "Roy, are you enjoyin' your nap?"

Roy's eyelids fluttered. "What, boss?"

"Just checkin' to see if you had your wits about you. Go back to sleep."

"All right."

Will turned to Linnea. "He'll be okay." They headed back to the kitchen and he poured himself a lukewarm cup of coffee. "Nice job with the stitchin'."

"You'll need to mend the outhouse tomorrow," she said.

He raised a brow in question.

"The roof is a little burned."

"What happened?"

"Lightning."

"You saw it hit? Lord, no one was in there, were they?"

"Corinne and I were on the porch. I ran to see what had been hit, and the roof was burning."

"Rain put it out?"

"It wasn't raining much yet, so I threw a few buckets of water on it. Didn't want to take any chances."

Will looked her over, from the loose tendrils of hair that had escaped to her wrinkled dress and the exhaustion on her face. "Hell of a storm. Came up all at once," he said.

Linnea was not the fragile china doll he had once believed her to be. Oh, she was small and delicate, physically. But her incredible strength of character was a muscle most people couldn't even claim to have used.

Her courage had been evident all along—in her willingness to forge a new life in a land she'd never seen, in her nurturing nature and her stubborn refusal to give up.

"You're ready to drop," he said.

"Corinne and the children are in my room," she said. "I kept them downstairs during the storm."

"That was the right thing to do. You're a level-headed thinker. Will you sleep upstairs then?"

She nodded. "If it's okay, I'll get Rebecca and lie down in Corinne's room."

"Why wouldn't it be okay?"

She shrugged and went for the baby.

Carrying two lanterns, he placed one on the bureau in the room where she would sleep and backed out through the doorway without another word. What could he say to change anything?

Will had spent a lot of energy resenting the fact that everyone had taken to Linnea like bees to honey, but they'd all seen what he'd refused to recognize.

And now it was too late.

He'd fallen in love with her, and she wanted to leave.

Which one of them was really the strongest? Which one would put these past months behind them and move on?

Which one would think of the other every night and day for the rest of their life…and regret that they hadn't known what to do?

Which one…?

Chapter Twenty-Six

One day was all they could keep Roy on his back in the other room. The next day he insisted on getting up and sitting in a kitchen chair, with his leg propped.

Corinne took over seeing to him, and Linnea gave them as much time alone as she could. That morning she moved Aggie's rocker to the porch and took the children to pick berries. In the afternoon she supervised their riding lesson with their uncle.

Will was tirelessly patient with his niece and nephew, even when they begged to ride outside the corral and he had to lead the horses.

He walked them back to where Linnea stood holding Rebecca. Corinne had sewn the baby a matching hat and bonnet, and Will admired her fashionable attire. "You haven't ridden the whole time you've been here," he said to Linnea. "Do you ride?"

She nodded. "I haven't had an opportunity. Cimarron and I take the wagon when we go to town."

"Want to now?"

She glanced at the horses he led. "What about Rebecca?"

"She and I will get along for a few minutes."

She smiled. "Okay."

He reached to lower Margaret to the ground, then asked her to sit with Rebecca on her lap for a moment while he assisted Linnea into the saddle and adjusted the stirrups.

Her skirts rose up her calves, but he acted as though he didn't notice. He stepped away and leaned over to take Rebecca from his niece. Linnea turned the animal's head with the reins, used her heels to gently kick its flanks, and rode away.

She urged the horse into a gallop and traveled the outer perimeter of the corral, across a grassy meadow and back.

She hadn't ridden for a long time, and never just for pleasure, and she enjoyed the sense of freedom and the time to free her mind.

She returned to find Zach and Margaret gone,

and Will walking along the corral fence with Rebecca in one arm. The sight made her chest ache.

"How did I know you'd be a good rider?" he asked, smiling up at her.

She stood in one stirrup to swing her other leg over and step to the ground. "Where are the children?"

"Probably pesterin' their mother for lemonade."

Linnea handed him the reins and reached to take Rebecca from his hold. Her hand brushed his arm, and she pulled the baby away a little too fast to avoid the disturbing contact. "I'll go help her make it."

She felt his gaze on her back as she made her way to the house.

Corinne didn't seem as cheerful as she had only an hour or so ago; in fact, Linnea thought she looked downright upset. Her face was flushed and when she smiled, it was forced. Linnea helped her finish making lemonade. Corinne didn't offer Roy a glass, so Linnea poured one for him. Roy didn't meet Linnea's eyes.

The rest of the afternoon stretched out uncomfortably, and Linnea was glad for supper, when the men arrived and their talk filled the room.

Afterward, Roy thanked both women for the

care they'd given him, gathered his belongings, and hobbled out after the men.

Linnea waited until she and Corinne were alone to speak to her. "Whatever is the matter?" she asked.

Corinne was helping her lay out a pattern for another baby dress on fabric she'd brought from Saint Louis.

Corinne stopped pinning and sagged onto a bench. "I'm just as confused as when I was a girl," she said. "It's all still there between us. The feelings." She turned a tortured expression on Linnea. "He feels it, too, I know he does." Impulsively she reached out and grasped Linnea's hand. "His kisses are like nothing I've ever known."

Linnea's heart went out to her, for she understood those confusing feelings.

"But he doesn't say anything," she said, frustration in her voice. "He pretends like it didn't happen, like it was nothing."

"Maybe he doesn't know what to say," Linnea said, not knowing how to comfort her.

"He could tell me he loves me," she said on a half sob, but collected herself and steadied her voice. "God knows I still love him as much as I ever did. That man broke my heart once, and he'll do it again if I let him."

The floor creaked behind them, and both women turned in surprise. Roy stood just inside the door, hatless, a look of shock on his face.

Corinne covered her face with her hands in embarrassment.

Roy limped forward. "Do you mean those words, Corinne?"

Face flaming, she lowered her hands and raised her chin. "I meant them, you fool-headed, rock-hearted man. I loved you when I was a girl and you left me so you could chase cows."

"I left so you could marry a rich man," he contradicted. "A man with family and money and your pa's approval."

"I didn't want a rich man," she said, her voice shaking now. "I wanted you."

"I always had feelin's for you, Corinne," he said. "That never stopped. I never wanted another woman. After I left and I heard you got married, I got drunk and shot up a saloon in Oklahoma. I sat in jail for a week."

Corinne stared at him.

Linnea edged toward the door, though neither of them seemed to notice she was still there.

"You told me to marry Edward," she said.

"Because he could give you everythin' I couldn't. I wanted you to be happy."

"You stupid man," she said, angry now. "*You* would have made me happy."

Linnea reached the door and bolted into the night. She escaped into the yard and breathed the refreshing air, her heart pounding at what she'd overheard. She pressed a hand to her breast.

"What's goin' on in there?" Will asked from beside her.

She jumped and turned to face him. "Roy's in there with Corinne."

"Oh? Is it gettin' good?" He took a step forward, and she stopped him with a hand on his sleeve.

"Leave them alone, Will, it's personal."

"Maybe we can hear."

"I heard enough."

"Tell me."

"She loved him when they were young. Roy told her to marry Edward, because he thought the man would make a better husband."

"So did my father. Thought he knew what was best for everybody."

"Did Roy really shoot up a saloon?"

Will grinned. "Yup."

Crickets chirped from the nearby bushes. In the distance a coyote howled.

"If I can't talk you into listening, let's walk," he said.

She hesitated.

"Just a walk, Linnea. I know you want to leave."

"Okay."

They strolled to one of the corrals.

"Watch this," Will said. He gave a warbling whistle. Seconds later, a magnificent stallion pranced forward, neck arched, mane flying. The animal bobbed his head and Will spoke to him, but he didn't come nearer the fence.

"I caught 'im last spring. For months, whenever I tried to get close, he'd rear up or run."

"What made him change?"

"Patience. Getting used to my voice. Learning I wasn't going to hurt 'im."

Linnea understood perfectly.

"I call 'im Whiskey, because he's that color."

They walked along the fence, and the stallion followed. Eventually their steps led them back to the house.

Hesitantly, Linnea placed one foot on the first step. With his hand spread firmly over the small of her back, Will urged her forward.

She never had a chance to reach the door, because the screen burst open and Corinne rushed out. "Linnea! Will! Oh, Will," she said, seeing her brother. "The most wonderful thing has happened!"

She flung herself at Will and he grasped her waist in surprise.

Over her shoulder, he looked from Linnea to the man in the doorway. Roy stepped out onto the porch, favoring one leg.

"Roy has asked me to marry him!" Corinne said, her voice breathless with joy.

"He has?" Will returned her hug, and after she'd released him and stepped back, asked, "And what did you answer?"

He was looking at Roy with amusement when he asked the question.

"Why, I said yes, of course," she replied. "I've never wanted anything so much."

Will stepped forward and shook his friend's hand. "None too soon, was it?"

Roy chuckled and Corinne moved to press herself against him and gaze up into his face. Roy wrapped his arm around her and smiled down, and seeing their happiness, Linnea's heart rejoiced with them.

"Now, you must give Roy some time off to join me in Saint Louis," she said to her brother. "We have a wedding and a honeymoon to plan."

"Am I losin' a foreman, then?" Will asked.

"Corinne and I have a lot to think about," Roy replied. "She has her business investments to see to, and that's important."

"But you'd never be happy in the city," she said. "I can sell my house and hire someone to handle my affairs. With the right help, I could handle them from wherever I choose to live."

"You sure you'd wanna do that?" Roy asked.

Corinne studied him. "It doesn't matter where we live," she said softly. "I'll be happy anywhere."

"I've saved some," Roy told her. "'Nough to buy a spread of our own, that is if you wanted to be a rancher's wife. I've had my eye on the place to the west, and the owner could probably be talked into sellin'."

"Looks like I'm losin' a foreman, either way," Will grumbled, but his tone wasn't the least perturbed.

"And gaining a brother-in-law," Corrine replied cheerfully.

The four of them laughed at her giddy happiness.

Linnea barely slept that night. Corinne was already making plans to leave, and Linnea had determined that she would leave with her.

With steely determination, she distanced herself from the men's nightly activities, from her lessons with Cimarron, from Aggie's knowing looks and—with the most difficulty—from Will.

"Why are you leavin'?" Cimarron asked her one evening, when he'd stayed in the kitchen after supper. Roy and Corinne had gone for a ride.

"I don't belong here," she said simply.

"I don't believe that," he said. "You've done a good job ever since you first got here. You were so determined that you could do the work, and all the hands were pullin' for ya."

"I do thank you and the others. Everyone made me feel welcome. That's something I never had before."

"Then why go?"

"Because…" She took a breath and confessed, "Will asked me to marry him."

"I figured it was somethin' like that. You don't wanna marry him?"

"I'm all wrong," she said, vigorously drying a pan. "Nobody knows the life I lived before I came here."

"Nobody cares here."

The words hung in the air.

She examined Cimarron's face.

"This country is about fresh starts," he said. "Out here a man don't ask another man about his past. Women ain't no different."

Linnea couldn't explain to Cimarron any more than she could to Will. It wasn't so much what she'd *done* before, but how she felt about who she was and where she'd come from. It was the lack of value that was bred in her bones.

Will kept his distance, too, no doubt preparing himself for her absence and not wanting to make their parting any more awkward or painful.

The morning they planned to leave dawned as ordinarily as any other. Linnea woke and painstakingly packed her belongings in a bag Aggie had given her. Linnea now owned more than she had when she'd arrived, counting her dresses and the baby's clothing and gifts. She stowed Rebecca's flannels and sheets and dressed her in the dress and bonnet Corinne had given her.

Corinne had offered Linnea a place to stay until she could find work, and Linnea had assured the woman she would earn her keep. "You could stay and work for me indefinitely," Corinne had told her, "but I don't know how long I'll stay in Saint Louis. Roy and I might move back here to Colorado soon."

So far, just having a place to go when she left the Double T was better luck than she'd anticipated, and Linnea was grateful for the chance to get a new start.

"I feel responsible for sending you here," Corinne had told her. "I thought for sure the position would work out."

The men ate breakfast without their usual vitality, and one by one, they wished Linnea goodbye.

She gave each one a heartfelt hug. Most of them bent over the cradle to grin or wave at Rebecca one last time. Cimarron stayed to carry her bags and help Roy and Will load the wagon.

She picked up Rebecca and her daisy hat and walked to where Aggie sat in her chair. She knelt in front of her, holding the baby where Aggie could see her. "Thank you for everything. For the hat and the aprons and the satchel. And for being my friend. Mostly for that."

Aggie's eyes filled with tears behind her spectacles. "Thanks for the glasses, girl. And for showing that ornery polecat he wasn't so tough. If he had half a brain, he'd hang on to you."

Linnea smiled through tears that blurred her vision and leaned forward to give Aggie a hug. "I wrote a letter to Mavis, saying goodbye," she told her. "If you see her, will you tell her I wished I could have said it in person?"

Aggie nodded. She reached out and affectionately touched Rebecca's smooth white cheek with a wrinkled hand.

"And," Linnea told her, "I mentioned to Mavis that she should come this way once in a while, so you can have your baths."

Aggie sniffed and waved her off.

Will came in the door and paused to pick up

Rebecca's cradle. He carried it out the door to the wagon, and Linnea observed from the doorway as he wrapped the bed in a tarp and placed it beside the trunks. Finished with the task, he stood to the side of the wagon.

Cimarron came for Linnea and walked her out behind Roy and Corinne. Corinne hugged her brother and Roy shook his hand. Will hugged Zach and Margaret and settled them on blankets in the back of the wagon.

"You're sure you want to do this?" Cimarron asked her.

Avoiding looking at Will, Linnea nodded. She cleared her throat. "I can never thank you enough," she said. "For being my friend and for teaching me to read. You gave me something that has changed my life forever."

"Aw, I was happy t' do it," he said, his voice gruff. He helped her up to the wagon seat and chucked Rebecca under the chin. "Bye, squirt. Take care of your mom." To Linnea he said, "You'll write to me?"

She smiled through her tears. "I'll write to you."

Roy assisted Corinne to the seat and climbed up beside her. Corinne took Linnea's hand and squeezed it. "Ready?"

Linnea nodded.

Roy picked up the reins.

Linnea's heart hammered in her chest. She hugged Rebecca to her breast. An unseen force drew her gaze, and against her will, she turned her head and found Will Tucker.

Chapter Twenty-Seven

Will stood, thumbs in his pockets, a look of calculated indifference on his face. He wore the familiar black Stetson, which shadowed his eyes, but she could see the set of his jaw, the hard line his mouth made.

Her heart felt as though a hand was squeezing the life from it. Linnea pressed her lips to the top of Rebecca's bonnet and held back a cry.

He hadn't said goodbye. Hadn't looked twice at the baby. Linnea knew his distance was to make her leaving easier on both of them, but it hadn't. Nothing could have eased the bone-deep pain she felt at this moment.

Dozens of memories assailed her: Will dabbing ointment on her burned hand; Will placing a lock on her bedroom door; she and Will dancing under the starlit sky; the two of them alone in the darkness of her bedroom—*Linnea, I love you;* her finding him in the barn and telling him she wouldn't stay and be his wife.

At the thought of never seeing him again, Linnea felt as though her soul was being torn from her body. A lifetime without him stretched out before her, and the realization made it hard to draw sufficient breath.

Her brief time on the Double T flooded back to her in a hundred vivid memories. She didn't have much to be ashamed of when it came to her accomplishments here—her only faults had been in initially deceiving Will about the baby and in being afraid to tell him she couldn't read. She'd made those poor choices because of her past. And he'd forgiven those mistakes.

She'd never before had a choice over her life. As a child, she'd been dominated by her heartless father. As a young girl, she'd been turned over to another man who controlled her every movement. Shame was a constant part of who she was.

For the first time she had a choice in what happened to her. Will hadn't held her against her wishes, hadn't coerced her, hadn't blackmailed her, hadn't bribed her, hadn't bought her—hadn't sold her.

Will had given her the freedom to choose.

She couldn't change the past. The past had made her who she was, good or bad, right or wrong.

What was it Cimarron had said about her past? *Nobody cares here.*

Well, she cared. And Will would care if she told him. But would he hold it against her? Would he be ashamed of her? She would never know unless she took a chance.

No, she couldn't change the past. But she could work on the present. And the future.

I'll be a good father to Rebecca, she'll be my own...I'd be proud for her to have my name.

He wasn't a man to make promises lightly. He wasn't a man to speak his heart or ask her to marry him unless he was deadly serious. Unless he truly loved her.

And she loved him. She hadn't allowed herself to think it, let alone say it, because a lifetime of experience taught her not to want anything. Not to hope.

Roy and Corinne, sitting beside her on this wagon seat, were proof of what happened when one didn't admit what they wanted, and instead imagined what was best for the other.

"Wait!" Linnea shouted the word, startling Corinne. "Stop! Stop the wagon!" Linnea handed Rebecca to Corinne.

Their eyes locked and Corinne smiled encouragement. "Yes," she said and touched Linnea's cheek.

Clumsily holding her hem to keep from plunging headfirst to the ground, Linnea climbed down from the wagon. The moment her feet touched the ground, she started running. The daisy hat fell behind her.

Will saw her coming. He took a step forward. Another. And in the next heartbeat, he was running, too.

Skirt hem flying, her heart racing, she reached him and he held her by her upper arms. Will stared down into her upturned face.

She caught her breath. "I can't change what happened to me in the past," she said, discarding her shame for the sake of hanging on to her first glimpse of hope.

"It doesn't—"

"No." She placed her fingers over his lips. "Listen."

He nodded and she dropped her hand.

Linnea drew a breath. "My father sold me to my husband for two hundred dollars and a box of Havana cigars."

She'd just admitted her most shameful truth, and her heart fluttered with the pain of that secret. Will's expression didn't change, but his jaw tensed.

"That's not much of a price for a person's life," she went on, baring her soul. "My value lessened once he missed the money and the cigars. My husband thought he'd paid too much for me and never let me forget my lack of worth. I never knew I was worth having someone love me. Especially someone like you, Will—a good man like you. You work hard and take care of people. You're honest and straightforward. And you'd never deliberately hurt anybody."

She looked Will in the eye. "My husband forced himself on me. Every time. I never knew anything different. If you can forget that, maybe I can."

"It's not your shame, Linnea," Will said. "It's your father's. Your husband's."

"You said you love me, Will. But you have to love me enough to forget my past. And there's more. Pratt was a thief. He and his friends robbed people. They held up trains. They shot people in cold blood. I spent most of the years of my marriage on the run or waiting in a shack. We didn't have a home. We lived in hideouts—caves and back rooms and woods."

Will cupped her cheek, and she realized there were tears trailing down her skin.

"I ran away once."

"He found you?"

She nodded. "He hurt me so bad I never tried again."

"I'm sorry," Will said, his voice a ragged tone.

"And I'm sorry I ever frightened you. Or raised my voice. Even once."

She shook her head as if there was no comparison.

"Finally Pratt got shot trying to rob a bank. I doctored him for a week, but we had to keep on the run, and he died. I helped dig a hole and bury him in the pouring rain. Kansas somewhere."

"And his partners?"

"They rode off. I went the opposite way and found work wherever I could. Then I found out I was gonna have a baby. And you know the rest." She looked up at him, pleading with her eyes. "That's who I am," she said. "Do you love me enough to forget my past?"

"I love you..." he said, with emotion choking his usually strong voice "...enough for anything. And I'll spend the rest of my life making *you* forget."

She loved this man so much it hurt.

He kissed her with a love and passion neither had ever known, kissing all traces of tears from her cheeks and absorbing them as if to take her pain.

Revealing her ugly past to Will made her feel as though she'd dropped a lead weight that she'd been carrying her whole life. The burden was gone. She took a breath, and even breathing was easier. If he hadn't been holding her, she'd have floated off the ground.

Linnea clung to him, to his strength and the heady promise of his love, to the bright promise of their future.

Will hugged her soundly, knocking his hat to the ground. A joyous laugh bubbled up from deep inside her and carried across the land, startling a jay from a clump of chokecherry bushes.

From their observation point at the corner of the barn, the hands sent up a cheer.

Will lifted his head and called to Roy. "Turn that wagon around and bring our baby girl back here!"

Roy and Corinne hugged and Roy led the team in a circle, heading the horses back toward the house.

Will and Linnea walked with their arms around each other's waists, carrying their hats and smiling into each other's faces. The Colorado sun beat on their shoulders. In the corral, a horse whinnied. Four hands came running to help unload the wagon.

And on the front porch of their house an old woman rocked…and cackled.

* * * * *